MAZIE BABY

JULIE FRAYN

DEDICATION

This book is for anyone who suffers abuse, be it physical, verbal, or emotional. Abuse can be in your face and violent — or it can creep in on tiptoes, subtle and slow. Either way, the tendrils of abuse infiltrate the victim, not just their bodies, but their psyches, until the effects take up residence. It is a poisonous and evil tenant that is hard to evict. I will never understand the perpetrators.

DEDICATION

This book is for anyone who suffers abuse, be it physical, verbal, or emotional. Abuse can be in your face and violent — or it can creep in on tiptoes, subtle and slow. Either way, the tendrils of abuse infiltrate the victim, not just their bodies, but their psyches, until the effects take up residence. It is a poisonous and evil tenant that is hard to evict. I will never understand the perpetrators.

ACKNOWLEDGEMENTS

Nothing I do is possible without the love and support of my children. Thank you, Brynn and Charlie, for being so wonderful, so funny, so sarcastic. And for cooking me dinner and bringing me beer when I am locked in my writing cave (a.k.a, a dark corner of my bedroom).

A million thanks to my dear systir, Carolyn Frayn (www.carolynfrayn.ca / www.artofbreastcancer.ca), for the gorgeous and very personal cover for *Mazie Baby*. She found the strength to create beauty while enduring the pain of chemotherapy, and used my own baby girl, Brynn, as a model for Mazie. This will always be my favourite cover. ♥

Many thanks to my brother, John Frayn, for his insights to all things police-related and for reading an advance copy. To Britta Kristensen, Crown Prosecutor, for educating me on the nuances of murder trials and ensuring the courtroom details of this story rang true (especially since the first draft stank of my obsession with American crime drama). And thanks to Kelly Killick-Smit for introducing me to Britta! Thanks to Tracy Todd for her enviable eagle eye and enduring sweet ways, and to Shauna Cooper for her first-hand recollections of trials in Calgary.

Countless thanks to my wonderful editor, Scott Morgan (www.write-hook.com), for not one, but two full edits. He makes me a better writer, and I'm glad I found him.

MAZIE BABY

Cool pavement kissed the soles of Mazie Reynolds' bare feet. Beads of shining dew, caught in that nether-moment between breaking dawn and the sizzle of a spring heat wave, clung to clipped blades of grass. The world smelled clean and fresh. Smelled of open air and endless horizons. Smelled of freedom.

The rusty bolt that secured the red flag to the mailbox whined when she forced it up. She shot a glance over her shoulder. The house remained still, her morning reprieve uninterrupted. The eerie quiet lulled her into a sense of normal.

Whatever that was.

She pulled a small stack of mail from the box, the envelopes like sandpaper against her fingertips. Bill, bill, flyer, pizza menu. The last bulky and colourful piece announced that Cullen may have already won two million bucks. She snorted. As if.

She glanced at the van sitting in the driveway before turning her gaze on the mountains in the distance, all lilac and orange in the rising sunlight. How easy would it be to just drive away? Never look back? Do something different. Something new. Something better?

The hair on the nape of her neck stood on end at the crack of wooden heels on concrete. She tensed her shoulders and set her jaw. She hadn't heard the door open. And why was he wearing those old cowboy boots on a work day?

"Surprise!" Soft, pale, freckled arms encircled her waist and squeezed.

Mazie laughed. "Well, good morning, Miss Simpson. You are definitely not who I was expecting." Mazie reached her arm around the girl's shoulder, gave her a small hug, and planted a light kiss on her frizzy, copper hair. "What are you wearing?"

Polly, the neighbour's daughter, stepped back and stomped the sidewalk with wooden clogs painted bright yellow. "Grandma sent them from Holland. They're klomps." She twirled. Her short skirt flew in the air and flashed a bit of pasty, plump ass cheek and white cotton underpants. "Can I go show Ariel?"

"She's still in bed. How about later?"

"Morning, Mazie. That's a lovely scarf."

Mazie donned a wide smile and turned slowly. That smug half-grin sat there on her neighbour's round face, all prepped for another day of sticking her stupid nose in everyone else's lives. "Hello, Rachel." Mazie touched the thin material around her neck and pulled the scarf higher before drawing her sweater tighter across her chest.

Rachel jerked her head at her daughter. "Polly, honey, get back inside and eat your breakfast."

Polly slipped off the klomps, picked them up, and skipped across the dewy grass, her wet footprints darkening the wooden front stoop before disappearing into the house next door.

"She's growing up so damn fast." Rachel plopped her balled-up fists on the sides of her ever-expanding muffin-top.

"Too fast. Just last year all boys had cooties." Mazie sighed. "Now those cootie-carriers are all cute. And Ariel asked if she could wear makeup."

Rachel nodded. "Well, today's twelve is our generation's fifteen."

"I suppose. Kind of scared for my future grandkids."

Rachel raised an eyebrow. "Getting a little warm for scarves and long sleeves. You must be boiling all bundled up like that."

Mind your damn business, Rachel.

"I'm fine. I like to be warm."

"And you're looking a little thin. You dieting again?"

Damn this woman and her incessant need to pry. Always peering over the fence, eyeballing Mazie's family from her deck, standing on her tiptoes and craning her stubby neck, listening to Cullen's phone conversations. Though, that was his fault. He shouldn't drink and take private calls in the backyard. He was so much louder when he drank.

"I'm always dieting." Mazie slipped her index finger under the flap of one envelope and tore it open, her focus anywhere but on Rachel's questioning gaze.

The paper sliced into her finger. She winced, squeezed the tip with her thumb and watched a droplet of crimson ooze from the tiny scratch.

"Any plans for summer vacation this year?"

Mazie nodded. "Maybe a trip to the mountains. Or east to visit Mom. Cullen will go fishing, of course."

"Without you and Ariel? You used to go all the time."

"He likes his solitude." And so did she.

The screen door squeaked on its hinges. "Mazie?" The air stilled after Cullen's voice boomed across the front yard. "Oh. Hello, Rachel." He said her name as if it were poison he had to spit from his mouth before it killed him.

Rachel's nosy eyebrow shot up. She crossed her arms. "Cullen."

"Mazie. Baby, come back in. Your coffee's getting cold." His voice lost its boom, took on an average volume, like what she imagined a normal husband would sound like.

She looked at her feet. "I'll be right there." She turned and headed toward the house.

"Well, have a nice day," Rachel called as Mazie retreated. "Come for coffee sometime."

Mazie waved over her shoulder, stepped inside the door, and bolted it against the outside world.

In the kitchen, Cullen leaned against the counter, his arms crossed in front of his chest, chin down, eyes dark and brows pinched. "Why do you talk to that stupid bitch?"

Anger spewing from his mouth was nothing new. But when his voice became a low growl, her skin crawled.

She dropped the envelopes onto the counter, turned on the tap and squirted dish soap under the stream of hot water. "I don't. She talked to me. She always does, you know how nosy she is." Mazie's voice was casual, almost sing-song. But even she could hear the underlying strain, like a too-taut piano wire about to snap.

The scratch of Cullen's work boots against the gleaming floor neared. She tensed, her hands immersed in soapy dishwater.

He rested his chin on her shoulder. The stench of his cigarette breath soured the air. Her scarf tightened around her neck.

"Just keep to yourself." His voice was gruff in her ear.

She nodded, willed the tears he so loathed — or feared — not to pool at the corners of her eyes. She held her breath against the pressure on her throat.

"Daddy?"

He let go of the scarf. Mazie grasped the sink's edge and struggled quietly for air.

"Morning, pumpkin. Shouldn't you be getting ready for school?"

The familiar shuffling of Ariel's slippers on the linoleum neared. "Mom, are you okay?" Her thin arms circled Mazie's waist.

"Of course she is." Cullen put one hand on Ariel's shoulder and pulled her away.

Mazie grit her teeth. "I'm fine, bug. Do as your father says and get ready for school. I'll make you pancakes." She didn't turn around. Didn't want Ariel to see that the tears had won again, and were dripping down her cheeks.

"All right." The whisper of slippers against linoleum disappeared at the living room carpet.

In Mazie's peripheral vision, Cullen scanned the grocery list on the fridge, ran one permanently grimy finger down the clean paper. "Are you going today?"

"Yes."

"You need more woman shit already? Didn't you just buy tampons?"

She swallowed. "That was last month."

"Fucking stupid bullshit. Maybe we ought to just get you fixed. Would save me a lot of cash." He yanked bills from his wallet, counted out five twenties, and slapped them on the counter. "Where's my lunch?" He yanked the fridge door open and leaned into it, shoved the food around. Glass containers crashed against each other as if they would crack open and spill their contents onto the shelf and the floor below. It would be his fault if they did. But she'd get the blame.

She sucked in a deep breath. "It's packed in your pail. On the sideboard." Like every other day.

He nodded, didn't even look at her. "I'll be late tonight. Going for a few beers." He turned his back and slammed the door. The aura of sweat and grime that never came out of his plaid work shirts no matter how many times she laundered them, no matter how much soap and softener and deodorizer she poured into the machine, fouled the air.

The truck rumbled to life. He gunned the engine and roared out of the alley.

She exhaled.

How did she get here? A prisoner in her own home. She should have taken Ariel and run years ago. She dropped her chin to her chest and wept at the sink.

"No." She stood straight. "Stop it, you stupid, weak woman." She pounded her fists against the counter's edge, spraying soapy water onto her clothes. "Damn it." She snatched a dish towel and dabbed at her shirt. "Can't you do anything right?"

~~~~~~~~~

Mazie's footsteps echoed in the near-empty aisles of the grocery store. A few women roamed the store that afternoon, dumpy in stained sweat pants or pyjama bottoms. They shuffled around, hair greasy, feet clad in brightly-coloured rubber clogs or flip-flops.

Cullen would kill her if she left the house looking like that.

She scanned her list and ticked off each item as she placed it in the cart. Exactly as noted, not one thing more. Only tampons remained. She searched the shelves for the most expensive product in the largest box, tossed it on top of the canned tomatoes, and headed for the cashier.

"Afternoon, Mrs. Reynolds."

"Hi, Lucy." Mazie pulled groceries and toilet paper from the cart and piled it onto the conveyor.

"You're in a good mood today."

"It's a beautiful day, sun is shining." And she got to be out of her cell for a few hours. Shopping days were the best.

"Well, I'm stuck here until six." Lucy dragged each product across the scanner. "Ninety-one seventy-two."

Mazie counted out the five twenties.

"And your change, eight eighteen."

Mazie hesitated. "No, that's not right." The pulse of her pounding heart bounced off her ribs.

"Sorry?"
~~~~~~~~~

"The change. It should be eight twenty-eight. Not eighteen."

Lucy ran her finger down the tape. "Oh, right."

Mazie's fingers trembled. "Every dime counts, right?" Her eyes darted about the store, landing anywhere but Lucy's face.

Lucy opened the cash drawer and handed her another dime. "Yes, of course. Sorry."

"Thank you. See you next week."

Mazie packed the groceries into the back of the van, fumbled with the door latch, sat in the driver's seat and gripped the steering wheel with both hands. The skin of her knuckles was taut against the bones, her fingernails dug into her palms. She eased her hands from the wheel, pulled open her purse and counted the change, did the math in her head. Eight dollars and twenty-eight cents. Exactly. She put her head back and took three deep breaths, then turned the key until the engine came to life.

Her purse vibrated against the centre console. She dug her cell phone out. The mid-day check-in with her jailer was particularly late that day.

Where you at?

She flashed her thumbs across the keyboard. *Grocery store.*

You're behind schedule.

She grit her teeth. What did it matter if she scrubbed the toilet first, or went to the store first? *Thought I'd pick Ariel up from school.*

You spoil her too much.

Her thumbs hesitated over the keys. What did he want her to say?

Right?

Of course. That's always the correct response.

Right.

She eyed the green glow of the dashboard clock. Two forty-five. Just enough time to run to the drug store before school was out.

Ariel would be so surprised. She hated the school bus. And some one-on-one time with her daughter before Mazie had to make dinner and vacuum was just what she craved.

She pulled into the parking lot of a Shoppers Drug Mart she hadn't been to in at least a month. She retrieved the box of tampons from a grocery bag, peeled the price tag from the bottom, and stuffed the box into a reusable tote. She took a few breaths, climbed out of the van, and ran one hand over her hair. In the store she made a beeline for customer service.

The lone clerk glanced up at her and motioned with two fingers for her to approach. "What can I do for you?"

"I bought these tampons last week and realized I bought the wrong brand." Mazie pulled the box from the tote and placed it on the counter.

"Receipt?"

"Sorry, I've lost it."

The clerk raised one eyebrow. "I can't give you a refund without a receipt. Just store credit."

Mazie nodded. "That's fine."

The clerk scanned the barcode. "Those are twelve ninety-five." She ran a gift card through the magnetic stripe reader and pressed a few buttons, then handed the card to Mazie. "There you are, thirteen sixty with tax."

Mazie took the gift card, tapped it against the counter and leaned in a couple of inches. "Thank you," she whispered and tucked the card into the back pocket of her jeans. In the van she pulled the grocery receipt from her purse and ran her finger down the list until she found the tampons. Not bad, almost three dollars profit on the return.

She reached below the driver's seat and tugged on the billfold duct-taped to the underside, added the gift card to the growing cache of other cards and money.

It looked like a lot, all stacked together like that. But was it enough?

~~~~~~~~

A line of SUVs battled for position in front of the school. Mazie pulled into an open spot just seconds before the final bell. Ariel skipped down the school steps holding Polly's hand, Rachel right behind them. Damn, she was volunteering again?

Mazie ducked down in her seat. Screw it. Her personal stalker could drive Ariel home. Mazie checked the side-view mirror and put on her left signal. She shook her head and clicked it off.

No. She wouldn't let Rachel steal her alone time with Ariel. Mazie pressed her fingertips to the horn, one long beep followed by three quick ones — their secret code.

Ariel spun around. When their eyes met, she waved and smiled. She said something to Polly and ran towards the van, her backpack bouncing against her shoulders.

Rachel waved. Mazie ignored her.

"I was hoping you'd pick me up!" Ariel tossed her backpack into the back next to the grocery bags and crawled into the passenger seat. "Can we get ice cream?"

"Sorry, bug. There wasn't enough left over from groceries today. Maybe ask Daddy if he has any spare change and we can go on the weekend?"

Ariel pouted. "No fair."

"I know, honey." She ran her hand over Ariel's raven hair. "Seatbelt, please. Watch you don't get your hair caught in the latch."

Ariel pulled her long locks to the other side.

"Maybe it's time for a trim, eh?"
~~~~~~~~

"Daddy said no. He likes it long."

Of course he did.

"It's not fair, it's my hair." She crossed her arms.

"Maybe I can talk to him. See if he'll change his —"

"No, that's okay," Ariel blurted out, the space between her eyebrows creased. "I don't want him to be mad at you." She turned away and stared out the window.

Mazie's eyes burned with unspent tears and she turned to look out the driver's window. "Speaking of Daddy, he's going to be late. Want to watch a movie before dinner?"

"Yes! *Madagascar*?"

"Again? We've seen that at least five times."

"Six. Can we?" A childlike gleam glowed in Ariel's eyes. She was caught in that twilight zone between child and young adult. Little girl and grown woman. Boys were high on her list of the most important things in the world. Begging to wear makeup had been a near daily occurrence until her father laid down the law with a boom in his voice and a wagging finger in Ariel's face. No daughter of his was going to get all slutted up before she even hit high school. She was months past needing a training bra, too young to look so, so .... sexual, as Cullen called it. But she just wasn't ready to let ice cream and animated movies slip from her life. Or pouting.

"All right, we'll watch one more time. But only if we can do the move it-move it dance."

"Can we close the drapes first? The neighbours already look at me funny when I'm in the yard."

~~~~~~~~~

Mazie sat in the living room, a cup of tepid tea on the side table. She stared at the television, her thumb on the remote, and flipped
~~~~~~~~~

through channel after channel, her mind on autopilot.

She'd tucked Ariel into bed after they'd worn each other out, dancing and singing and filling the house with laughter. The second she flicked off the light and clicked her daughter's bedroom door closed, the light-heartedness evaporated and the burden of what was to come smothered her.

With the sound of every engine that roared by and every footstep that clopped on the sidewalk as someone passed out front, her heart raced.

She waited in the incandescence of the floor lamp, the three-setting bulb on its lowest wattage. The streetlamp on the corner threw its orange glow into the room, the decorative window bars casting a checkerboard shadow over the family portrait that hung on the opposite wall. The cuckoo clock ticked and tocked, ticked and tocked. Its hollow marking of time echoed in the empty kitchen.

Her head hurt. She was tired of waiting for him to come home. To tell her what to do, what to think, who she was or wasn't allowed to speak to.

Her chin dipped to her chest, her eyelids thick with sleep. The roar of Cullen's truck jolted her awake. She jumped from her chair and scurried into the kitchen, stripped cellophane from the plate of cold meatloaf, mashed potatoes and steamed carrots, all smothered in dark brown gravy. Six beeps of the 'quick cook' button and his dinner was on its way to hot while she threw out the plastic, polished off the droplets of condensation it had left on the counter, and fetched a fork and knife from the cutlery drawer.

He walked in the door and sat at the table as the microwave announced that his food was ready. She slid the hot plate in front of him and stood still, just to his left.

He barely breathed between the forkfuls of food he shovelled into his mouth. Hops and barley emanated from his pores.

"You pick her up from school?" He spoke through a mouthful of potatoes.

"Yes."

He paused, his fork mid-air, turned and raised one eyebrow at her. "I told you not to spoil her."

"I was already so close. Why make her take the bus?" She stared at her feet.

"Because she'll expect it, that's why." He shook his head. "Stupid."

His work boots sat in the back landing, one on its side near the closed door, the other right smack in the middle of the tile. She armed herself with paper towels and a spray bottle of all-purpose cleaner, aligned the heels of his boots against the wall and placed them on the rubber shoe mat. She wiped the dust and polished the tile.

When she was finished and the soiled towels were safely in the garbage, she took his plate. He had tossed a napkin over what little remained of the meal, his silent cue that he was finished and she should hurry up and clean up after him.

She turned her back, scraped and rinsed the plate, placed it in the dishwasher, and set the machine to wash.

She took a deep breath and turned to face him.

He held out his hand.

She pulled the grocery list and receipt from her pocket and handed it to him, along with the change.

He ran his finger down the receipt, compared it to the list she'd written out. He counted the change, nodded and pocketed it, then ripped up the papers and handed them to her.

She slipped the garbage into the bin under the sink.

He looked her up and down, "C'mere." His voice was raspy from too much beer and nicotine. He reached out and grasped her wrist and yanked her into his lap. He wrapped his arms around her, crushing her in an embrace, her arms pinned to her sides. The smell of the cigar bar oozed from his hair and clothes, a sickly sweet stench like gym socks dipped in fake vanilla and lit on fire. Her head spun and her stomach lurched. One of his hands slid between her legs, the other up her shirt and under her bra.

She shivered and swallowed the bile that rose in her throat. The calluses on his hands scraped against her soft skin. There'd be fresh scratches under her breasts or across her backside after he finished with her.

She squirmed. "I … I have my period."

He stiffened. "Shit. Again?" He pushed her off his lap.

She reached for the counter, caught it with one hand, the other hand on the linoleum, and steadied herself. Better than landing on her ass on the floor. She used the countertop as leverage, stood and turned to him.

He was already halfway up the stairs.

~~~~~~~~~

Earls restaurant buzzed with the anonymous conversations of dozens of strangers. Mazie sat in the booth, Ariel at her side. Cullen sat across from them, the birthday crown Ariel had made him out of gold construction paper askew atop his head.

"Can I get you another beer?" The skinny blonde server with the micro-mini-skirt sidled up to him and put one hand on his shoulder.

He grinned up at her. "Sure. The birthday boy deserves another brew." He gunned the third of a pint still left in the Albino Rhino glass and handed it to her.

"And you, ma'am? More water? If you're the DD, I can get you some pop or iced tea, on the house."
~~~~~~~~~

Mazie shook her head. "No, thanks."

The server cleared the empty plates and smiled at Cullen. He watched her walk away, his gaze firmly planted below her waist.

"You want your present now, Daddy?"

"I didn't see a box or bows. What present?" He smiled at his daughter, his eyes alight with the game. Same game, every year. He bought tickets online, paid for them himself, printed them out and handed them to Mazie to give to him for his birthday. As long as he got what he wanted, he didn't mind not being surprised. And he always played along with Ariel, who was none the wiser.

Mazie slid the envelope to Ariel under the table. She pulled it out and handed it to him. "Happy birthday."

He ripped the envelope open and grinned at two tickets to the Calgary Stampeders' game in June. He nodded at Mazie and Ariel. "Thank you, my ladies."

"Can I come?"

Cullen's brow creased. "To a football game? I always take Jerry."

Ariel sank in her seat and looked at her lap. "Okay."

Mazie slid her hand across the leather of the bench seat and patted Ariel's arm.

"Happy Birthday, to you," a crowd of wait staff gathered beside their table and sang the birthday song. Skinny Girl placed a large piece of warm chocolate banana cake ablaze with a sparkler in front of Cullen and handed him a fork.

His toothy smile lit up his face, his laughter lit up Ariel's. Mazie grinned. It had been a fun night, light and easy. For the most part.

When they finished singing, applause popped around the room, other patrons joining the fun. "Thank you, thank you," Cullen called out to the nearest tables and waved.

He leaned across the table and took Mazie's hand.

She flinched.

"Did you hear the pipes on the tall dude with the long hair?" he whispered. He looked around the room, pointed at a young man taking orders three tables over. "That guy." He turned back to her, squeezed her hand. "He sounds a lot like I used to, don't you think?"

Mazie nodded. "I guess so. It's been so long since I've heard you sing."

"Yeah, well, that life is over."

His phone chimed and a red light flashed. He picked it up, grinned at the screen and ran his thumbs across it. Seconds later the phone chimed again. He let out a small laugh and responded.

Mazie sipped her water, hacked off a bit of cake and stabbed it with the fork then handed the fork to Ariel. "Yummy cake, eh?"

Ariel nodded with her mouth full.

Cullen texted back and forth with someone who did a better job of making him happy than Mazie was doing. After the fifth chime, she sighed.

He glanced up at her. "What's your problem?"

She looked at the table. "Nothing." She took a breath. "Just that, whoever it is, maybe the texts could wait until after dinner?" She lifted her eyes to his.

His one eyebrow shot up and he squinted. Mazie looked away.

"Daddy, can we get ice cream on the way home?" Ariel to the rescue.

He smiled at her. "Sure we can. It's my birthday, after all."

Ariel slid the side door of the van closed, chocolate ice cream stained her upper lip and dripped from a waffle cone.

Mazie clicked the passenger door shut and waited for Cullen to pass in front of her before falling into line behind and heading for the front door.

"Evening, Reynolds clan." Rachel's husband, George, stood on his front lawn in checkered shorts and a ratty old T-shirt. He held the garden hose and sprayed a fine mist over Rachel's beloved rose bushes.

Cullen ignored him.

"Hi, George." Mazie waved.

Rachel jumped out through the front door. She was like a damn jack-in-the-box and Mazie's presence was the hand crank. The second she was in range, surprise! Rachel popped up.

"Beautiful evening!" she yelled. "Ariel, want to come play with Polly?"

Cullen spun around. "No, she doesn't. It's my birthday and she's spending it with me."

Rachel cocked her head. "Well, sooorry, birthday boy. I didn't know this was the day the world was graced with your presence." She jerked her chin at Ariel. "Maybe another day that isn't so special, 'kay sweetie?"

"Okay, Mrs. Simpson. Thanks."

Ariel took her ice cream into the living room and turned on the television.

Mazie clicked the front door shut. "Don't drip on the carpet, bug."

Cullen went straight to the cupboard over the fridge and pulled out the bourbon. He sloshed a few ounces into a tumbler and turned to her. "I swear, one day I'm gonna kill that bitch." He kept his voice low.

Mazie placed her purse on the kitchen table. "She's snoopy, but harmless."

"And for future reference, who texts me and when I choose to reply are none of your damn business."

She looked at her feet. "Sorry. We don't get many nights out. Just thought it would be nice to focus on that."

"I don't care what you thought." He snatched her purse and rummaged inside. "Let's see who you've been texting, huh?" He pulled her phone out and slid his grease-stained fingers all over the screen. The same thing he did at least once a week. He pressed his lips together and threw her a withering look. "Good. Just me." He tossed the phone on the table, took his drink, and joined Ariel in front of the television.

At ten, he sent Ariel to bed. At ten-thirty, he took Mazie by the arm. She followed him up the stairs, her wrist aching in his grip.

In the bedroom, he stripped and tossed his clothes on the floor.

Mazie got undressed, hung her pants in the closet and put her shirt and underwear in the clothes hamper with the other dirty laundry. She picked up his clothes from the carpet, along with his filthy work shirt and jeans that lay where he'd dropped them after work — shag the colour of applesauce had seemed the right choice thirteen years ago — and tossed them into the laundry basket she kept in the room for his things. Kept them away from her clothes so his filth didn't infect her.

He stood by the head of the bed, hard and anxious. "Hurry up already."

She approached from the other side and lay on her back.

He crawled on top of her, ran his sweaty, stinking, sticky skin all over her. She closed her eyes and turned her head. He wouldn't care. He never kissed her on the mouth anymore.

He pushed her legs apart with his knees and forced himself inside. The weight of him knocked the breath from her.

She clamped her lips closed, shut her eyes, and imagined an idling river, a quiet meadow at the base of the mountains, the scent of daisies and pine needles. Ariel played in the distance. Molly, their golden retriever, frolicked in the grass. The dog she'd always wanted. A dog they'd never owned. Ariel tossed a stick to Molly and the dog fetched and returned flawlessly.

Cullen's breathing became laboured. He shifted his body until he loomed over her and encircled her throat with one hand.

As the air left her, she opened her eyes to glare at the monster he had become.

He grunted and groaned and thrust into her harder and harder, his grip on her neck tightening with each creak of the bed, each thud of her head against the headboard, the headboard against the wall.

Creak, thud, gasp, thud, creak.

Sparks of light exploded in her periphery. She clawed at his arm.

"No! I'm not done fucking you yet."

Mazie gasped for air, prayed for his grip to falter, to allow just one small slip of oxygen through. Her vision blurred and she closed her eyes. He was going to do it this time. She was going to die. Tears dripped onto the pillow.

His body went rigid and his grip relaxed. He toppled onto her and breathed garlic and liquor onto her cheek. "Oh yeah." He rolled off. "That's what I needed." He swatted her thigh with the back of his hand. "Go shower. You're disgusting." He turned off the bedside lamp and stuffed his pillow under his head.

Mazie slid from the bed, her movements robotic and stiff. She clicked the bathroom door shut and opened the one drawer that was hers and hers alone. He would never peer where tampons and pads and hair removal products lived, nauseated as he was by the whole 'woman thing.'

She pushed the contents aside and tugged the false back away. The Polaroid camera lay at the ready.

She ran the shower, inched the door open a sliver and peeked out. He was unconscious. Bourbon-fuelled snores grunted from his nostrils.

She snapped two photos of the fresh hand print on her neck, the cumulative damage redder and brighter than before, the contrast against her ashen face a stark reminder of why her drawer was full of scarves. When the pictures popped out, she wrote the date on the white border of each and returned everything to the drawer, replaced the false back and slid the drawer shut.

She stepped under the near-scalding shower. The loofah found every inch of her skin. She ran the bar of herbal soap over her body again and again, lathered her fingers and slid them inside herself, stroking and rubbing to purify where he'd stained her. Masturbating in the shower used to be a relaxing, exciting, release. But this wasn't masturbation. It was cleansing. She felt no pleasure. Only relief to know that as much of him as possible was out of her body.

When she was as clean as mere soap and water could get her, she sat in the tub and wept. No matter how hot the water, no matter how long she scrubbed, no matter how many bars of soap she went through, she could never wash him off.

She climbed into bed and turned her back to him, the slice of mattress between them a glacial chasm. She fell into a fitful sleep, her body on the brink and her arm hanging, fingertips pressed into the carpet. They were all that kept her from going over the edge.

Like any normal day.

<div style="text-align:center">~~~~~~~~~</div>

Mazie perched on the edge of her chair and sipped her sweet tea. The dinner dishes were washed and dried and put in their place where they belonged. The lingering comfort of roast pork pulled at her senses, quickly losing the aroma argument to the yeast of too many lagers poured down Cullen's throat.

Ariel sat on the carpet, her face too close to the television, its glow illuminating her black tresses with strands of neon blue. Mazie reached out with her foot and gave Ariel a gentle poke in the butt. "Time to get ready for bed."

"Not yet!" Ariel swiped at Mazie's foot with one hand. "My show's not over."

"Ariel!" Cullen pushed his newspaper down, crumpling its pages. "Do as your mother says and get your ass upstairs."

"Daddy, please? It's almost finished."

Mazie winced at the whine in her daughter's voice. "It's okay. She can finish watching."

"It is not okay." He slammed his beer bottle on the table and tossed the paper aside. He stood, grabbed Ariel's arm and yanked her to her feet.

Mazie's legs went cold.

"Ow, Daddy that hurts!" Ariel gazed up at her father. Fear and defiance glinted briefly in her eyes before the tears came.

"Then do as you're told." He threw his hands open. Ariel stumbled backward.

Mazie stood. "Cullen, leave her be. She's just a child."

He turned to her, eyes squinted, upper lip trembling.

Ariel rubbed her hand over the giant red fingerprints on her arm.

"She's not a child, damn it. Look at her! She's got tits for Christ's sake. About damn time she grew up."

Mazie took a step back and guided her daughter away. "I just don't want you to hurt her. It's not her fault."

"It's not her fault." His face twisted and his voice raised an octave. "It's not her fault, it's not her fault." He put his hands on his hips and laughed once on a heavy exhale. "You're right."

Mazie hesitated and looked back at Ariel.

She was right?

Ariel gaped at her father and inched toward the stairs.

"Yup. You are so right." One side of his upper lip lifted in a sneer. He took two steps and poked her collar bone with one finger. "It's your fucking fault." He raised his right hand across his chest.

She closed her eyes.

The back of his hand slammed into the side of her face.

"Daddy, no!"

He swung around and stepped toward Ariel. She screamed and ran up the stairs.

He turned back to Mazie and punched her in the stomach.

The wind left her and she doubled over onto the floor. She gasped for air and willed her dinner to stay put.

"Get that little bitch in bed now, before I give her a real lesson in behaving."

Mazie crawled to the staircase and looked up to the landing. Ariel stared at her mother, her eyes red with tears and double their normal size.

Mazie grasped the railing and forced herself to stand. She smiled at Ariel. "It's all right, honey. Mommy's all right. Come on, I'll read you a story."

She looked back at Cullen. He was hidden behind the newspaper, his beer near-empty. She climbed the stairs, gripped the railing for balance.

That wasn't normal. He'd never hit her in front of another living soul. Had never really harmed Ariel. Not with his hands.

At the top of the stairs, she touched a finger to her cheek and winced. Her eye had already swollen, her fingers stained with blood.

What lie could she come up with this time?

Mazie took her daughter's clammy hand and led her to the bathroom. Her fingers trembled in Mazie's grip.

She squeezed toothpaste onto Ariel's toothbrush and handed it to her, gave her a weak smile and brushed strands of shiny long hair away from her emerald eyes.

Ariel's hand trembled. Half the toothpaste slid off the brush and landed on the counter.

"It's okay, bug. You brush. I'll clean that up."

Ariel nodded and stuck the brush in her mouth, making feeble attempts to clean her teeth. She spat into the sink and rinsed her brush, then wrapped her arms around Mazie and hugged her hard.

A pang shot through her bruised belly. She kissed the side of Ariel's head. "Come on, let's get you into bed."

When Ariel had changed into pyjamas, Mazie fluffed her pillow and pulled back the covers. Ariel climbed in, not the usual run and jump and bounce. Just dragging feet and quashed spirit. It was all so damn familiar, like looking through a window into her past, witnessing those first signs of giving in. Giving up. Acknowledging that this was what her life was going to be. And that she had no power to fix it.

Mazie pulled the covers up to her daughter's chest and chose a book from the shelf. "Clementine?"

Ariel allowed a shy grin to cross her face but quickly wiped it away.

They hadn't read the Clementine books in over a year. They used to read them every night, the pages so worn they almost fell from the binding. But the adventures of a plucky red headed third grader didn't cut it anymore. That night they found comfort between the covers of a well-loved story. A reminder of a time before Ariel bore witness to the grown-up realities that happened in her home every day.

Halfway through the book, Ariel sighed. Mazie could see her daughter peering up at her at the end of every page.

"Why did Daddy do that?"

Mazie closed the book and put her arm around Ariel's shoulder. "I don't know. He has trouble dealing with anger sometimes, so he lashes out. But usually only at me." She squeezed Ariel's shoulder. "I'm so sorry he hurt you." She set the book on the nightstand and feathered her fingers over the handprint on Ariel's arm that had blossomed with purple tendrils where her husband's thick fingers had crushed the flesh of his own child.

"You always have bruises everywhere. He does that, right?"

Tears sprung to Mazie's eyes. "You've seen them?"

Ariel nodded.

"Well, you know what a klutz I am." She took Ariel's hand, stared at their entwined fingers.

"You're not a klutz. I know you wear long pants and sweaters to cover it up. I'm not stupid, you know."

"I never said you were," Mazie whispered. She wiped her cheek dry.

Ariel laid her head on Mazie's shoulder. "I'm sorry, Mom," she whispered. "I'll be good from now on."

"This was not your fault, you understand?" Mazie sat up and cupped Ariel's chin in her hand. "It's my fault. You just be you. But maybe in front of Daddy, no sass, okay?"

Ariel nodded, her chin quivered. Mazie gathered her in her arms and lay with her, rocking her and singing an old tune she used to sing to her every night.

Playmate, come out and play with me/And bring your dollies three/Climb up my apple tree...

When Ariel fell asleep in her arms, Mazie slid out of the bed, turned off the light and clicked the door shut.

She tiptoed down the stairs and peered around the corner. Cullen was passed out in his chair. His loud, drunken snores punctuated the silence. She sneaked back upstairs, retrieved the camera, snapped duplicate photos of the new damage and dated them. In her bedroom closet, she dislodged a cardboard box that was taped to the inside wall where Cullen would only see it if he cleaned out the closet, stood inside, and closed the folding door. Safe bet he'd never clean anything. That was her job, after all.

She took the photos from that night, and the ones she'd taken last time he choked her, and added them to the pile she'd been accumulating the past two years. She made identical notes in two journals. Date. Damage done. Escalation to the abuse of Ariel.

Ariel.

Mazie tiptoed into her daughter's room, drew the blanket down and pointed the camera at the hand print on Ariel's arm. She hesitated, her finger on the trigger. No. No pictures of Ariel.

Mazie covered Ariel back up, crept back to the closet, tucked the photos and journals into the box and reapplied the tape.

~~~~~~~~

Mazie polished left to right, a habit from her childhood when her mother insisted there was a process, a specific order that must be maintained. Start in the corner of the room and work left to right so there was no cross-contamination of dust and finger prints. Mirrors gleamed when polished counter-clockwise with a soft cloth. Clockwise left streaks on the glass.

Mother was nuts.

Yet here was Mazie, more than twenty years later, following those same rituals. They'd served her well for life with Cullen. A life where he was the only thing allowed to be less than perfect.

She picked up the first framed photo on the mantle, one of many that bore witness to their shared lives. To the unaware, they appeared normal. Happy, even. And they were. Once.

She ran her dust cloth over a candid Polaroid of the two of them on vacation, walking on the boardwalk in Atlantic City just a few
~~~~~~~~

months after they'd started dating. Some random guy had snapped their photo and then stepped in front of them.

"Hey, mister. Carry this moment with your beautiful lady forever." He waved the tiny photo in the air until it developed, then handed it to Cullen.

Cullen leaned his head next to hers and shared the photo with her. They strolled arm-in-arm, her head on his shoulder, her long hair blowing in the breeze. He was so handsome — emerald eyes, dark hair that normally hung free below his shoulder blades was pulled back into a ponytail. His guitar, that ever-present giver of music and joy, was slung over his shoulder. His other hand gripped the black guitar strap that she'd bought him, tiny, bright beads of yellow, red, and blue embroidered along its length. Cullen's broad smile lit up his face.

He had laughed with such ease.

"Look at you, baby. You're gorgeous." He turned to the man. "How much?"

"A mere twenty dollars."

Mazie rolled her eyes. "Twenty bucks? That's ridiculous."

Cullen dug his wallet out of his pocket and paid the man. "Totally worth it. I want to remember this day forever." He kissed her right there in front of total strangers, then tucked the photo into his breast pocket.

Later that evening, after a beautiful dinner in a fancy restaurant he couldn't afford, they shared a bottle of cheap wine under the boardwalk. He played his guitar and sang to her. And he proposed. She gifted him with an enthusiastic yes, and even more enthusiastic lovemaking in the sand, the sounds of their passion drowned out by carnival music and the hollow footfalls on the boardwalk overhead.

A dull thud echoed in the front entry. Her visit to a happier time was cut short by the daily sound of the morning newspaper hitting the front door. She peered at the clock on the kitchen wall. The paper boy was way late. Three damn hours late. The missing paper that morning had been her fault. Everything was her fault.

Mazie placed the polished frame back on the mantle. Her reflection in the glass stared back at her, the difference between now and then was jarring. Long hair was the only consistency, but now it was flecked with too much grey hair for a woman of thirty-seven. Lines on her face bore witness to life's stresses, to the change in Cullen's feelings for her over the years. The black eye spoke of his hatred.

~~~~~~~~

Cullen stormed in through the back door as Mazie placed his dinner on the table.

"Ariel," he screamed from the back landing.

Mazie cringed. "She's upstairs doing her homework."

"Ariel, get your ass down here." His face was crimson, that tell-tale vein over his left temple pulsed in time with his heavy breath.

Mazie set her jaw, her shoulders tense, and braced for the coming storm. "What's wrong?"

"She left her goddamn bike in the driveway, that's what. Ran over the fucking thing. If she's lucky, there won't be a hole in my tire."

Ariel ran down the stairs and slid on sock-covered feet across the polished kitchen floor, her hands out like a surfer vying for balance in the curl of a twenty-foot wave. When she stopped, she turned her smiling face on her father, a trick that used to melt his heart and garner her anything she wanted. "What, Daddy?"

Cullen reached out and laid his paw on her shoulder. He shoved her toward the back door. "See that?"
~~~~~~~~

"My bike! Why'd you break it?"

"You left it there. You made me run over it."

She looked up at him, tears in her eyes. "I forgot. I — I'm sorry." She began to cry. "Can you fix it?"

"Fix it?" He turned his glare from Ariel to Mazie. "You hear that? She's as stupid as her mother."

"She is not stupid!" Ariel pushed against his chest and wrested free of his grip. She ran for the stairs.

He caught up with her, spun her around and lifted one hand.

"No!" Mazie screamed and ran across the room. She stepped between Ariel and her husband, inched backwards until Ariel found the stairs and raced up to her room.

Her heart in her throat, Mazie found her voice. "Cullen, what the hell is wrong with you?"

He dropped his hand, squinted, and stared at her. "I beg your pardon?"

Mazie glanced at her feet, swallowed, then raised her head to meet his gaze. "You were going to hit her. She didn't do it on purpose." She planted her feet, prepared for the blows to come.

He turned away and ran his hand over his face. "You want to know what's wrong?" His voice was deadpan, barely audible. Not normal. "Another round of layoffs today."

A pang of fear sliced through her chest. "Did you lose your job?"

"Not yet." He turned back to face her, his eyebrows pinched together, his jaw clenched. "But it's just a matter of time."

Mazie nodded. "Okay, but you haven't yet. And even if you had, how is that Ariel's fault?"

Cullen's eyes clouded over and his stare bore into her. "What did you say to me?"

Mazie grasped the railing. She scanned the room for an escape, but he blocked her path. The only way was upstairs, and all that waited there was certain pain. She swallowed hard and dropped her gaze to her feet. "I just don't understand why you're taking it out on her. She's not to blame."

"You're right."

Shit. She glanced up.

He bowed his head and looked at her from under heavy lids, his eyes ablaze, like a wolf about to pounce on its prey. "You're both to blame." He took a step forward. "If you hadn't got knocked up with her I'd never had to do this shit work. I'd be writing music, performing. Maybe touring. Maybe I'd be on the road. Maybe I'd be just a tiny bit happy." He held the thumb and index finger of his right hand a half-inch apart and took another step forward. "Maybe I'd feel a little proud of myself. But you know what I feel instead? Disgusted." Tears dripped from his eyes. "I can barely look in the mirror. This was not supposed to be my life, you know that? My back hurts. And look at my fucking hands!" He held them both up and shoved them toward her face.

Mazie flinched and stepped onto the first stair. She was very familiar with his hands. How they looked. How they smelled. The sharp sting of their slap and pain of their punch. Like sandpaper when they encircled her throat and tried to choke the life from her.

"I used to make music with these hands. Now my fingers are nothing but thick stumps. They're stiff and sore. I bet I can't even strum a damn guitar." He turned and shuffled to his chair, sank into it, put his face in his hands, and wept.

Mazie stared at him. She glanced up the staircase to the landing above, turned and eyed the front door. Was there time to grab Ariel and get out? Was this her moment to escape?

But her feet were bolted to the floor. And she'd she never make it to the threshold before he caught up with her.

After minutes of his anguish filling the otherwise still room, she let go of the railing and inched toward him. She kneeled by his chair and placed one hand on his knee, ran her other hand through his hair. "Cullen," she whispered.

He lowered his hands, wiped his nose on his sleeve and looked into her face with red-rimmed eyes.

They shared a momentary connection. A silent understanding.

Neither of their lives had turned out as they had planned.

He wrapped his arms around her and sobbed.

Mazie froze. Anticipation churned in her stomach and she braced herself.

But he just cried and held on, buried his face in her hair. "I'm so sorry, Mazie Baby. I'm so sorry."

His breath was hot on her neck. She shut her eyes and swallowed. A shiver ran through her and goose bumps chilled her skin. She fought the urge to push him away. With a trembling hand, she stroked the back of his head. "I know you are."

~~~~~~~~~

Cullen's snores punctuated the two-in-the-morning silence. Mazie ran her palms down her restless legs. He hated it when she twitched and turned. Hated to be bothered in his sleep, awakened before he was ready. But she could find no peace. She inched out of bed, put on her robe, and tiptoed down the stairs.

She poured herself a rare drink of brandy and warmed it in the microwave. Alcohol loosened her tongue. Heightened her bravado — and her risk. Sober was the way to go, the only way to be sure she kept her wits about her. But with him dead to the waking world, she let her guard down, just for a moment. The warm liquor calmed her shaken nerves.
~~~~~~~~~

In the dark of the living room, stillness engulfed her. She closed her eyes against her life, but behind her eyelids she couldn't prevent memories of how she ended up here from invading her respite.

Cullen had thrown the back door open with such force that the doorstop snapped off and skittered across the floor. There was a hole in the drywall where the doorknob slammed into it. They'd celebrated their first anniversary the week before.

He was late for dinner and she'd watched for his arrival. Before he spoke, she snapped at him. "Damn it, Cullen! That's the second hole in the wall this month." Two weeks before, he'd been upset over a cancelled gig and punched the bedroom wall. An indent in the shape of his fist remained there for weeks before he spackled and painted over it.

He glared at her and tossed his guitar case onto the landing. "It's just drywall, for Christ's sake." He let out a heavy exhale, ran one hand over his head and along the length of the ponytail that hung close to his waistline.

"It still has to be fixed."

He held his palm toward her face. "Just don't. Not today."

She had learned when to stop talking. He was upset about something that had nothing to do with home. Nothing to do with her.

He pried his shoes off with the toes of the opposite feet and kicked them toward the rubber mat against the wall. They landed askew on the linoleum. He brushed past her and grabbed a beer from the fridge, popped the top and drank most of it in three long gulps. He stood with his back to the counter, one hand gripped the edge.

"Well, are you going to tell me what's going on?"

He wiped his mouth with the sleeve of his denim jacket. "You know that agent," he made air quotes, "that was going to shop my demo around?"

Mazie nodded. "The one you paid the three grand to for studio time and expenses?"

"Yeah, that guy." His lips pressed into a thin line. He looked at her, his eyes heavy-lidded. "He won't return my calls. There won't be any studio time." He shook his head. "Guy's a goddamn shyster."

"How do you know?"

"Because I called the studio. It's a scam. He's not a real agent." He rubbed his forehead with the arm of the hand that held the beer. "Three fucking thousand dollars. That's five shows, not counting costs. And to top it all off, another gig got cancelled. They got a better act." More air quotes. He pulled out a chair and slumped into it, leaned his arms on the table and rested his head on his arms. "I think it's time to give up. Time to get a straight job."

Mazie sat next to him and rubbed his shoulders with one palm. "Don't say that. Cullen, I can get a second job. You're too talented to give up yet."

He sat up, his face red, jaw clenched. "Yet? You already planning for me to fuck this up permanently?"

Her brows furrowed. "That's not what I meant."

"You don't think I can take care of my own wife? You have to take care of me, support me? What am I, a child?" He stood and paced the kitchen. "What kind of man do you think I am? You think I'm a gigolo or something?"

"No, Cullen." She jumped up from her seat and tried to put her arms around him. "I love you. You'll make it, it's just a matter of time. I'll do anything to help you see it through."

He pushed her away and she staggered against the table. She regained her footing just as the back of his hand slammed into her face.

She covered her cheek with one palm and stared at him, her mouth agape.

His face contorted and tears sprung from his eyes. "Oh, God. Oh, God." He reached out for her and engulfed her with both arms. "Mazie Baby. I am so sorry. You know I didn't mean it, right?"

She pulled away and nodded. "I know."

He slumped to the floor and pressed the heels of his hands to his eyes. His entire body trembled. "You're all I have, Mazie. You're everything that is right in my life." He rested his head against the cupboard door and looked up at her. "I am so, so, sorry. You believe me, don't you?"

He was so vulnerable, so broken. With his parents long dead and no brothers or sisters, he was completely alone. Except for her.

Her heart melted at the sight of his red and swollen eyes. She dropped to her knees and slid up to him, placed her hands on either side of his face. "It's okay. I believe you." She kissed him and brushed aside an errant strand of hair that had come free from the elastic shackle.

"I'd be lost without you, Mazie." He wiped snot from his nose with the back of his hand. "If you got another job, that would be okay. Just for a few months. I just know something is going to come along."

She smiled. "Me too."

~~~~~~~~

Mazie stuck Ariel's report card to the fridge with the heart-shaped magnet her daughter had made out of clay four years before. She ran her fingers over the page. Grade seven, and all of Ariel's marks were excellent, nothing under eighty percent. Except math. Damn math.

She called up the stairs. "Ariel, dinner will be ready as soon as your father comes home."
~~~~~~~~

No answer.

Mazie leaned against the wall, one hand on the railing, and stared up the stairwell. "Are you doing math homework?"

Footsteps shuffled overhead. "Yes," came the tentative reply.

Mazie smiled. Like mother, like daughter. Some book had caught Ariel's imagination and taken over her every waking moment. For Mazie it was Goosebumps. Her mother had hated that she'd loved those books.

The truck engine reverberated against the house and rattled the window of the back door. She never understood why he had to have it so souped up, like a teenage boy. It wasn't like he needed to compensate for anything. Wasn't that the saying? Big engine, small penis? Maybe in his case it was big engine, small heart.

"He's home, Ariel. Come now, please."

Mazie pulled the macaroni and cheese casserole from the oven and placed it on a trivet in the middle of the table. Ketchup between Cullen and Ariel, hot garlic bread still in the foil, steaming and savoury, to the left of the casserole, and bowls of salad, already dressed, beside each place setting.

He walked in the back door, slid off his shoes and placed them on the mat, the heels lined up against the wall. He took the short steps two at a time, and met her at the fridge door where she'd just pulled out a cold beer. He was smiling. A big, genuine-looking smile, and his eyes glinted with joy.

He kissed her cheek. "Happy Friday, darling."

She smiled at him. It was hard not to when he looked like the old Cullen. Like the man she fell in love with. "You're in a good mood."

He took the beer from her and rummaged through the drawer for the opener. He popped the top and raised the bottle. "Last day of layoffs and I'm still standing." He grinned and took a long pull on the beer.

"That's wonderful."

"Damn straight it is." He tucked two fingers in his front pocket, pulled out a fifty dollar bill, and held it up in front of her. "Maybe take Ariel to a movie or something." He looked her up and down. "Or maybe a manicure, just for you." He took one of her hands and inspected her fingernails. "You've got to take better care of yourself. I might start wandering or something."

She swallowed and glanced at her feet.

He lifted her chin with the fingers holding the cash and winked. "I'm just shittin' ya. Go on, take it. Do something nice for yourself."

She reached to pluck the bill from his fingers.

He whipped it away with a flick of his wrist.

She started at the sudden movement.

He laughed. "Jeez Louise, take a chill pill."

She flinched at the sound of her middle name. Jeez Louise. Mazie Baby. At least he amused himself.

He pulled her toward him and hugged her hips to his, then tucked the bill into her back pocket. He whispered in her ear, "You can make it up to me later."

Ariel ran down the stairs. She hesitated at the threshold to the kitchen. "Hi, Daddy."

"Hey, pumpkin." He held out one arm.

She glanced at Mazie.

"Well, come on. Give your dad a hug."

She inched toward him and put her arms around his waist, a slight grimace on her face.

He squeezed her to him and smiled. "You hungry?"

"Yes."

"Well all right then," he clapped his hands, "let's eat."

They sat at the table in their normal seats. But unlike any normal day, the tension in Mazie's shoulders had infected Ariel. And for once, Cullen was immune.

She sat straight in her chair. Her gaze shifted from her daughter's uncertain smile, landed imperceptibly on her husband's genuine grin, it's presence on his face almost as disturbing as the scowl that normally lived there, then followed a familiar path to her plate, the tabletop, a scan for dirt on the floor, to the napkin in her lap and back to Ariel.

Her daughter's eyes were electric, her movements animated. She was trying too hard. Or was lulled into believing that the glimpse of his monster personality was just a blip, and she was relieved he'd returned to some sense of normal.

When Ariel told of her day at school, about how the teacher had read her story in front of the whole class as an example of the right way to write a story, Cullen interjected with a few 'atta girls' and something about always being better than everyone else.

When Cullen finished eating, Mazie cleared the plates and took a tub of ice cream from the freezer.

"Isn't it report card day?" Cullen finished off his beer, reached behind, and retrieved another from the fridge.

"It's on the fridge." Ariel pointed.

Mazie took a deep breath. Please ignore the math mark. Focus on the rest of it, the higher grades, the teacher's comments about what a wonderful student Ariel was, the effort she put into trying to get math right.

"Well, go on pumpkin, bring it here. What was our deal?"

"Ten dollars if I got all eighties and better."

"Right. So how'd you do?"

Ariel glanced at her mother before sliding the paper out from under the magnet. She hesitated and sighed. Her eyes shimmered with the threat of tears.

Mazie placed a bowl of ice cream in front of Cullen, another for Ariel was cool in her hand. She rubbed her daughter's shoulder. "It's all right, bug. It's a great report card."

Cullen looked up at Mazie, one eyebrow arched.

Ariel handed the paper to her father.

He scanned the page, nodded with his lips pursed and eyebrows raised in appreciation. Then his face shifted and clouded. He didn't move, but his eyes turned on his daughter. "Sixty-two in math?" He didn't raise his voice, but there was no atta girl in his tone.

"I tried, Daddy, honest I did. I just don't get it."

Mazie tapped the paper with one finger and pointed to the teacher's comment. "Look, he says she puts in the work, does all the assignments. She tries her best, but she just doesn't have a math mind." She mussed her daughter's hair. "Must have inherited that from me." She smiled at Ariel.

Her daughter's face calmed and she smiled back.

"Bullshit." He threw the report card on the table. "She's as lazy as you are, that's what she inherited. She has to try harder."

Mazie stared at the report card and swallowed. "We could get her a tutor."

He crossed his arms and stared at her. "A tutor? You think that's what I do in the bathroom every morning, shit out money?"

"Well, then maybe you could help her. You were good at math." Mazie placed Ariel's ice cream on the table.

He backhanded the bowl and sent it flying off the table. It hit the fridge and bounced onto the tile. Ice cream flew everywhere, but the bowl didn't break. Small mercies.

"She needs to get her sorry ass up to her room and study. And no ice cream."

Mazie pressed her lips together. Stand your ground and don't cry. Not this time. She rubbed her hands down the front of her pants in a vain effort to make them stop trembling. "Maybe she'll be a writer, or a journalist. Not everyone can be good at math." She stuck her chin up and looked into the eye of the storm. "And even if she were, she might not use it later." She stood straighter. "You never used it, so what does it matter?"

He raised that one eyebrow, the omen brow, the precursor to all things painful. His hands flat on the table, he inched his chair back and stood. He crossed his arms and walked to the sink, stared out the front window, his shoulders near his ears. He was either trying to keep his shit together, or about to fling it at the fan. "Ariel," he said, his voice low, his back to them. "Go upstairs."

Ariel slipped her hand into Mazie's and tucked her body against her mother. "Mom, come with me. Help me with my homework. Please?" She never took her eyes off her father's back.

"Your mother has to clean up that mess she made. Go, Ariel." He looked at her over his shoulder. "Now."

Mazie pulled her hand away from Ariel's grip and kissed the side of her head.

"Go, bug. Do as Daddy says, remember?"

"But, Mom…"

"No buts!" Cullen smacked the edge of the counter with both palms and spun around.

Ariel backed away. "Okay. I'm going." She glanced at her mother, turned, and took the stairs two at a time.

Mazie stared at the floor, at the ice cream that dotted her jeans, at her big toe that stood in a sticky puddle.

"Tell me again." His shadow neared her feet. "Tell me how I never use math."

"I was just pointing out —"

"What? What were you pointing out?" He stood inches from her, but her gaze never left the floor. "That I'm a failure? That rig pigs and garbage men don't need no stinking math?"

She swallowed. "You haven't worked the rigs for years."

"Yeah, that was my point. Fuck."

"Ariel wants to be a writer. Or a dancer. Does it matter if she gets good grades in math?"

He shook his head and rolled his eyes. "She needs to be more practical. There's no money in dancing. Unless you want her hanging naked from a pole."

"So we don't encourage her to follow her dreams?"

He threw her a withering look. "Dreams die. They suck the life out of you until you're a fucking zombie. You want that for her?"

She winced.

"If I hadn't married someone so stupid, maybe I could have lived out my dream, huh? Not be schlepping other people's trash day in and day out."

She mustered enough courage to look him in the eye. "You have to stop blaming me for your life."

His fist swished through the air and connected with her temple. A flash of light illuminated his face before everything went dark.

~~~~~~~~

Mazie sat in the dim bar, her eyes riveted to the stage. She took a long inhale, intoxicated by the haze of cigarette smoke that wafted around her, the pinch of it at the back of her throat, the darkness interrupted by a single white spotlight aimed at the singer.

It was the first time she'd seen him and she was hooked in an instant. He sat on a stool, another stool beside him. A lit cigarette rested in an ashtray, a wisp of smoke curled into the air, past the beam of the spotlight, and disappeared into the blackness of the rafters overhead. He sipped from a tumbler between songs. Not
~~~~~~~~

water. No, he wet his lips and tongue and throat, kept those sultry vocal chords supple, with amber liquor. Whiskey perhaps.

That first Friday night she sat in the periphery, just outside the circle of stage light that he shared with a few chosen admirers. She admired from afar. But not too far. Close enough that the whisper of his guitar strap across the shoulder of his black leather jacket caressed her ears, the clink of ice cubes in the tumbler punctuated the din of the bar. His audible inhales of cigarette smoke made her long to light one up. Even though she'd never put one to her lips before.

He strummed the guitar, stared at his hands, watched his own fingers stroke its neck and pluck at each string. His chocolate hair hung in front of his face like a stage curtain about to go up. He built anticipation in her like a skilled lover brings his partner to the edge of orgasm. She held her breath until the climax, until he began to sing.

The first lyrics filled the room and he looked into the faces of those who sat close by. His style was an odd but intriguing mix of soul and blues with a touch of country twang. No covers, all original songs he'd told his anticipating audience.

His voice pierced her heart. She couldn't take her eyes from his, though his were looking anywhere but at her. Under the cover of the dark room she felt like a stalker, watching his every move, lost in the deep emerald of his eyes that glowed with golden fire when the spotlight hit him just so. His olive skin was luminescent, sweat beaded on his forehead.

He removed his jacket and laid it on the stage. He lifted the guitar strap back over his shoulder. The muscles in his arm rippled and took her breath from her. When the set was finished, he leaned into the microphone and thanked the audience, reminded them to stick around for the main event, and hoped they enjoyed their night.

He gathered his jacket and stood to his full height. She immersed herself in his black T-shirt, the sleeves bisecting his pronounced biceps, admired the cut of his Levis and the black boots with three-inch heels.

He held his cigarette between his lips, squinted to keep the smoke out of one eye, snatched his drink, and walked off stage, his back to her.

Her heart beat heavy in her chest.

"Mazie?" A hand tapped her thigh.

She shook herself from the trance this man held her in and looked at her date for the evening. Allan. Nice young man. Cute, if not a bit too skinny. Accountant in the making. Terribly polite and chivalrous. Boring as hell.

"He was pretty good, I guess. Can't wait for the main act, though. They're really going places."

When the date ended, Allan took her home. She didn't invite him in. Turned one cheek to him when he leaned in for a kiss. Said she'd call him. But she never would.

The next night, she returned to the same bar. She sat alone at a table just inside the glow of the stage lights, off to the right, directly in his line of vision. She wore her lowest-cut top, her impressive cleavage impossible to miss. Her short skirt and highest black patent stilettos accentuated her legs. And she wore her hair down for a change, parted in the middle. Her raven locks draped over her shoulders and hung almost to her waist. Only a bit longer than his.

What a striking pair they would make.

A man stepped on stage and took the microphone in hand. "Good evening, folks. Please give it up for our opening act, Mr. Cullen Reynolds."

Scattered applause popped pitifully around her, but Mazie clapped with enthusiasm. The crowd was thinner, the audience preoccupied with each other, their cell phones, the silent hockey game on televisions that dotted the bar.

Cullen stepped onto the stage, put his drink and cigarette down in their rightful place, and sat on the stool. He reached his guitar strap over his head and adjusted the microphone.

Mazie leaned forward, her elbows on the table, and ran one finger around the rim of her glass. The clatter of dishes and murmur of voices disappeared and the bar went silent in her ears except for the clink of ice cubes in Cullen's drink.

He strummed his guitar, his hair hanging in his eyes. A replica of the night before. When he lifted his head and sang the first words, his eyes met hers. He hesitated, missed the second line. "Fuck," he said under his breath. He let out a small laugh and tapped his fingers against the guitar strings to stop the music. "Sorry, folks. Got a bit distracted there." He said it to the room, but stared at her. He smiled, winked, dropped his head, and started again.

This time he didn't miss any words — but he watched her like she was the only one in the audience and he was singing just for her. About her. About them.

Near the end of his set, he shot the rest of his drink and repositioned the microphone. "Going to try something different tonight. Something I've been toying with. Bear with me, folks."

He launched into an acoustic, bluesy version of Rush's *In the Mood*. Instead of the rocking, up-tempo song she'd grown up with, it was slow, sensual. And aimed directly at her.

When he sang that he wanted to rock and roll her until the night was gone, he flashed his eyebrows up and down at her.

Heat rose in her cheeks and flooded her belly. She crossed her legs and wiped a bead of sweat from her upper lip.

At the end of the set, he came straight over and asked if he could join her. They made small talk, learned each other's names. He was from out west, doing a cross-country tour of small bars and pubs, anywhere that would let him play. North Bay was just one stop on a long list. Toronto and Montreal were next. He had demo CDs in the hopes that agents or music industry professionals would hear him and be interested, but hadn't had a bite yet.

She got stoned off his cologne, the fire in his eyes, off his dreams and dogged determination. She could barely look away. But she had to pee.

She excused herself, turned back to catch a glimpse of him. He watched her, their eyes met. From across the bar, the arch of his one eyebrow was as obvious as his satisfied smile.

When she came out of the bathroom he was right outside the door. He took her hand and led her to the end of the hall, leaned her against the wall and brushed her hair back from her face, his finger trailing across her neck and shoulder and down her arm.

Her heart nearly jumped from her chest. Heat seared between her legs and sliced through her abdomen. She licked her lips and leaned in. Their kisses were furious and passionate and wet. The taste of his cigarettes and bourbon, yes, bourbon for sure, heightened her arousal. He was a complete departure from her usual, steady, predictable, clean-cut guy. She barely drank and she hated cigarettes. But he pushed every button she had, and a few she didn't know existed.

He ran his hands behind her and pulled her hips to his, guided her along the wall, through a door, and into a supply closet. In the darkness of that tiny room, the air thick with dust and bleach and spilled beer, he hoisted her skirt, slid off her thong, and fucked her silly. His lips moved from her neck to her cleavage and back to her mouth where he buried her in kisses, his whiskers leaving a scratchy trail of goose bumps in their wake.

After he climaxed, he zipped his pants while she pulled up her underwear and shifted her skirt down.

"Wow." He ran one finger between her breasts. "Can I see you again?”

A pen on a string dangled from a clipboard hanging next to the door. She wrote her phone number on his palm and dotted the 'i' in her name with a heart.

He smoothed her hair, placed one finger under her chin and kissed her with a simple tenderness that would stick with her for years to come. Then they made their way back to the table so he could gather his guitar and 'work the room.'

"Gotta say, I fucking hate that part, but you've got to do it if you want people to remember you. Maybe to buy a CD." He signed the jewel case of one with a sharpie, handed it to her, and kissed her cheek. "Thanks. It was really great to meet you," he whispered in her ear. Then he turned and walked away.

She arrived home sated but aroused, loopy with his sex and his smell. The next morning she was nothing but embarrassed. She didn't know where he was staying. Had no idea how long he'd be in town. She was probably just one of a string of back-room trysts. And she hadn't even been careful about it, didn't use a condom.

When her period arrived a week later, the relief was overwhelming. She felt like a fool calling bars in town to see if he was playing. But he was gone. And she was an idiot.

~~~~~~~~

Strange voices called out. A cacophony of clicking and beeping and honking and wailing assaulted Mazie's ears, each noise like another punch to her head. Her hand found a metal bar running alongside her body. She blinked against the bright lights, focussed on a thin clear tube hanging above and followed it to a needle stuck in her arm. She lifted her head. Stars exploded behind her eyes. "Shit."

"Mommy?"
~~~~~~~~

Her eyes sprung open. "Ariel?" She pulled herself up, but a firm hand on her shoulder kept her down.

"Try to relax, Mrs. Reynolds."

She looked up into the face of a young man, a stethoscope dangling from his neck. The room swayed and jerked. No. Not a room. She was in an ambulance.

"Ariel?" Mazie twisted her head until she found her daughter sitting across from her, eyes swollen and nose red. Dread filled her. "Where's your father?"

"Ma'am," the baby-faced EMT patted her arm. "He's being kept in holding. Domestic violence."

"Oh no. No, no, no."

"Ma'am?"

"How?"

"Your daughter, ma'am. She called nine-one-one."

"Ariel, why?"

Ariel started to cry. "I thought he was going to kill you."

Mazie closed her eyes. "Damn," she said under her breath. "I want to talk to the police."

"They're meeting us at the hospital. They'll take your statement there."

She looked over to Ariel and held her hand out.

Ariel took her hand. "I'm sorry, Mommy."

"No, don't be sorry. It's not your fault. Nothing is your fault. We'll go home and have a bath. Maybe you can sleep with me tonight."

"What about Daddy?"

"I won't press charges."

"You don't have a choice in that, Mrs. Reynolds." The EMT pressed a finger to her side.

She cried out against the pain that shot through her torso,

gasped and turned to glare at him.

"Charges are automatic, he's already being processed. He broke a couple of ribs. I thought your eye socket was broken too, but it looks like it's just swollen. We'll get it X-rayed to be sure. You're lucky it wasn't worse."

She squinted. A stab of pain shot through her eye. "Do I look lucky to you?"

"Sorry, ma'am. That's not what I meant."

~~~~~~~~~

Cullen's shadow filled the window of the back door. Mazie's feet were frozen to the floor. He'd been released on his own recognizance, pending a court date six weeks out. And here he was, the day after getting out of jail, standing on their back porch.

At least he knocked.

She unlocked the deadbolt and inched the door open. "You're not supposed to be here."

His eyes were red-rimmed, his hands tucked firmly in the front pockets of his jeans. "I know. I just had to see you. See Ariel."

"If they catch you, you'll go back to jail. Is that what you want?"

His eyes darkened. "Are you going to call the cops on me?"

She averted her gaze. "Cullen, what do you want me to do? They gave you conditions. You can't just ignore them."

"I know that." He closed his eyes and took a deep breath. "Can I come in? Please?"

Every instinct told her to slam the door, dial nine-one-one. But her training won out and she stepped aside.

He slipped off his shoes and lined them up neatly against the wall, strolled into the kitchen and stood at the sink, staring out into the front yard.
~~~~~~~~~

She stood still, clasped her hands together and rested them on her belly. They made a knot, like a human heart. She squeezed them together in time with her staccato heartbeat. One. Two. Threefourfive.

"Do you want coffee?" Her voice cracked and her hands shook.

He huffed. "No." He glanced back at her. "Thanks," he whispered. "Where's Ariel?"

"She's spending the weekend with Polly."

He nodded.

Mazie cleared her throat. "She's afraid that you're angry with her."

He turned, his eyes misty. "Afraid?" He wiped a tear from his cheek.

For minutes, absolute silence screamed in her ears. The standoff ended when he pushed off against the counter. The sudden movement made her jump, sending a jolt of pain through her ribs.

"I just wanted to say that I'm sorry. I really am." He touched her arm.

She flinched.

"I'll go now."

He sat on the step and tied his laces.

"Where are you staying?"

"A guy I work with. Sleeping on the couch." He looked over his shoulder. "They almost fired me, did you know that?" The edge in his voice sliced the air. He stood. "But that's not your fault. I know that." He put his hand on the knob. "I do love you, you know that, right?"

She said nothing, stared at her feet.

He turned and left without another word. Left the door ajar.

She pushed it closed and pulled the drape aside. His truck rumbled away. Rachel's face popped over the fence, then ducked out of sight when she caught Mazie's eye. Maybe she'd get the bat out of the shed and play neighbour Whac-A-Mole.

~~~~~~~~

Mazie caught her reflection in the mirror. The bruise around her swollen eye extended over her brow and down her cheek. She pulled her shirt up and followed the purple contusions that spread from the confines of the tape around her ribs and snaked up her back toward her shoulder blade and down to her hip. She peeled off the bandage, winced at the sharp pull of sticky tape from her tender skin, and crawled with trepidation into a steaming bath.

With dinner in the oven, she poured a coffee and sat at the table. Half an hour passed with no sound except the ticking clock. The band of her silver ring with the tumbled garnet cut into her right ring finger. She twisted it, stared at the stone. It meant new beginnings, he'd told her. A gift shortly after Ariel was born. During the best year of their marriage. Before he devolved into a now-familiar cycle of anger, resentment, violence, justification, and repentance. That last part of the cycle showed up rarely these past couple of years. Justification became the norm. It was her fault, Ariel's fault, his boss's fault that he hit her. If that guy hadn't cut him off on the freeway and nearly caused an accident, he wouldn't be so upset. When she was stupid, it added to his stress. She made him snap. All her fault.

That ring had been a life raft and her marriage was a sinking ship. Over the years, the shining crimson stone looked less like hope, and more like a tiny pool of her own blood, frozen in time.

A key scratched in the front door lock. Her heart leapt into her throat and she held her breath.

"Mom?"
~~~~~~~~

Mazie exhaled and gripped her mug of cold coffee with both hands. "In the kitchen, bug."

That evening, Ariel cleared the dinner dishes while Mazie put leftovers in the fridge. They chatted about school, about Polly, about anything except the hard realities of the past week, the evidence of it written all over Mazie's bruised and cut face.

Mazie listened to Ariel make light of her day, her forced cheerfulness a poor imitation of a normal young girl. The false breeziness of the evening was cut short by a knock at the back door.

There he was again, ignoring police orders. Showing up unannounced. Uninvited.

"Mom, it's Daddy." Ariel stepped behind Mazie. "What do we do?"

"I'm not sure."

"Should I call the police?"

"Not this time. It would only make him angry."

She opened the door. "Why are you here?"

"I brought some things for you and Ariel." He looked over Mazie's head into the kitchen. "Hi, pumpkin. Daddy brought you something."

Ariel froze in place, glanced at her mother then averted her eyes and stared at her feet.

A guilty ache jabbed Mazie's heart. Ariel was mirroring her own actions, had probably seen Mazie in that same stance so many times. It was her coping mechanism. But she had no idea that Ariel was watching. Maybe it was ingrained in all women, that apologetic, guilty response. Even though they'd done nothing to deserve it. Hell, maybe it was genetic.

He arranged his shoes in their proper place, slipped his socked feet up the steps and dropped a grocery bag on the counter. The familiar clink of glass told her it was either beer or bourbon. Or both.

Couldn't he go one night without drinking? She had blamed much of the early abuse on the alcohol. It changed his personality, made him angry. Poisoned his spirit. But as the years wore on, he didn't need booze to be abusive. Or maybe the alcohol was never cleansed from his system. He never gave it a chance to be.

He reached into the bag. There was a second of absolute stillness, anticipation for what he would pull out. Like a rapt audience waiting for the magician to pull a rabbit out of a hat, but then, ta-da! It's a dove.

Mazie watched for the neck of the Jack Daniels bottle.

Ta-da! It was a small box. The kind that jewellery comes in.

He turned to Ariel and held it out to her. "Here, pumpkin. For you."

Ariel shot a fleeting look at her mother, then raised her eyes to her father's face but didn't move, didn't lift her head.

"It's okay. Take it." He didn't take a step forward. It was as far as he ever went with conciliation. Hold out the carrot, have the abused make the first move.

Ariel inched around the table and held out her hand. He dropped it into her open palm. She opened it, and a subtle smile crossed her face.

Cullen plucked a delicate chain from the box, a cursive capital A dangling from it. "It's gold. Big girl jewellery." He undid the clasp and placed it around her neck. She pulled her hair out of the way while he did it up.

Ariel held the A in her fingers and ran her thumb over it. She grinned.

He stroked her hair. "Will you take care of it?"

She nodded. "Yes, Daddy." Ariel stepped forward and went to put her arms around his body, but only got her hands to his waist. She touched her head to his chest. Not the usual Ariel bear-hug.

"Thank you," she mumbled.

He hugged her hard and kissed the top of her head. His eyes glistened. But with what? Love? Relief? Or satisfaction that he'd perpetrated the same ruse with his daughter as he had with Mazie time and time again.

Did I hurt you? Here's a piece of jewellery. Won't happen again. Did I do it again? Here's a bunch of flowers. Won't happen again. It was your fault. You made me hit you, made me choke you, made me break your ribs. Will it happen again? Can't make any promises.

It's a lie! A trick! Don't believe it Ariel! Mazie's screams never left her mouth. How could she ruin her daughter's moment? No matter how brief this respite from their normal lives would be?

He reached into the bag again. Flowers. He held them toward her. "I'm sorry. You know I don't mean to do those things." An actual tear ran down his cheek.

She made no move forward, just stared at the flowers. The kind you get at the grocery store checkout. Or from that woman who sells them in front of the liquor store.

He shook the bouquet. "Are you going to take them?" The tear dried up and his eyes had that frustrated glint — the forecast of the storm ahead.

She reached out and snatched the bunch from his hand. "Thanks."

"You should put them in water before they wilt."

No shit.

She pulled a small vase from the top shelf of the cupboard next to the sink. The place she kept consolation prizes from past beatings that gathered dust, but that she hadn't thrown away. Not because of sentiment. Because he would have noticed them missing and flipped out. The ice cream boats for banana splits that he bought when Ariel was just three. An apology for 'accidentally' pushing Mazie down the stairs. Ariel had loved those treats, but the boats hadn't been used in four years. There was the sushi set and the mini-doughnut machine. And the vase. An actual crystal vase. He'd bought her that after the first time he choked her during sex. An experiment in erotic asphyxiation, he'd said. But even he didn't buy that lie. So he rewarded her with a dozen roses in the crystal vase. Red roses. Blood red roses.

She filled the vase with cool water and pulled her sharpest chef's knife from its sheath. The sun caught the stainless steel and flashed a spark of light in her eye. She stared at the blade like she'd done hundreds of time. Imagined it slicing through the delicate skin of her wrists, releasing her from this hell she lived in. But Ariel's face always got in the way. Her baby girl finally grew out of her fear of monsters under the bed only to discover the worst monster slept right down the hall.

Perhaps she should slice his wrists instead. Free them all from the torment that every normal day brought. She squeezed the handle, her fingernails bit into her palm. She lifted her face to the warm setting sun that streamed in the window. She sighed, sliced off the ends of the rose stems with one fluid motion, and slid them into the water. She put the vase on the table, so he could admire his vague and lame apology.

He maintained a watchful eye on her and reached into the bag again. Ta-da! Bourbon. Of course. He couldn't help but get himself a gift. And that was the gift that kept on giving.

He pulled one last thing from the bag. "I got you brandy. You haven't had that in a long time." His smile proved how pleased he was with himself. That his generosity astounded him. That he'd allow her this small bottle of brandy once or twice a year while he went through a two-six of Jack almost weekly. "I thought we could sit and talk. Maybe have a drink."

She took the bottle from him and placed it in the cupboard over the fridge. "Maybe."

"And maybe I could help Ariel with her math homework. How does that sound, pumpkin?"

"If you want to, Daddy."

Cullen sat beside Ariel at the table, her textbook open, pencils sharpened. He kept his shit together, didn't yell when she didn't understand, and found ways to show her how to do it right. She didn't get it all, but he had made a difference.

Mazie picked up the last dish and turned to watch them do homework while she dried it with the damp dish towel. She froze. He'd slid their chairs together, his arm around Ariel's shoulder. He stroked her hair, his cheek resting on the top of her head. Every few seconds he buried his nose in her hair and inhaled.

He glanced up and caught Mazie watching. He straightened his back and scooted his chair away, his gaze shifted from the math book to the floor to his hands. Anywhere but her face.

"It's getting late," she said through grit teeth. "Ariel, say goodnight to your father. He has to go."

"What about our drink?"

She shook her head. "No. Not tonight."

~~~~~~~~~

The subsequent week brought daily texts filled with apologies and declarations of Cullen's undying love for Mazie and Ariel, and one that body-slammed her with guilt.

I'm nothing without you. If I lose you, I'll just kill myself. There'll be noting to live for.

He dropped in to visit, to cut the grass, to offer his handyman services. Something he'd not done for years while actually living
~~~~~~~~~

there.

Inch by inch he wormed his way back home. She ignored the conditions of release, ignored the red flags and her own voice screaming inside her head, *it's a trick, he's a liar, run away*, and let him in.

He remained quiet and polite. Hell, he was downright pleasant. By the end of the second week, she allowed him to sleep on his own couch in his own living room. By the end of the third, they were sharing their bed again. But only the bed. They lay with their backs to each other like normal. But something had changed. Sleep found Mazie more than usual. The edge she clung to grew less sharp as each day without pain or anger passed.

She watched him around Ariel. He kept a polite distance, only touching her for good night hugs and the occasional high-five. Perhaps what she thought was inappropriate was simply a father missing his little girl. She'd overreacted. Over thought. He would never cross that line. But no matter how often she tried to convince herself, that damn gold A dangling from Ariel's neck whispered a different story.

Three Saturdays after being arrested, Cullen ran some errands and arrived home hours later, his arms laden with packages. Another shopping apology, trading stuff for forgiveness. Product for understanding. Material things for love.

He yelled for Ariel to come to the living room. Mazie stood at the sink and dried dishes. The sound of ripping cardboard and crinkling plastic was punctuated by the screech of the television stand being dragged against the hardwood. She cringed. Would he blame her for the damage that little trick would cause?

Ariel's footsteps bounded down the stairs. "What, Daddy?" Her old self had eked back in. She could relax in her home, not spend her energy anticipating the next time her father would hurt her, yell at her, or punch her mother.

Ariel's scream pierced the air. Adrenaline coursed through Mazie's veins. The plastic bowl fell to the floor and she raced to the living room.

Cullen and Ariel stood in the middle of the room, her arms around his waist, a huge smile on his face.

Mazie stopped short, her chest tight.

"Thank you, Daddy, thank you, thank you, thank you. Can we play?" Ariel looked up at him, adoration for her father back full strength.

Cullen caught Mazie's eye. "Sure, pumpkin." He winked at his wife, stood aside and jerked his head toward the television. A new video game console sat on the ottoman. Wires snaked across the floor and into the TV. Packaging debris littered the floor. "It's a Wii. For Ariel. But we can all play." He picked up a white remote, stretched his arm to bridge the gap between them, and handed it to her. "You use your body to play. How about bowling, pumpkin?"

"Yes!" Ariel took another remote.

Cullen turned on the television and put a disc in the console. They created their own avatars, Ariel's with long raven locks and denim capris, Mazie's with the same hair but long pants, and Cullen's with long dark hair and a smiling face. Like his old self, he said.

Mazie glanced at him every few seconds.

His old self.

She should have had him arrested years ago.

Cullen showed Ariel how to aim, how to use the remote to simulate the action of tossing the ball down the virtual lane. He did the same for Mazie, stood behind her, held her hand that held the remote, and drew her arm back with his. She knew how to bloody well bowl, she didn't need guidance or a tutorial. But he smelled of cologne and toothpaste, and the rasp of his afternoon beard sent a shiver down her spine. Was she aroused by him?

For an hour, the sound of fake pins hitting a fake hardwood floor filled the room. Real laughter bounced off the walls.

After Ariel won the bowling tournament, she asked to play tennis.

Cullen glanced at Mazie. "But only two can play that game."

"It's all right. I'll go get us more soda." Mazie gathered up their empty glasses and filled each with ice and cola.

Cullen and Ariel volleyed the ball back and forth. Or at least they looked pretty silly swinging remotes around while their avatars ran around the virtual court.

Mazie passed behind him carrying a tray laden with full glasses. He pulled his arm back and smacked her in the cheek. A soda tipped. She caught the glass before it hit the floor, but cola sprayed everywhere.

He swung around and stared at her. "I'm so sorry. I didn't mean it."

She stared at him.

"Come on, don't look at me like that, you know it was an accident." He put his hands on his hips and raised that damn eyebrow.

She stood frozen in place, her gaze quickly shifted to the floor.

"Shit." He threw the remote at the couch.

Ariel's eyes filled with tears. "Daddy, please." Her voice was barely audible.

He turned to his daughter and kneeled on the floor in front of her, held her arms with his hands. He turned back to Mazie. "It was an accident this time. Honest." His grip on Ariel's arms was gentle. His gaze filled with regret.

She touched her fingertips to her cheek. "I believe you." She was surprised to realize that she actually did.

He smiled and nodded once. He jogged into the kitchen and returned with a roll of paper towels and a bottle of all-purpose cleaner.

Mazie held her hands out.

"I'll do it." He kneeled on the hardwood and wiped up the sticky spill.

Mazie took the tray to the kitchen. She peered at him out of the corner of her eye, watched him spray the floor and mop up the mess. She smiled, rinsed the tray and wiped the spilled soda from the glasses.

Once Ariel was asleep, Cullen took Mazie's hand and led her upstairs. He stood at the foot of the bed, brushed hair from her neck and unbuttoned her blouse.

She closed her eyes and willed her hands to stop trembling, her stomach not to refuse dinner and spew it all over his face.

He kissed her neck, her collarbone, her lips. He found a tenderness she thought he'd lost forever, and guided her into bed.

She began to relax, to allow herself a moment of enjoyment, an instant of passion and love for a man she'd grown to hate. Was this real change? Was her body responding to his sex with more than just stiff resignation? She wasn't sure, but she couldn't look at him. She shut her eyes to the sight of the monster hovering above her, and remembered the Cullen of old. It was like cheating on her husband with a better version of him.

His hand brushed against her throat. Her eyes sprung open. Her body stiffened and she stared into his face.

He was frozen in place, his palm against her neck. He inched it away. "I'm sorry," he whispered.

He pulled away, grabbed his robe and left the room. The sounds of a good, stiff drink clinked up the stairs. An hour later he sneaked back into the room and slipped beneath the covers.

She pretended to be asleep.

~~~~~~~~

"Mr. Reynolds, how do you plead?"

"Guilty, your honour."

Mazie closed her eyes for a full two seconds and let that admission sink in. He was taking responsibility. Admitting he had hurt her. Not exactly saying it was his fault, but it was the closest he'd ever come.

The judge scanned the papers in front of him. "Mrs. Reynolds, I understand you are willing to take your husband back?"

Mazie stood. "Yes, your honour."

The judge harrumphed. "Well, Mr. Reynolds, this is your lucky day. Since this is your first offence ..." He eyed Cullen over his glasses. "First official offence ..." He shook his head. "Time served, two years probation." He pointed at Cullen. "If I see your name cross my desk again, there won't be forgiveness, and there will be no bail, you understand me?"

Cullen's shoulders tensed and inched toward his earlobes. With his back to her, Mazie could only imagine the look on his face. Defiance. Anger. Fuck you, Judge.

"Yes sir. I understand."

~~~~~~~~

The next few days passed in relative silence. Life seemed normal — the good kind of normal. Cullen hadn't tried to have sex with Mazie again. Maybe he knew he couldn't fuck her without hurting her. That he couldn't get off without bringing her to the brink of death. That if he did it again, he'd land his ass back in jail.

Mazie remained on edge, walked as if broken glass littered the house but she wasn't allowed to let her feet bleed. Everything made her jump, every noise, every knock at the door, every ringing phone, every alarm on her cell that warned of his texts. But each one was polite — the *Sorry, I'll be late, Do you mind getting me a pack of smokes* kind of polite.

His drinking continued unabated, but he'd found the strength to rein in the terror. To control his emotions. Why couldn't he have done that all these years? When would the elastic waistband of his emotional big boy pants snap? When would he be fully exposed again, the real him, the only one he knew how to be?

Each day, sharp edges of his anger began to scratch at her. His words started to bite, his displays of affection, as awkward as they'd become, waned. *I won't be home after work. Have dinner waiting* started appearing on her phone. *Where you at?* crept back in.

One night he walked in the door, an hour late for dinner. No text that day. No phone call. No consideration.

She pulled his plate from the fridge and put it in the microwave, punched the EZ-cook button four times, watched the plate spin and the timer count down from two minutes.

He brushed past her, his hair reeking of smoke, the rest of him stinking of bourbon. And perfume.

She pinched her eyes shut. The night he'd traipsed in thirteen years ago, three hours after the bars closed, niggled at her. She'd confronted him in the kitchen on her way out the door for work, exhausted from working too many hours at two different jobs. Part of the act was being friendly with the fans, he'd always said. "If they want to give you a hug and get a picture with the gorgeous lead singer," he jerked his head to flick his hair back, "then you let them. That's how you make sure they come back."

"Yeah? So casual hugs here and there with more than one

woman, and the result is that you reek of Chanel? Only Chanel?"

"I don't know what kind of perfume it is."

"I do. It's my brand. The one you buy me every Christmas." She stood with her arms crossed, her cheeks on fire. "And I guarantee you, it's not mine."

"Come on, Mazie. It's just part of the act." He put his hands on her hips and wiggled them back and forth, his pelvis against hers. "You believe me. Right, baby?"

She turned her face from the stench of his bourbon breath. "I used to." She pushed him away, grabbed her purse, and bolted out the door. She peeled out from the curb and turned the corner before pulling over and crying against the steering wheel. He'd never admitted to cheating, and she'd never figured out if he had, but the thought that he might sleep with another woman and then come home to her made her gut lurch. The fact that he was a liar stung.

The microwave beeped. She opened her eyes but didn't move.

"Hey, wake up." His voice grated in her ear. "It's done."

She pulled out the hot plate and dropped it on the table, a fork and knife clanged against the wood where she tossed them.

"What the hell?" He raised that damn eyebrow like he was all innocent and shit and she was the bloody problem.

She glared at him. "I'm going to bed."

She turned and walked away. She'd lost the will to give a damn. He could fuck whomever he wanted. Choke them for shits and giggles. As long as he left her the hell alone, what did it matter?

~~~~~~~~

Mazie pushed peas around her plate then poked at her pork chop. She glanced up at Cullen. His plate was nearly empty, three fingers of Jack over ice already gone from his tumbler.
~~~~~~~~

She cleared her throat. "Are you taking time off when Ariel starts summer break?"

"Thought I'd go fishing. Get away for a bit."

She nodded.

He glared at her. "What? You want to come, right? Damn it Mazie, it's the only time I get to myself!" He pitched his fork onto his plate and grabbed the bottle of bourbon. Another three fingers went down in one gulp.

Ariel sat next to her father, frozen in place, staring at her plate.

Mazie reached across the table and patted her hand. "No, me and Ariel don't need to come." Trapped in the woods in a shitty one-room cabin with no phone, no television. No escape. No, she wouldn't do that again.

"Oh." He nodded and picked up the fork, shoved the last of his mashed potatoes in his mouth. "Good," he said through the food.

"I was thinking I could take Ariel to see my mother."

"Do whatever you want. As long as I don't have to see the old bat. She can't die soon enough. Bitch hates me."

Ariel peered at her. "Is Grandma going to die?" she whispered.

"Not yet, sweetheart." She plastered a fake smile on her face to hide the clenching of her jaw. "But she is sick and we can't visit her often." She cleared the plates and stacked them next to the sink. Rachel's daughter rode her bike past the front of the house. "Ariel, why don't you go out and play? Polly's out there."

"Can I, Daddy?"

"Sure, pumpkin. Whatever you want."

Ariel's face lit up. "Thanks, Daddy." She ran to the entry, slipped on her runners, and bolted out the front door.

Mazie stood at the window and watched Polly jump from her bike and hug Ariel. The joy on her daughter's face melted Mazie's heart. She closed her eyes and tried to conjure the face of her childhood best friend, but Sherry's memory had become another bit of blurry flotsam in the emotional turbulence that churned in the wake of her life. She opened her eyes to find that the Johnsons' twin sons had joined the girls. The four of them stood on the manicured front lawn beside the spirea bush still waiting for its white flowers to bloom. Sunshine caught the gold A of Ariel's pendant and flashed a glint of light into Mazie's eyes.

She blinked, ran the water, squirted the dish soap into the stream, and slid the dirty dishes under the surface.

Cullen shuffled around the room, ice cubes clinked into a tumbler, bourbon glugged from the bottle.

His footfalls neared until he stood beside her, a cigarette in one hand, bourbon in the other. He stared out at the children and sucked on the cigarette until a long ash dropped onto the counter. He flicked it into her dishwater, held the butt under the suds, the hiss of its dying heat just another fuck you.

He rested one hand on her shoulder. "Look at our little Ariel."

Mazie glanced at him and caught herself smiling. Bathed in the yellow light of a spring sunset, he almost looked his old handsome self. His long, soft, chocolate hair was now clipped above the ears and peppered with grey. His tanned face bore evidence of the passing years, the smile lines and soft skin now weathered by years of hard labour in the hot sun and cold wind, the rain, the snow. The deep furrows between his brows and frown lines that cut alongside his drawn lips proof of the transition from easy-going and loving partner to taskmaster with a heart filled with contempt.

He should have sold a million records by now. Won a Grammy or two. Not foundered on the bottom rung of a too-tall ladder, with more talented, more driven, more connected musicians stepping on him as they clamoured past on their way to the top. His hatred for her was borne of his own bitter disappointment in himself. Mazie knew it. But she could never make it any better. He wouldn't allow her to.

"She's starting to look like you," his voice rasped in her ear.

He set his tumbler on the counter and slid behind her, brushed her hair from the nape of her neck and leaned over her shoulder, his cheek touching hers. "You know, when you were younger. When you were pretty." He pressed into her back.

Mazie froze. It was the only thing she knew to do. The lump of his erection rested between her ass cheeks.

"She's so tall. Must have got that from me. But the tits, those are all you, Mazie Baby. All you." He reached his left arm around her, slipped his hand under her shirt and bra, and massaged her breast. His right hand bounced against the seat of her skirt.

Mazie forced back a lump of bile that rose in her throat and gripped the sink's edge with both hands while he masturbated against her.

"Look at her hair, Mazie. Black like yours, shiny and thick like it used to be." His hand left her breast and lifted her skirt, then yanked her underpants down.

She swallowed hard. "Not here, not in the kitchen." He didn't mean it. He couldn't be thinking about their daughter that way. "The kids might see."

"Yeah, they might." He rested his chin on her shoulder and held her hip. With each stroke, he slapped himself against her bare flesh and grunted in her ear. "I'm almost done with you, Mazie. Bored in fact." His breath was laboured and his words were punctuated by the wheeze of too many cigarettes. "Time to move on, right? To someone younger. Someone prettier. Like you used to be."

His breath was sweet with syrupy bourbon. She shut her eyes and steadied her breath, tried to prevent the convulsions that were threatening to explode her dinner all over the kitchen window.

"Cullen, no. You wouldn't."

"Oh, yes."

Mazie opened her eyes. Ariel spun in circles on the lawn. She stopped and staggered about. Laughter lit up her face.

He groaned. The warmth of his climax hit her lower back and dripped into the crack of her ass.

She grit her teeth. "She's just a little girl for God's sake! Your own daughter, Cullen!"

One hand covered the back of her head and pushed her face into the dishwater. Her arms flailed and knocked something off the counter. The muffled sound of shattering glass broke through the splashing and her silent screams. Her legs went numb and her mind blanked. Familiar glints of bright light flickered behind closed eyelids. And then nothing.

~~~~~~~~~

"Breathe, Mazie Baby. Breathe."

The chrome bar was cold in her hand. Her screams filled the room.

Cullen stroked her sweaty head and bent forward, his lips pursed, eyes wide. He puffed air at her to show her how to breathe, just like the Lamaze instructor had taught him.

The contraction eased. Giddy from nitrous oxide, she laughed into the mask on her face. "You look like a constipated monkey."

A glint of anger flashed across his eyes. Then he broke out in a loud laugh.

It had been a long, hard day. And one of the best in their marriage.

Two hours later, there was Ariel, squirming atop Mazie's stomach, still tethered to her mother by the umbilical cord.
~~~~~~~~~

Cullen ran his thumb over their baby's head, gross and sticky with placental fluid, blood, and white chunks like so much spilled cottage cheese. He rested his chin on the edge of the bed and stroked Ariel's hair, stared at her eyes, not yet open, not yet aware of her parents' faces.

And he cried. Not sad or angry or resentful tears. Just streams of water dripping down his cheeks. Like he was being cleansed from the inside out.

The doctor handed him scissors and held the umbilical cord.

Cullen hesitated. He looked so helpless and afraid. "Will it hurt her?"

The doctor smiled. "No, neither of them will feel any pain."

Cullen kissed Mazie's knuckles, then hacked through the tough cord tissue until mother and daughter were no longer one.

For months he was happy. And mostly sober. He smelled of soap and freshly brushed teeth. Of cologne and promise and hope. He bounced out of bed to pick up the baby when she cried in the night. He stared at mother and daughter during feedings, desperate to be part of a bonding that no man could ever experience. Ever understand. He changed diapers and fetched fresh onesies.

Was it true change? Were they going to be all right?

Whoever said bringing a child into a bad marriage would not fix it was wrong. Ariel had been their saving grace.

<div align="center">~~~~~~~~~</div>

Mazie blinked against the pain in her head and the blinding light of the hundred-watt bulb above. She lay on the floor gasping for air, her hair and clothes soaked with dishwater. Drops of blood dotted the linoleum where broken glass cut into her skin.

Cullen squatted in front of her and pushed wet hair from in

front of her eyes. "Clean this up."

The stench of whiskey and cigarettes turned her stomach.

He stood, grabbed the bottle of bourbon by its neck, and sat in his chair in the living room.

Her entire body quaked. She gripped a chair and dragged herself to her feet. The blood rushed from her head, her feet numbed and she sat in the chair and put her head between her bloody knees.

She turned to glare at the monster she'd married.

He sat in his recliner, remote in hand, flipping through television channels like nothing had happened.

Nothing.

Ariel's laughter came through the window. Mazie stood and gripped the counter's edge. The setting sun caught the steel of the chef's knife and shined a glint of light in her eyes. She stared at the blade, then gazed out the window at her smiling daughter.

<center>~~~~~~~~</center>

Cullen remained silent the rest of the day. Mazie kept Ariel busy in the kitchen, baked cookies and talked about the trip to visit grandma. Anything to prevent her from being alone with her father.

Cullen went to bed early, his drowsiness fuelled by half a bottle of Jack. He slept soundly, no remorse for his actions to keep him awake, no guilt for the harm he had done, the threats to his child. His snores reverberated in the bedroom.

The street light danced shadows of the thirty-foot poplar across the bedroom walls. Her eyes flitted along with the quaking leaves until the trunk loomed closer and pinned her to the bed. She shook her head and sat up, her throat tight.

The money would have to be enough. The time was now. Before it was too late. Before he ruined Ariel. More than he already had.

Mazie glanced at the clock radio. Two thirty-eight. She slid from beneath the sheets and tiptoed to Ariel's room and lay on the floor in front of her bed. Mazie closed her eyes, and listened to her daughter breathe.

A thud shook Mazie from a shallow sleep. She sneaked back into her bedroom and glanced at the alarm clock. Five fifty-six. She pulled the drape aside and peered out in time to see the paper boy toss an elastic-bound newspaper at Rachel's house. Mazie slipped back into bed, turned her back on Cullen, and feigned sleep.

Cullen rose at six sharp to the screech of the alarm, threw the covers off them both and onto the floor, and walked to the bathroom without so much as a glance in her direction.

She cinched the belt of her robe, the long sleeves shielding Ariel from the scabs and bruises of the day before. She retrieved the newspaper from the stoop, brewed coffee and poured his in a to-go cup with cream and three sugars. She packed his lunch pail with leftover dinner, cookies, two water bottles, and a Coke.

He tromped down the stairs, showered and shaven, looking his best for the men he worked with. He took the coffee and newspaper from her, snatched his full lunch pail from the sideboard, and walked out.

Mazie rubbed her hands up and down the sleeves of her robe. His last day of work before his summer break. Before he'd be in the house every day. All day long. Standing over her, pointing out each spot she missed, the right way to scrub his shit stains from the toilet. Eyeing Ariel as if she were a potential conquest, not a child. His child.

She watched the truck peel out of the back alley and race to the corner. He turned right at the stop sign without hitting the brakes. She clicked the back door shut, squeezed her eyelids together, rested her forehead against the cool windowpane, and struggled for steady breath.

When her nerves eased and she was ready to open her eyes to the reality of life, the back yard came into focus, his messy tool shed and oil stains from his precious truck. She wiped her forehead smudge from the glass with the terry-cloth of her robe sleeve.

Rachel's eyes and forehead appeared over the edge of the fence. When she saw Mazie, she ducked, then reappeared a second later waving her pudgy hand.

Mazie squinted and bolted the door. Of all the potential BFFs out there, why did Ariel have to pick Rachel's kid?

Like hell would she stay cooped up in this prison just waiting to be wailed on again. Waiting for her daughter to be raped. And all under the ever-watchful eye of the nosy gossip-mongering neighbour. She'd let it go on too long. Should have run the first second he'd hurt Ariel. What kind of mother sits on the sidelines and allows her child to be abused?

Mazie yanked the garnet ring from her finger and flung it into the garbage bin. She yanked a mug from the cupboard and poured a cup of coffee. Steam from the sweet, creamy brew curled into her nostrils and brought her a slice of peace. A moment of clarity. She fished the ring from the garbage, pulled a meat mallet from the drawer under the knife block, and crushed the garnet against the cutting board. Bits of red stone scattered across the counter, like blood spatter after a good beating.

She lifted her head, closed her eyes, and took a long breath.

Fuck, yeah.

~~~~~~~~~

Mazie leaned against the jamb of her daughter's bedroom door, stared at her sleeping form and listened to her deep inhales and tiny
~~~~~~~~~

whimpers with each exhale. She glanced at Ariel's bedside clock. Time to get on with it. She sidled up to the bed and placed a gentle kiss on the back of Ariel's head. "Sweetheart, wake up."

Ariel rolled on her side and opened one eye. "What time is it?"

"Eight-fifteen."

Ariel pulled the pillow over her head and moaned. "Gawd, Mom. It's summer vacation. Let me sleep."

"You're going to spend the day with Rachel and Polly. Have a sleepover tonight, too."

Ariel tossed the pillow aside, sat up and rubbed her eyes. "Why?"

"I have some errands to do, and packing for our trip. You'd be bored. We'll leave early tomorrow morning. Just you and me, kid."

"Like Thelma and Louise?"

Mazie raised her eyebrows. "Where'd you hear about that?"

"Mrs. Simpson was watching it once. They drive off a cliff."

"Yeah. We're not going to do that."

Ariel giggled.

"Go brush your teeth. I'll pack you an overnight bag. Grandma is going to be surprised how tall you've grown."

Ariel yawned and padded to the bathroom.

Mazie tossed a shirt, jeans, and fresh underwear into a small tote bag, and placed Darryl, Ariel's favourite floppy-eared rabbit with the purple corduroy overalls, on top. Since the first time she'd seen him that Easter morning ten years ago, she'd never slept without him.

The toilet flushed and Ariel exited the bathroom, peered into the tote. "Mom, it's all messy. You didn't fold them right."

Mazie hesitated at the scorn in her daughter's voice. "I'm sorry."

Ariel froze and stared at her mother, her eyes glistened with pending tears. "It doesn't matter. Things can be sloppy once in a while." She swallowed. "Right?"

Mazie nodded. "Right."

Ariel stuffed her toothbrush into the side pocket of the bag, made her bed and ran her hands over the bedspread to flatten out the wrinkles.

Mazie turned away, pinched her arm to fend off tears. When had Ariel picked up that need to be sure everything was perfect? That was Mazie's job. Make it just so. Keep the peace. Protect her daughter.

She'd failed at that too.

~~~~~~~~

At the drugstore, Mazie ran one finger along a row of sleeping aids. She picked one up and read the package, then another. They were virtually identical except for the logo on the box. And the price. She chose the cheapest and headed to the checkout.

The cashier ran the box over the barcode reader. "Seven ninety-five. How are you paying?"

Mazie dug the billfold, sticky with duct tape residue, from her purse and pulled out one of the gift cards from her tampon returns.

When the transaction was complete, the woman handed Mazie the bag, a receipt, and the gift card. "Three fifty-five still left on the card."

At the bank, she stood in the long line, arms crossed, toes of one foot tap-tap-tapping against the tile floor.

Twelve-nineteen, the clock behind the teller said. Damn these normal people, all crammed in on their stupid lunch hour. Her days didn't have the same markers as the working world. She just ran her errands when she was told.

When a teller became free, Mazie slipped up to the counter. "I need to make a withdrawal."

"Swipe your card and enter your PIN please."
~~~~~~~~

"I don't have a card."

The teller stared at her. "All right. What's your account number?"

Mazie reeled off the numbers and waited while the teller's fingers flew across the keyboard.

"Okay, Mrs. Reynolds. How much would you like to withdraw?"

"What's my balance?"

The teller clicked her mouse and typed a few keystrokes. "Checking account has just over fourteen hundred." Click, click. "Savings has fifty-three ninety-two and change." The woman looked up at Mazie with an expectant look.

More than five grand in savings? And he couldn't spare enough for a tutor for Ariel? Well, screw him. "Give me the balance in the savings, and six hundred from checking." She kept her voice low, glanced at the customers on either side of her.

The teller typed and clicked the mouse. "Do you care what denominations? We can do hundreds and fifties for most of it."

Mazie nodded. "Fine. Whatever."

The woman slid papers and rubber stamps into a drawer and stepped to a machine along the back wall, swiped a card through a reader and typed on the keypad. Bills flew out of the machine, like a master card sharp shuffling a deck of playing cards. The woman returned to her station and placed the first bill on the high counter in front of Mazie. "One hundred, two —"

Mazie put her hand over the woman's and leaned in. "Do you think you could count that down there in front of you, and quieter? I'd rather the whole place not know how much cash I'm carrying around."

The woman's cheeks pinked. "Sorry, ma'am. Of course." She counted out the cash and slid the bills into an envelope, then handed it to Mazie. "Sign here, please."

Mazie tucked the envelope into her purse and signed the receipt. She tapped the counter twice with an open palm and smiled at the teller. "Thanks."

At home, Mazie prepared a roast for the oven, loaded Cullen's dirty work clothes into the washer along with his favourite flannel fishing shirt that had gathered dust over the winter. She folded clean towels and stocked the linen closet, pulled the luggage from the crawl space in the basement, and filled the bags with her and Ariel's clothing and toiletries. When everything was packed, she hid the luggage in Ariel's closet, transferred Cullen's work clothes to the dryer, and went out to the shed. His fishing gear was where he'd left it when he came home from his last trip the summer before — tossed into a corner, the scaling knife sticky with scales and rotten with fish guts. She lifted the latch on his tackle box. The flies were strewn about, fishing line tangled and shoved into the bottom. Mazie untangled the line and wound it onto the reel, separated feathers from hooks and sorted the flies and lures. She soaked the knife in soapy water, scrubbed it until it gleamed and set everything on the porch outside the back door.

She put the kettle on, sat at the kitchen table, and pulled the small drug store bag from her purse. As she sipped black tea, she read the inner pamphlet, the dosages and warnings. *Avoid taking with alcohol.* Yeah, right.

Four of the tiny blue oval pills popped easily from the confines of their foil bubbles and bounced into the mortar. The pestle soon crushed them into powder. The grinding of marble against marble kept time with the ticking of her mother's old cuckoo clock. The bird had died a violent death at the hands of her husband two years before. He'd yanked it out by its neck and crushed its head under the heel of his boot shortly before slamming her into the wall and breaking two ribs. He hated that clock. And that was her fault.

She glanced sideways at it. Four forty-seven. A full hour before he'd storm the house.

About seven ounces remained in the opened bottle of bourbon. She twisted the cap off, sniffed and recoiled at the smell of anger and pain. She tipped the bottle to her lips. The amber liquor hit the back of her mouth and she swallowed hard against her gag reflex. The booze burned down her throat, a shiver ran through her body and warmth filled her stomach.

Tonight called for some liquid courage, even if it meant drinking from the enemy's flask.

She set a funnel in the bottle's neck and poured crushed sleeping pills into the bourbon. She swirled the liquor in the bottle and watched the alcohol dissolve the powdered pills. A smirk crossed her lips. She recapped the bottle and placed it on the table next to an empty tumbler at Cullen's regular seat. Even if he was in a beer mood, he could never pass up a finger or three of J.D.

The aroma of perfectly slow-roasted beef filled the house. Mazie pulled out the pan for one last check, basted the meat with the drippings and set the roast on the cutting board to rest. She turned the potatoes, so perfectly brown and crisp on the outside, poked one of the carrots to check that they were done, their natural sugars caramelizing the scrubbed skins to perfection. Just the way Cullen liked it. She extracted some of the drippings and made gravy. When the brown liquid thickened and bubbled, she eyed the clock. Ten minutes to go.

She puttered about the living room, tidied the spotless space, dusted the polished furniture. An odd sensation overtook her. Calm, with a side of anticipation.

The roar of the truck announced his approach long before he backed into the driveway. At the sight of the bronze bull's testicles dangling from the towing hitch ball, she retreated into the kitchen and pulled the rest of his dinner from the oven.

While she sliced the meat and scooped potatoes and carrots into serving bowls, the sound of him entering the house brought a chill to her spine. His boots hit the wall before landing with a familiar thud on the linoleum. She envisioned him kicking them off, aiming to mar the drywall and scuff the paint. Purposeful, hateful. He would demand she clean it up after dinner.

Like any normal day.

His lunch pail clattered against the counter. The scrape of the chair legs against the floor was her cue. She turned and placed the food in front of him, a bowl of gravy already at his elbow, buttered bread stacked on a plate in the middle of the table.

He didn't look up. Made no attempt to speak, to make any form of polite contact. He scooped food onto his plate, crushed potatoes under his fork, buried everything in gravy, and poured half the remaining bourbon into his glass. He gulped a mouthful of it down, screwed up his face and sniffed the glass.

Halfway through the meal, he glanced up at her. "Why's my fishing gear on the porch?"

"I cleaned it out for you. So you could go anytime you like."

He huffed. "In a hurry to be rid of me? Am I that bad?" He grinned at his plate before shoving a forkful of beef into his mouth.

She set her jaw and held her tongue. That had been an easy task for most of these past ten years. Keeping quiet probably saved her from countless beatings. But it was time she found her voice.

She pushed food around her plate with her fork, her appetite non-existent, nerves a-tingle. "It's not that." She sighed. "You wanted some time alone. Needed a break from work. From Ariel." She shot her eyes at his face for less than a second before concentrating her gaze on her plate. "From me."

He nodded and drank the remaining bourbon. "I could use a

break from everything." He reached out and patted her hand. "Thanks."

For years she'd yearned for any glimpse of his old self, for one empathetic touch, one loving gesture. Now she fought not to recoil when his skin touched hers. Fought not to push him away, to run and scrub his filth from her. That pat on the hand wasn't appreciation. Wasn't love. It was just another lie.

He rubbed both hands over his face. "Man, I'm beat." He filled his tumbler with the last of the Jack Daniels and sipped it before thrusting another forkful of gravy-laden dinner in behind it. "Where's Ariel?"

"She's sleeping over at Polly's. First night of summer break and all, I figured why not?"

"You should have asked me. If I do go in the morning, I won't see her for days."

"Sorry, I never thought of that."

"That's your problem. You don't fucking think." He gunned most of the remaining bourbon and slammed the glass down on the table. "I'm staying home tomorrow." He pointed one finger at her. "Maybe I'll go the next day. Maybe I'll just take Ariel with me." He ripped a piece of bread in two and dragged one half across his plate, sopping up gravy. "Just the two of us. What do you think of that, Mazie Baby?" He filled his disgusting mouth with gravy-soaked bread and stared her down.

She'd die before she'd let her daughter spend a week in the woods alone with him. She wanted to scream, claw his eyes out. Instead she stared at him, her tears in check. "We're going to visit mother, remember?" She breathed steadily until she couldn't bear his scrutiny any longer. Her gaze hit the untouched food on her plate and she berated herself for being so damn weak. "Ariel doesn't like the cabin. Too many spiders."

"Little bitch needs to toughen up." He shoved his plate away, leaned back in the chair, and pressed the heels of his hands to his eyes. He sat forward and shook his head.

Mazie glanced up at him without lifting her head. "Are you all right?"

"Not really." He rested his head in his hands. "I'm exhausted. Really dizzy."

"Maybe you're coming down with something."

"Maybe. I'm going to go lie down for a bit." He threw the rest of the bourbon down his throat and made his way to the stairs. He stumbled on the first step, grabbed the banister.

She watched him. "Do you need my help?"

He glared at her over his shoulder. "No, I don't fucking need your help. I'm not a damn baby." He grasped the railing and staggered up the stairs.

His uneven footsteps thumped down the hall, the slammed bedroom door cracked against the jamb. His ridiculous oversized belt-buckle hit the floor above her head with a loud thud and the bed creaked under his weight. Then there was blessed silence.

She put the leftovers in the refrigerator, cleared the dinner dishes, filled the dishwasher, and wiped down the countertops until everything gleamed.

She snatched a new bottle of bourbon from the cupboard, twisted off the top and took a long pull before heading to the stairs. With each step she mounted, with every inch she drew closer to their bedroom, the stench of sweat and motor oil that emanated from his pores married the cloying scent of pine cleaner and the sharpness of bleach. The whole house stank of a lifetime of her accumulated failures. Failure to make his dreams come true. Failure to prevent pregnancy. Failure to stand up to him. Failure to leave. To protect her daughter from his anger and abuse. To be happy. To be normal.

Her hand trembled against the cool of the doorknob. She turned it and peered in. He lay on their bed on his back, covers on the floor. His naked body that she'd once found so enticing, now repulsed her. The only sound was his breath, the only movement the rise and fall of his chest.

Why hadn't she thought of drugging him before?

She approached the side of the bed and pulled the thin sheet over him, blocked his exposed private parts from her view. She poked his cheek with one finger. He didn't flinch. She smirked and dropped the bourbon on the nightstand.

She pulled the only two neckties he owned from the closet. The coarse hair on his legs rasped against the satin finish of the material as she wrapped each tie around his ankles and tethered them to the bedposts. He slept through the caress of polyester against his skin, through the shifting of the bed sheets when she dragged his legs into place. A sour odour emanated from his feet. He'd never let her put charcoal insoles in those old work boots, complained that they made his feet sweat even more. He tromped those smelly feet all over her clean floors. The sweat infiltrated the carpet, hung in the air like a permanent, inescapable cloud.

She released the scarf from her neck, touched the tip of her fingers to the bruise that ran parallel to her collar bone and winced. Her upper lip quivered and she narrowed her eyes. The silky fabric slithered around his right wrist. It was too good for him, too soft. He didn't deserve such comfort. Why didn't she think to get rope?

No. The scarves were perfect. She'd hidden behind them for years. It was time they were put to better use.

She tied a French bowline knot around his wrist like she'd practiced, then secured the scarf with as many half-hitches as the length of fabric would allow. The other end was tied to a slat in the headboard with an anchor bend knot. It worked better during trial runs, without his damn arm attached to the other end.

"Shit!" She tossed the untied end aside and stood, arms akimbo. A cow hitch would have to do. When she yanked it tight, his hand flopped into the air and slapped the mattress. The knot held. And he kept snoring.

She dug into her scarf drawer, all the way to the back where the old scarves were. Her hand brushed something cold and hard. Her flask. She'd forgotten about that. She shook it, still more than half full of brandy. She set the flask on the dresser, chose her least-favourite scarf, and secured his other arm.

She emptied the pockets of his pants and dropped the contents on the dresser. She pushed the items aside with one finger and wrinkled her nose. Used Kleenex stained with the dirt and grime that he breathed in every day, a gas receipt, and a few coins. She fished his wallet out of the front breast pocket of his work shirt and flipped open the billfold. His debit card was right there on top. She slid it free from the leather turned it over. Six-two-six-nine. He'd written his PIN where the signature belonged. She glanced at him.

And he thought she was stupid?

She tucked the card into her back pocket along with the few bills he was carrying. Something purple glinted from the fold in his wallet. With her index and middle fingers, she pulled out a foil packet. A condom? In his wallet? He had her on the pill for years. To make sure her mistakes didn't come back and haunt him again, he'd told her. Like she wanted to bring another innocent child into this war zone.

"You sorry bastard." She shook her head. "It's not enough that you're an abusive prick? You have to fuck around on me too?" She rummaged in the bathroom drawer until she found the smooth steel of her hair scissors. The packet yielded to the blade, like a hot knife through ice cream. She slivered the foil and rubber and sauntered back to his bedside.

"I don't give a damn how many women you've slept with. Better them than me, right?" She tossed the scissors on the dresser next to his empty wallet, and strewed the remains of the condom across his body and the bed.

The box in the closet came loose from its duct tape shackles. She sat in the chair in the corner of the room and flipped though the duplicate Polaroids, reread her notes and the dates, relived every abusive blow, every choking hold on her throat, every cut, every scratch. Every broken bone.

She paused at one photo. Her first black eye. The first time the abuse took a public form. And the first time she documented what he'd done to her. She held the picture up. "Look at that, Cullen," she waved it in the air. "Remember that day? I do." She stood and hovered over him. "Like it was happening this very second. The same way I remember every time you've hit me. Beat me. Demeaned me." She paced around the bed. "Every time you glare at me, raise your voice. Even when you're silent. Hell, those are the worst times of all. Silence is the eye of the Cullen storm." She chewed on her thumbnail and stopped at the foot of the bed, her other arm around one footboard post. The smell of his foot, lashed to the bed, wafted up to greet her. She wrinkled her nose and continued to pace.

"Do you know what it's like? To live your life in fear of someone who is supposed to love you?" She paused at the head of the bed and slapped his cheek. "To never know if what you do or what you say is good enough? Is right?" She resumed pacing. "It fucking sucks, that's what it's like. I can never relax, except when you go fishing without me. But when you made me go? That was the worst. I hated those trips. Just there to gut and fry the fish, clean your gear, and fuck your sorry ass."

She kneeled beside the bed and rested her arms on the mattress, poked at his shoulder. "But the worst is when you apologize. I used to feel so sorry for you, happy that you were sorry for hurting me. Relieved. But you were always sorry, weren't you? And it was all a big fat lie. Were you ever truly sorry, Cullen?" She stood. "Were you?" Tears streamed down her face and she swatted them off her cheek. "No. No damn tears tonight. Because I'm done with you." She stabbed one finger toward him with each sentence. "I'm over this shit. Finished with this life. Wake up, damn you! I want to see your face when I leave. When I take Ariel away from you."

The room darkened as dusk turned to night. The digits on the clock radio glowed eleven fifteen. He'd been asleep almost five hours. Her body vibrated, and she hopped around the room to shake off the adrenalin. She drank a long gulp of brandy and sat the flask, uncapped, on the dresser.

As time wore on, she wearied from the wait. Maybe she should've only put two pills in his booze. But maybe that wouldn't have been enough. She closed her eyes and leaned back in the chair.

The bobbing of her head jarred her awake. She eyed the clock. Three fourteen. He was snoring now, and his legs twitched and pulled against the tie bindings. He moaned and turned his head, pulled on his arms. His eyes crept open. It seemed to take minutes for him to focus. Then clarity crossed his face. He jerked his head back and forth, looked from one tethered wrist to the other. "What the fuck?" He lifted his chin to his chest and stared at his legs, then his gaze found her. "Untie me, you crazy bitch!" He yanked on the scarves, twisted his head around to reach for the knot with his mouth.

She stood and stepped toward him at a glacier's pace. "What's the matter? I thought you liked a little bondage." She reached up under the shade of the floor lamp and tugged the string. Soft light bathed the room.

He laid his head back and laughed. "Oh, I get it. You want to get kinky with me? That's a first." He eyed her up and down. "Get these off me and I'll show you how to do it right."

Her heart hammered in her chest and her knees shook. But she was out of his reach. For the first time in years.

"What's your plan here, Mazie? Just going to piss me off more and more? Wait 'til you see what I've got planned for you when I get free." He yanked on the ties and kicked his feet. "Let me loose, you fucking whore!"

The sight of him tied down, unable to get loose — at her complete and utter mercy — along with brandy still warm in her veins, bolstered her bravado. She edged up to the bed and leaned her face toward his. A sneer crossed her lips. "Make me," she said, her voice a low growl.

He jerked his head forward. She jumped back and covered her face with her hands. Her heart pounded, legs trembled.

In the quiet of the room, his laugh cut right through her.

She lowered her arms.

He grinned at her. "You chicken-shit bitch. It doesn't matter what you do, I'll always have you. Always."

Her peripheral vision blurred and his face came into clear focus. She spun around, snatched the scissors from the dresser and plunged them into his thigh.

He screamed. His mouth and brow contorted and he thrashed his arms against their restraints.

She retreated, one hand over her mouth, and stared at the black plastic handle sticking straight up from his leg. Blood oozed from the wound, dripped onto the cotton sheets.

That would leave a stain.

When she backed into the bookshelf opposite the end of the bed, she stumbled and landed on her ass on the carpet. She laughed

— a snicker at first. Soon she was lying on the floor, doubled over, killing herself laughing.

"Mazie, it hurts."

She stopped laughing and sat up, her back against the rows of books that had kept her company these past years, when friendships waned and her isolation grew. When she couldn't find the energy to lie about the damage to her body and simply hid from the world, covered head to toe in clothing, and buried beneath a landslide of self-doubt and guilt.

She stood and edged closer, stared at the scissors, at bright blood juxtaposed against creamy sheets. The black plastic handle, the stainless steel blades buried in his olive-toned flesh. "Mazie, it hurts." She scrunched up her eyes and spit his pitiful plea back at him in high-pitched baby-talk. She touched the handle of the scissors, drained her face of emotion and looked him in the eye. "I think that's the point." She turned the blade.

He gasped. His eyes went from dark and angry to pinched and pleading. Frightened and in pain. "Stop. Please."

She cocked her head. He was vulnerable and wide-eyed. She'd never seen him like that.

She neared the head of the bed, transfixed by the pain in his eyes. By his need for her to save him. To rescue him. She kneeled down and touched his chest with one hand, rested her chin on her other arm, and watched his expressions change.

His breath was heavy and laboured, his chest rose and fell in fast rhythm with each inhale and bourbon-scented exhale.

"Mazie." His voice was gravelly. A hoarse whisper. "Baby."

She used to love it when he called her that. Mazie Baby. It spoke of his love for her, his desire to take care of her, protect her. Like a mother is supposed to keep a child safe from harm. It morphed into a taunt, like a schoolyard bully mocking a weak kid crying for his mommy. What's the matter, baby? You gonna cry, baby?

"Come on, baby. Untie me. You've made your point." He smiled one of his fake smiles. "You know I love you, right?"

How many times had he said that? After he hurt her. After the apologies that used to mean something but now rang as hollow and untrue as most every word he spewed.

He took a deep breath, his cheeks ruddy and splotchy. "Let me go now," his voice had turned from sweet and conciliatory to low and growling. "And I promise I won't hurt you."

She narrowed her eyes. "You promise?" She pushed off against his chest and stood. "You promise?" Her voice gained strength with the understanding that no promises would ever be kept. That he would hurt her if he wanted, whenever the whim struck. "How many times have you promised you would stop? Then what happened, huh? I'll tell you what. You beat me. Again. And again." Tears streamed down her cheeks. "It's never going to end, is it?"

"If you don't take those scissors out of my leg and untie me," his voice grew stronger and louder with each word. The pleading and fear in his eyes dissolved under the weight of the hatred and fire that returned with a vengeance. "I'm going to fucking kill you."

Every emotion drained from her. She turned and snatched the brandy from the dresser and took a long drink.

"It fucking hurts, damn it! Can't you see that?"

She spun around and threw the flask against the wall behind his head. It hit with a thud and bounced onto the floor. Sticky alcohol sprayed the wall and the bed and his face and chest. She crossed her arms, twisted her face up, and bent toward him. "It hurts." She imitated the mocking tone he'd turned on her countless times these past years. "It hurts, it hurts, it hurts!" She grabbed the stack of Polaroids and held them up. "You want to know what hurts?" She flung each picture at him, like dealing a deck of red-hot cards. With each photo that landed on the bed, she reminded him of the damage done. "A black eye, that hurts. And a broken arm. Two broken ribs. Yeah, that hurt too. Oh, remember this?" She held the picture up and shoved it in his face until it was pushed up against his nose. "That's what my lower back looked like after you beat me with an empty Jack Daniels bottle because I forgot to get you a new one!" She paced and shook her head, derision huffing from her nostrils. "Yeah, that fucking hurt, believe me." She turned back and yanked the scissors from his leg.

He cried out and clenched his teeth. Deep crevasses were carved into his face. He looked old and weathered, drained of every last shred of the handsome man he once was.

She yanked down the collar of her shirt and jutted her chin in the air. "How about this, Cullen? When you choke me? Again and again and again. How long before you get it right, huh? Before you suck every last ounce of life out of me?"

A half-smile crept onto his face.

She stepped toward the bed. "That fucking hurts." She plunged the scissors into his other leg.

He screamed. "Fuck, fuck, fuck. You stupid fucking bitch."

She put one hand over his mouth. "Shut up. You trying to wake the whole fucking neighbourhood?"

He tried to bite her but she snapped her hand away. She sidled up to the window, moved the drape aside with one finger and peered out. Every house across the street remained in darkness. Typical. They sure never heard anything when she screamed.

His damn blood stained the drape. She held her hands out and inspected them. More blood tarnished her fingers and pooled under her nails. She wiped it on her pants.

He glared at her. "I should have kept choking you, killed you when I had the chance. You're a useless, stupid, waste of skin. Can't do anything right. Raising our daughter to talk back to me." He thrashed against the restraints then cried out. "God fucking damn it!"

"You sorry piece of shit." Her voice dripped venom. "You don't have the goddamn balls to kill me. You never could finish what you started. Gave up on your music, gave up on me. You'll give up on Ariel, too. If you don't ruin her first. Rape her, beat her, use her. That's the plan, right? Move on to a younger version of me? Just to get your puny rocks off. You don't give a damn about her. About anyone. You're a selfish, arrogant, stinking pile of dog shit!" She had inched closer and now stood over him. She jabbed one finger into his chest, punctuating each insult. "I'll die before I ever let you touch her."

"That can be arranged." He yanked on his restraints. The cow hitch shifted and came loose from the slat that held his right arm.

Mazie jumped on top of him, pinned his arm down and grabbed the scarf.

He squirmed beneath her and laughed. "Can't even tie a proper, knot you stupid cunt."

The slick material slipped through her fingertips.

He grabbed her hair, yanked her neck back until her face was an inch from his. "You're my bitch now."

She stared into his eyes. Something prodded her leg. Bile rose in her throat.

He had an erection.

She leered at him. "This is what turns you on, right baby?" She reached back and stroked him over the sheet. "Violence. Control. Pain." She swallowed. "My pain."

He smiled and narrowed his eyes, yanked her hair harder. "Untie me and I'll show you. I'll fuck your fat, ugly brains out."

She laughed. "Fuck yourself." She grasped the handle of the scissors. "I'm nobody's bitch anymore." She pulled the scissors free from his thigh and jabbed them into his shoulder. The blade crunched against bone.

He screamed and let go of her hair.

She jumped to her feet, raced to the other side of the bed, wrapped the loose end of the scarf around her hand and held it firm in her fist. She dragged his arm straight out to the side. "How about now, baby? That turn you on?"

"Fuck, fuck, fuck."

She eyed the sheet where it covered his groin. "Oh, poor Cullen. Can't get it up now? That's too bad. Because I'm aroused as hell."

"I'm going to cut you to ribbons when I get free." He turned his head and glared, sweat beaded on his upper lip and dripped from his forehead. "They won't even find the pieces."

"Free?" she shook her head. "I'm the one who's free. By the time you get out of this, we'll be long gone. You'll never hurt me or Ariel again, you hear me? Ever. Again." She filled her mouth with saliva and sent a ball of spit into the air. It landed on his neck, a few drops of spittle dotting his cheek and chin.

He closed his eyes and pressed his lips closed, turned and glared at her. "You can't even spit right." His voice had lost its edge. "You're pitiful." The malice waned, replaced by a false bravado. He'd lost his grip on her and he knew it.

A dark spot grew on the sheet. She raised one eyebrow, threw her head back and laughed. "What are you, three years old? Poor Cullen. Pissed his bed like a widdle baby."

"Fuck you."

Mazie yanked on the scarf. He resisted, but the damage to his shoulder had weakened him. She used a better knot and tied it tight to the slat.

She stood back and surveyed the room. The bed sheets were ripped, the cream canvas splattered with crimson blood, soaked with yellow urine, and punctuated by black mascara smudges from her attempts to secure his free arm. It was almost beautiful. Like a Jackson Pollock painting.

Mazie jerked the scissors free from his shoulder and tossed them on the dresser. She grabbed the bourbon and put the bottle to her lips, her eyes on his. She grinned at him and tipped her head and the bottle back. The booze heated her throat and her belly. She shook her head and marvelled at the cold shiver that trailed from the base of her neck to her tail bone. She ripped the sheet off of him and poured the alcohol into the open wound on his left thigh.

He pressed his head back into the pillow and screamed.

"You like that?" She set the bottle on the dresser and peeled her T-shirt off revealing her black bra with the touch of lace where her breasts met to create the ample cleavage he so loved. "How about this? This good for you?"

His breath was laboured, his face twisted, but he stared at her chest.

She mounted him, straddled his hips and rocked against them. She dry-humped him and ran one finger over her breasts. Despite his wounds, the pain, the blood, despite pissing himself just a moment before, his erection soon pressed against the crotch of her jeans. A crooked smile crossed her face. "Yeah, that's it. Come on, baby. You wanna fuck me?"

He didn't speak, but his lips parted and he stared into her eyes.

She put one hand to his throat and pressed.

His eyes flew open and began to water. He thrashed beneath her and gasped. "Mazie," his voice creaked through his constricted windpipe. "Can't. Breathe."

"Shut up!" She leaned forward, her face just a few inches from his, and smiled. "I'm not done fucking you yet."

She stopped humping and stared at his face, at the colour in his cheeks and the fear of pending death. His eyes rolled back and his mouth slackened. His body stiffened beneath her.

She released her hold on his throat and cocked her head.

An experiment the first time, he'd told her. Erotic asphyxiation. Was supposed to heighten orgasm. She'd fought it, said no, pushed him away. It heightened his orgasm all right. But as he climaxed, she had passed out cold. She awoke to him snoring beside her, physically spent and emotionally absent. She got online the next day and looked it up. The person being asphyxiated was supposed to get off. It was normally a lonely activity, one using a belt or a tie. Or a scarf.

His cherry cheeks began to pale, his mouth opened wide and he gasped for air, coughed, and swallowed. His eyes darted back and forth, coming to rest on her face, his eyes wide. The throbbing of his heart shook his body, bouncing her on top of him with each pounding beat.

So that's what she looked like every time he'd done that to her. Red-faced. Wild-eyed. Scared to death. Relieved to be alive. Now he really understood her.

He couldn't hold her gaze and turned his head to the side. He looked at her out of the corner of his eye, before moving his focus to the other side of the room. "Mazie, why are you doing this to me?"

She crawled off the bed, turned her back to him and pulled her shirt back over her head. Blood smears stained the inner thighs of her jeans, soaked through the fabric at her right knee and into her skin. Damn, why hadn't she thought to change first? Her favourite Levi's, ruined. She spun around.

"Look what you did! You wrecked my jeans. You can't even bleed right. Maybe you ought to scrub the stains out, huh? Think you could handle that, you simple bastard?"

He smirked at her and huffed air out his nostrils. "I get it." His voice was hoarse. Probably damage to his windpipe. She could sympathize. But she wouldn't.

"Yeah? And just exactly what do you get?" She stared at the bright red handprint on his neck. At the gaping wounds in his thighs and arm. His flaccid manhood dangling between his legs.

He swallowed and coughed. "You think you're showing me what it feels like." Tears dripped from his eyes onto the pillow case.

Another damn stain.

"A little payback, maybe." He was barely whispering now.

She crossed her arms. "There is no amount of shit I could do to you in one night that will ever make you 'get it.' Do you understand?" She paced the carpet beside the bed, shook her head, and grumbled unintelligible words. Her head was woozy from sucking on brandy and bourbon — more booze than she'd had to drink in years. More than she'd meant to have that night.

She stopped short and stared at the floor, at the stains of drying blood on her feet. She spun around, her eyes darting across the carpet around her. Her bare footprints stared back at her, the bloody toe marks diminishing as she'd wiped his blood from her feet with each step. Her heart raced and she took three steps toward the hall.

She had to get it cleaned up before Cullen got home.

When she got to the threshold of their bedroom door, awareness struck her like a fist to the side of the head. She turned back and found him still lying on the bed. Still tied up, one limb to each corner. Drawn and quartered.

How many times had she cleaned up his filth? Piss on the toilet seat, on the floor, on the side of the bathroom cabinet where he splashed because he couldn't bother to sit or wipe up after himself. No, that was her job. And his vomit all those times he got drunk and missed the bowl. That was her job too. What used to be just normal smells of human life had become the stench of him, a vile, inescapable odour that followed her every move. His sweaty armpits when he fucked her without showering, his stinky feet when he walked across the spotless linoleum and ground his smell into the carpet, coffee and cigarettes and bourbon and beer that he breathed, hot and moist, onto her neck when he held her hair, pulled back her head, and growled obscenities into her ear.

He was covered in blood, soiled with his own urine, stinking of the booze he'd drunk and of the bourbon she'd poured into his wounds. She cocked her head and smiled.

There would be no cleaning up. Not for him. Not ever again.

She paced at the foot of the bed, her arms crossed, her gaze fixed on his eyes.

He turned his head. "Stop staring at me."

He looked deflated. Like a balloon with a tiny hole that had lost a lot of hot air. She'd broken him, made him cry, hurt him and demeaned him. She should be elated. Satisfied. A tiny bit happy.

But she was none of those things. There was no joy in seeing him this way. No excitement, no release in causing him harm. There was only emptiness. The relief of that fact was overwhelming. She was not a monster. She'd never be what he had become. She took no pleasure in his pain, despite every hateful blow he'd heaped upon her, despite her own hatred for him. The stream of tears it brought to her eyes was unrestrained.

"Damn it, you've made your point!" His breathing became laboured, his chest heaved. His eyes lost their resignation and regained a familiar glint. He was angry.

Nothing had changed. If she let him loose she would suffer at his hands. He would overpower her, attack her. Break her. Kill her. That was the inevitable end to life with Cullen.

Death.

He pulled on the restraints and kicked his feet, his face contorted in pain. The bed creaked and the headboard hit the wall.

Thud, thud, thud, thud.

Her body rocked with the sound of their sex.

Creak, thud, gasp, thud, gasp, creak, thud.

She wiped one palm across her forehead, then covered her ears with both hands and closed her eyes. "Stop it!" She barely heard her own voice screaming over the incessant banging of wood against drywall. The room began to spin. Her eyes shot open.

The whole bed rocked with his attempts to rip himself free. "Let me loose. Now, so I can fucking kill you! I hate you, you fucking bitch. You hear me? I hate you!"

Mazie raced down the stairs to the kitchen. The thudding and creaking followed her with each step. Her eyes scanned every inch of counter space. She yanked open the knife drawer, touched the handle of each blade. Her fingers tingled when they made contact with the smooth surface of the black pakkawood handle of her favourite chef's knife. She raised it from the drawer and slid it from its sheath. Moonlight streamed in the front window and glinted off the sharpened edge. Her reflection in the steel was warped and twisted, like a funhouse mirror. She focused on the purple bruise around her eye and scabbed wound on her cheek. On the smear of his blood across her forehead.

She held the knife at her side, blade pointed toward the floor. Every footstep up the stairs, across the hall and into the bedroom calmed her. Her mind was lucid. Her intention clear. Her patience with him spent. She stood beside the bed and stared at him as he thrashed.

His efforts had opened his wounds. Fresh blood, bright and scarlet, dripped onto the bed sheet.

His gaze froze on the knife. His eyes darted from the blade to her eyes and back again. He shook his head. "Don't do it."

"Do what?"

His eyes narrowed and he smirked. "You can't do it, can you?"

"Do what?"

"You fucking nut job. You haven't got the stones for it."

She raised the knife.

He pressed his head back into the pillow, his eyes frozen open, tracking the arc of the blade.

She brought the knife down in one swift movement. It sliced though his abdomen, as easy as hacking up a summer watermelon. When the knife came up, a trail of blood flew from the tip, leaving an arc of red spatter across the bed and his chest. The second time the blade pierced his flesh, his screams disappeared amid the thrumming of her heartbeat in her ears. She brought her arm up three times, four, five. She stabbed and sliced, the room silent despite Cullen's open, screaming, bourbon-reeking mouth. There was only her heartbeat, the swish of metal through the air, and the spray of his blood.

Her arm wearied. She ceased the onslaught, her arm above her head. Drops of his metallic, stinking blood, like a rusted scouring pad left under the sink too long, landed softly in her hair and on her shirt. She dropped her arm to her side and poked his face with her other hand. His head lolled to the side, his eyes open, mouth agape. He'd stopped screaming. Stopped yelling at her. Stopped demeaning her.

He'd just stopped.

The time glowed on the clock-radio. Five forty-seven. Mazie wandered to the window and brushed the drape aside with the knife blade. The horizon was awash in red and purple streaks. The air was still, the cul-de-sac silent.

It was going to be a beautiful day.

~~~~~~~~~
~~~~~~~~~

Mazie sat in the chair at the foot of the bed and watched the clock radio mark the passing of each interminable minute. Leaden arms and legs pinned her to the seat, her mind a blank canvas, empty of thought and emotion.

A hollow thud shook her from her daze. She crossed the room and peered out through a crack in the blood-stained drape.

The paper boy rode his bicycle away from the house and stopped in front of Rachel's. He grabbed a newspaper from the wagon behind his bike, bound it with an elastic band, and tossed it toward the Simpson's porch.

Awareness seeped in. Her skin was sticky and crusty with Cullen's blood. She held out her hands. In the right was the knife. Her favourite one, so sharp and perfect for cutting through carrots and potatoes at a professional pace, for severing sinew from bone when she butchered a rack of lamb down to chops. In her left was her husband's flaccid penis. She recoiled and dropped it on the carpet. She spun around. His body was still. His angry mouth silent. He was covered in blood, sliced and diced. His crotch and torso were ground beef.

She looked at his penis on the floor. So small. So insignificant. A grin crossed her lips and soon she was laughing hysterically. How had this insignificant thing been the cause of so much pain and anguish? What power did it hold over him that satisfying it was more important than keeping his wife, the woman he used to love, safe and free from harm? She shook her head and stepped over it.

God, she needed a cup of coffee.

The screech of the six o'clock alarm clock made her jump. She raced to the other side of the bed and slapped the snooze button, turned and surveyed the room. Her arms and legs went cold, her mind numb.

Blood trails splattered the walls and the carpet. The bourbon bottle lay on its side on the dresser, its contents pooled on the pine. She raised her eyes and followed a roadmap of his death. Red sprays stained the ceiling and scarlet drops plopped onto the pools of blood on his body. She tossed the knife and held out her arms. They were soaked with him. Crimson taunted her from under her nails, from the grooves of her fingerprints where his blood had ground into her skin. She wiped her palms against her T-shirt to find it sticky as well, like a murderous tie-dye experiment gone horribly wrong.

She sank to the floor, and curled up on the carpet. Her entire body convulsed with shivers and tremors and dry sobs. What had she done? She'd only intended to hurt him and leave.

The snooze alarm sounded and her body jerked at the intrusion. Her gaze darted around the room. Six oh-nine.

She had to get ready. She had to go.

She reached up to the night stand, clicked the alarm off, stood and rubbed her hands down the front of her pants, her gaze fixed on the bloody sheets.

Cullen's cell phone vibrated against the wood of the night stand. With each shimmying alert, it hopped and bounced, nearer and nearer to the edge.

Mazie held her breath and cut her eyes to his face. She expected his arm to reach out and grab the damn thing. He just lay there, his eyes open and staring straight at her. She exhaled, leaned one knee on the bed and forced his eyelids closed with two fingers. She walked around the bed, her gaze never leaving his face, not fully believing that he was gone. Her nerves were on high alert, ready to cut and run if he sat up and tried to come after her.

She picked up the phone. A text. Her heart fluttered. She wasn't allowed to see his phone, to intrude on his life. But like hell would she not intrude on his death. She pressed the centre button and the screen lit up.

Hey man, what time are we heading to the cabin?

Damn. He'd made actual plans. Someone expected him. Her breathing came in short bursts and her arms went cold. Who the hell was J-Dawg? The phone vibrated in her hand and another message popped up.

Dude. Come on. If we're going today I need to get my shit together and call the girls.

Her eyes narrowed. The girls. She looked at Cullen. Needed some time alone. Away from everything. Right.

She put her thumbs to the keyboard and took a breath. *Sorry man. Not yet. How about next Friday?*

That would give her a week to get some distance. See her mother before she died. Then find a new life.

The phone buzzed. *Seriously? We'd only have the weekend then. Man, these chicks are good to go! You're gonna spend a week at home with that bitch instead?*

Her eyes were slits. He didn't just call her a bitch at home. He let his friends do it too. And just how many trips alone to the cabin involved chicks that were good to go? She glanced at his flaccid manhood lying on the floor, curled her nose at the smell of excrement that was seeping from his anus.

Want to spend time with my little girl. There will always be more chicks. She grinned and pressed send. *I'll let you know.* Send. She turned the phone off.

"Yup, those chicks would love you now, you sorry bastard." She swatted his foot.

Mazie stripped, gathered her soiled clothes and ran them down to the washer. She righted the brandy bottle and wiped up the spilled alcohol, but it had already started to take the finish off the dresser. She scanned the room. There was no way she'd be able to clean it up. What was the point? She couldn't move his body anyway. He was too heavy even when he wasn't dead weight.

She gathered the pictures, wiped drops of drying blood from them onto the sheets, and arranged one set of them on the bed in order of the beatings, from the first black eye to the last. She opened one copy of the notebook filled with proof — dates and damage done, lies and guilt. She added a final entry.

I, Mazie Louise Reynolds, have murdered my bastard husband, Cullen Reginald Reynolds. I didn't set out to kill him. I just wanted him to have a taste of his own medicine before I took our daughter away. To protect her from him, from being physically and sexually abused by her own father. He'd hit her. And he planned on raping her. I know because he told me so.

This notebook and the pictures document the terror he's inflicted on me for the past four years. It does not include anything he did in the seven years prior to that. I didn't think to document it. I thought he had a good heart. I thought we could make our marriage work. I thought he loved me.

If I hadn't killed him, it would be my body lying here. And Ariel would be irreparably damaged.

I do not regret my actions. But I do apologize for slicing off his penis. That was overkill.

She signed her name, dated the entry, and laid the book on his mangled torso.

She ran the shower until it was hot, climbed into the tub and scrubbed her skin and her hair. After two shampoos it was still caked with blood. She washed it three more times and left conditioner in while she took a nail brush to her fingers and feet. When she was finished, no trace of his blood remained on her body, but her skin was nearly raw. Pink drops of bloody water dotted the floor and stained the nylon shower curtain. She dried her hair and doused her skin with the same body lotion she'd used every day for years. A life lived on autopilot.

She tiptoed around blood, slid on her slippers to protect her clean feet, retrieved the clothes that waited, folded and clean and tucked safely in the bottom drawer of her dresser, that she'd set aside for the trip. The air left her when each piece — white bikini briefs, camel walking shorts, stretchy black tank, lightweight cornflower cardigan, and her ivory scarf — came out dotted with red spots.

"No, no, no." She licked her thumb and rubbed at one spot. It didn't budge. She clamped her eyes shut and held her breath. When she opened them, the spots had disappeared. She flipped the fabric and inspected every inch, but they were clean and blood-free. She buried her face in the soft cotton of the cardigan and sniffed the mountain freshness of fabric softener. Her shoulders shook. She lifted her head from the fabric and giggled. "Jeez Louise, Mazie Baby, don't lose your shit now."

She rushed to get dressed, held an un-bloodied corner of the bedroom chair for balance while she slipped each trembling leg into her shorts. "Get yourself together, girl. You can do this. Just a little change in plans, that's all." She glanced at the bed. Brandy and bourbon rolled up her throat. She fought back and swallowed the urge to vomit. She nodded. "Just a little change in plans."

She retrieved the packed luggage from Ariel's closet, sidestepped her bloody footprints in the hall and on the stairs, bounced the luggage down the steps and stood each piece at attention on the tile floor in the front entry. She ran downstairs, pulled her wet clothes out of the washer and piled them into the dryer.

Coffee. She needed coffee. She started a pot and filled a tote bag with water bottles and snacks while it brewed. She skittered about the house making last-minute preparations. A Thermos filled with fresh, creamy coffee joined the snacks in the tote bag while she ticked off necessities of a long trip in her head.

Food for the trip? Check.

Drained the account of cash? Almost.

Shut off the main water? Check

Unplugged the appliances? Check

Clothes, toiletries, lady products, makeup to cover her bruises and wounds, lots of scarves, all packed? Check.

House spotless?

She glanced around. The main floor was neat as a pin except for a few bloody toe prints. Almost normal. She looked at the ceiling above her and closed her eyes. "Good enough."

That was going to be her new mantra.

She pulled open the front door. The newspaper sat where it had landed earlier.

"Damn it." There was always something.

She snapped the elastic band off the rolled paper, found the contact numbers on the second page and made a quick phone call to put delivery on vacation hold. She smirked. Permanent vacation hold. She tossed the paper into the recycle bin and hauled the luggage and tote bags and extra shoes out to the van. After four trips, everything was set. She stood in the kitchen and took one last look around her home.

No, not home. Home is a safe place. Somewhere to find peace and comfort, to look forward to coming back to. This was just a house. A cell. Bricks and mortar and invisible iron bars. She'd never be coming back.

The clock ticked in the silent room. It wasn't even eight. She couldn't knock on Rachel's door this early on a Saturday. She poured the last bit of coffee into a mug, finished off the cream that remained in the fridge and threw out the container, then sat at her kitchen table for the last time. She held the mug with both hands and sipped, the ticking of that damn clock growing louder with each passing minute. She ran her fingertip around the rim of the mug, tapped one foot against the floor and let out a sigh. She had to keep busy.

She Swiffered the kitchen floor and dusted the living room furniture. She'd done both the day before. There was no dust worth cleaning up. She eyed the pink toe prints on the living room carpet, each stain growing more faint the farther from the stairs she had run, until they disappeared just before the kitchen tile. She dug a bottle of soda water from the fridge, poured it on a stain and pressed paper towels into it. It faded but persisted. Mocked her attempts to erase her tracks. She tossed the soiled towels into the garbage, put the bag out in the black bin in the alley, dumped the rest of the soda down the drain and pitched the can into the recycling container under the sink with the other soda cans and Cullen's empty beer and bourbon bottles.

She stood at the sink, her hands on her hips, and stared at the clock. Eight-twenty-seven. Seriously? Did it need a new battery? She pulled her cell phone from her purse. Nope, it was dead on. She smiled.

Dead.

Why was that funny?

The alarm on the dryer let out its pitiful mewls. She took the stairs at a snail's pace and stared at the red light that blinked and winked at her. Your bloody clothes are dry. Hurry up and fold them.

She pulled her jeans from the machine, held them up in the dim light of the concrete utility room. Palm-sized stains, rusty and pink, marred the thighs and the knees, and ran down the side seams and the back pockets where she'd attempted to wipe him from her skin. She ran her hands across the denim. Tears welled in her eyes. Total write off.

She was going to miss those pants. She dropped them to the cement floor, climbed the stairs, and left them behind.

She was so done with this house. It was time to get out.

She slipped on her sandals, pulled the front door closed with a quiet click, secured the deadbolt, and headed across the grass. She didn't look at the house again. Didn't glance up at the bedroom window where Cullen was growing colder by the minute. Colder than he'd been in years. Now that's good karma. Or perhaps a twist of sweet irony.

The morning dew still clung to the grass, the cool droplets on her bare toes refreshing. She scooped up the newspaper from Rachel's stoop and tapped on the door.

The door opened on the first knock. Damn nosy woman had been watching.

"Morning, Rachel." Mazie held out the paper. "Ariel ready?"

"Just finishing breakfast. Come in for a second."

Rachel took the paper and tossed it onto a small table near the kitchen as she passed. The flannel of her pyjama pants swished at the thighs with each step.

Mazie stepped across the threshold. In all the years they'd lived next to the Simpsons, she'd only been on their back deck, and that was just to recover Ariel's Frisbee.

A ball of fur bolted toward her, yapping and sniffing at her exposed ankles. She laid her fluffy little body at Mazie's feet and licked her big toe.

"Biscuit!" Rachel picked up the dog and shoved her away. "Sorry. She's usually more standoffish. You must have walked through something yummy." The woman's lilting laugh came easy.

Shoes littered the front entry, none of them lined up against the wall, no plastic mat to protect the floor. Dusty prints and clumps of mud crunched under Mazie's sandals. She pushed shoes aside with her feet, trying to make some small bit of order from the sneaker and sandal and winter boot chaos. Winter boots in the entry. In June?

"Hey, mom." Ariel sat beside Polly on a tall barstool at an island in the kitchen. It stood high, diner lunch counter-style. Ariel's hair was a tangled mess. Milk dripped from a spoon and onto her nightgown as she shovelled Cheerios into her mouth.

"Hi, bug. Are you about ready to go?"

"Almost. I just have to get dressed and brush my teeth."

"And your hair, please."

Ariel nodded, her mouth full of cereal again.

"You want a coffee?" Rachel had been eyeing Mazie. "Ariel will be a little while, you've got time."

It was the last thing Mazie wanted. Should she agree? An attempt to act normal? Though, normal would never include having coffee with Rachel. Or being inside her house.

Mazie rubbed a growing chill from her arms. "I'd like to get going soon. It's a long trip. Was hoping to make Regina before supper and spend the night."

Rachel grabbed her hand and tugged on it. "That's only an eight hour drive. Come on. You've never even stepped foot in my house before."

Mazie sighed. "All right, one cup." She went to slip off one sandal.

Rachel waved a hand toward Mazie's feet. "You can leave your shoes on."

Mazie swallowed before taking a tentative step onto the carpet. Her shoes would be covered with dirt and dust from the grocery store and the van and the sidewalk. It would get tracked onto the carpet and dull it with filth. One, two, three steps in. Nothing happened. No one yelled at her. No one swatted her and told her she was disgusting and should clean up her footprints.

Rachel's husband, George, crossed the living room, clad only in a terrycloth robe, a large mug of coffee in one hand. He raised the cup to her on his way by. "Morning, Mazie. Lovely day for a road trip." He slapped Rachel's ass.

Mazie stiffened. She looked at her feet, then raised her eyes to the couple.

Rachel jumped and pretended to slap him, her cheeks pink.

George flashed his eyebrows up and down at his wife and kissed her cheek. "I'm going to get dressed and clean up the dog crap." He turned to Mazie. "You want me to mow your lawn?"

"No thank you. I just did it two days ago."

"All right then. Just let me know if you'd like some help. I notice your husband is never out there."

"He works long hours. The house is my job."

George raised one eyebrow. "That's a load of bullshit, love. Tell me if you change your mind. And drive safe, hear?"

"I will, thank you." Mazie glanced around the room and pressed a hand to the growing knot in her stomach. The house wasn't filthy, but clutter was strewn about. The books on the bookshelf weren't lined up in a row, some were on their sides and some had the spines upside down. The furniture clearly hadn't been dusted in days. Tufts of long Lhasa Apso hair stuck to the carpet. Dishes from the night before still sat in the sink, and sugar crystals and drops of cream dirtied the countertop.

George didn't seem to give a damn that his home was untidy, or that it was almost nine in the morning and his wife hadn't even dressed yet. He seemed… happy.

Mazie took small steps toward the kitchen. She picked up the sink cloth, rinsed it under the tap, and began wiping down the countertop.

Rachel put both her hands over Mazie's and stopped the swirling motion of the cloth. "Honey, you don't have to do that. I'll get to it later."

Mazie let go of the cloth, pulled her hands away from Rachel's touch, and nodded. "Sorry."

"Go. Sit with Ariel. I'll get you a coffee. How do you take it?"

"Cream and sugar, please." She kissed the top of her daughter's head, mussed up Polly's already messy mop of copper curls, and sat at the counter.

Rachel placed a mug of steaming coffee in front of her. "Goodness me, you're trembling."

Mazie wrung her hands together. "I'm fine. Just a bit hungry."

"Want some of my Cheerios?" Ariel held up a dripping spoonful of cereal.

Mazie smiled. "No thanks, bug. Maybe we'll get some doughnuts on the way. There's a Tim Horton's in Shawnessy. We can make a quick detour before we hit the highway."

"Yes! Can we get maple cream?"

"Anything you want."

"Timbits too?" Ariel's eye nearly bugged out of her head.

Mazie laughed. "Anything at all."

Rachel climbed onto the stool across the island from Mazie. The woman's hair was kinked and tatted, her makeup smudged, flakes of day-old mascara dotting the skin under her eyes. Mazie touched her fingers to her own hair, clean and dry and sprayed into place.

"Is Cullen going fishing while you two are away?"

Mazie swallowed and looked at her hands. "He's gone." At least it wasn't a lie.

Rachel squinted at her. "But his truck is still in the driveway out back."

Mazie's heart thumped in her ears. She opened her mouth but no words came. She looked at the coffee mug, at the countertop. Anywhere but Rachel's nosy face. "He went with a couple of buddies from work. They took one guy's camper."

Rachel nodded. "Oh. I guess I didn't hear them go."

"Well, they left at some ungodly hour in the middle of the

night." Mazie did her best to sound casual and hoped that Rachel didn't notice the crack in her voice. "I guess they wanted to get a jump on weekend traffic."

Rachel nodded.

She looked at Rachel. "Cullen will be gone for at least ten days."

Ariel hopped off the stool. She grabbed Polly's hand and the two of them ran up the stairs. Mazie took their bowls to the sink, dumped the milk and remaining cereal into the garburetor, and rinsed them under the tap.

"Mazie, stop. You don't have to clean up after us."

She spun around. Rachel stood with her arms crossed over her chest, that snoopy look on her snoopy face.

"I... I'm sorry. It's just habit. I didn't mean anything by it."

"I know that. Just sit and relax for a minute. There's nothing you need to do here."

Mazie crawled back on the stool, stared at the mug, sipped at the coffee. For a few blessed moments, Rachel shut the hell up.

Ariel's and Polly's footsteps thudded down the stairs. They came into the kitchen, their heads close together, both looking at Polly's phone and laughing. "Mom, do you have your cell phone?"

"In the van."

"Good." She took Polly's phone and thumbed the keyboard. "Text me. All the time."

Polly nodded. "Ditto."

Mazie stood. "Ready?"

"Ready!"

"So, you're gone for more than a week?" Rachel stood, one eyebrow raised in that 'tell me everything so I can tell the world' way she had.

"Yes, ten days or so."

"And Cullen too? We shouldn't expect any movement in your

house for ten full days?"

Mazie stared at her, nodded slowly. "That's right. Ten days." She turned and started toward the front door.

"Mazie, wait." Rachel blew air from her lungs and glanced around her kitchen. Her face lit up. "Mail!"

"I'm sorry?"

"Your mail. Can I bring it in for you? And your paper?"

"I stopped the paper. But yes, the mail." Why hadn't she thought of that? "Do you mind?"

Rachel shook her head. "Not a bit." She made a move toward Mazie. "Look, do you need anything? For your trip I mean."

"No thanks."

"I have some spare cash. Do you have enough money?"

Mazie scrunched her face up and shook her head. "Rachel, we're fine. Are you okay?"

"Yeah, I'm good. Just, you know, call me if you need anything." She scurried over to the fridge and scrawled on a pad of notepaper stuck to it with magnets. "Here's my number. Anything you need. Anytime."

Mazie took the paper. Under the phone number, Rachel had scrawled 'I understand' in loose cursive. Mazie snapped her head up and looked at the woman.

She nodded again. "You take care of yourself, Mazie. You hear me?" She stepped forward and crushed Mazie in a long hug.

Mazie stood perfectly still, her arms pinned to her sides. She looked at Ariel and rolled her eyes.

Ariel shrugged.

~~~~~~~~

Three people stood in line in front of Mazie, each waiting for the
~~~~~~~~

slowpokes at the two ATMs to hurry the hell up. She tapped one foot on the dirty tile of the vestibule and ran her thumb over Cullen's debit card. The raised letters of his name taunted the pads of her trembling fingers and made the fine hairs at the base of her neck prickle and stand and on end.

Her gaze ping-ponged about the space and came to rest on a camera above one machine. She slid her sunglasses off her head and onto her nose, pulled up the hood of her jacket and tucked her hair back. Her gaze cast downward, she approached and withdrew the five hundred dollar daily limit. She would drain the balance the next morning, then slice his card to little bits.

Slice, slice, slice. She grinned. Why was that funny?

A block away, she pulled into the doughnut shop drive-through. A police cruiser was dead ahead. Her heart raced. She coughed and covered her mouth and most of her face with one trembling hand, glanced in the rear-view mirror. Another cop car pulled in behind her.

"Mom, are you okay?"

"What?"

"You're breathing funny. And sweating." Ariel pointed out the front window. "And the line moved up, like, two cars."

"Shit." She jerked the van forward then slammed on the brakes.

Ariel giggled. "Can I swear?"

"Only after you get your driver's license." She gripped the wheel with both hands and forced out a laugh.

Time to get her shit together. They wouldn't even have found his body yet.

She yelled their order into the speaker then inched up to the window after the first police cruiser had pulled away.

"Good morning. Your order was covered by the car ahead of you."

"I'm sorry?"

The clerk in the brown polyester uniform gave her a withering look. "You know, that whole 'pay it forward' thing that's been going on?"

"No, sorry. I don't know. The cops paid for our doughnuts?"

"Yes, ma'am."

Mazie shook her head. "Okay then. How about I pay for the police behind me?"

The clerk flashed a wide grin. "You bet! Two extra-large double-double and a twenty pack of Timbits. That'll be eight-oh-seven."

A bit of good karma couldn't hurt.

Mazie pulled the van onto Highway Twenty-two and headed east. The sun was brilliant, the heat penetrated the air conditioned space and warmed her face. She took a sip of coffee and popped a ball of deep-fried dough into her mouth. Sour cream glazed, her favourite.

Ariel wasted no time finding a radio station. She bobbed her head and mumbled the words to some song Mazie was unfamiliar with.

"Can we put on another station?"

Ariel covered the buttons with her hand. "No, please? Daddy never lets me listen to my music. He's always got that country crap on."

Mazie grinned. "Fair enough. No country crap. But maybe when the radio cuts out, we could put in the Beatles or Bon Jovi or something I know the words to."

"You're going to sing?"

"Yes." Mazie nodded. "Yes I am."

As they approached the city limits, a siren whooped behind them. Mazie glanced in the rear-view to find a police cruiser, lights flashing.

"No, no, no."

"Are you speeding?" Ariel twisted in her seat and watched out the back window.

"Nope." She signalled right, pulled onto the shoulder, and slowed to a stop. She watched the officer approach in the side mirror. She gripped the steering wheel, huffed a few breaths like she was in labour. Not that those idiotic breathing exercises actually worked.

She could floor it just as he got to her. Get a head start. She looked the rear-view, at the new black and white Interceptor, another cop in the driver's seat. She wouldn't even get half a kilometre.

He tapped on her window. She jumped, depressed the window button and waited for it to slide down. "Hi, officer. What's the problem?"

He flashed a bright smile at her. "No problem, ma'am. Just wanted to say thanks for the coffee and Timbits." He tipped his hat. "Where you all headed?"

"Just a summer road trip." Mazie's voice cracked.

"We're going to visit my grandma." Ariel beamed at the handsome officer.

"Here, young lady." He pulled a Tim Horton's gift card out of his breast pocket and reached into the van.

His arm was inches from Mazie's face, his shoulder brushed her hair. The smell of his cologne and sweat brought coffee and Timbits rolling up her throat. She swallowed hard. Could he hear her heart beating?

He handed the card to Ariel. "Wherever you're headed, lunch is on me and my partner." He tipped his hat again. "Drive safe, now."

"We will, thank you." Mazie watched him in the side view mirror until he disappeared behind the van and the patrol car pulled out and did a U-turn on the highway. She let out the breath she'd been holding and blinked a long blink. "All right then. Let's get on the road."

~~~~~~~~

The thrum of tires on blacktop, Matchbox Twenty at low volume, the utter boredom of the flat prairie horizon. The perfect storm for falling asleep at the wheel. Mazie's head jerked. She blinked and tried to focus on the horizon, to ignore the white lines painted on the highway zinging past her peripheral vision. She pinched her thigh, cranked the air conditioning, and pointed the air vents at her face. Regina's meagre skyline loomed ahead.

"Bug, we're here."

Ariel stretched and rubbed one fist against her eye. "Grandma's?" During her waking moments, the 'tween persona dissolved into the innocence and wonder of a sweet little girl. If only time could freeze and keep her there. Keep her from maturing and noticing boys. Boys who turn into men. Men who turn into monsters.

"Not yet. We're at a hotel in Regina. I'm done driving for the day. Maybe we can order in some pizza and watch a movie?"

Ariel straightened and glanced around, her hair stuck to one sweaty cheek. "Okay. I'm starved."

Hours later, sated by cheese and dough, they settled into their shared queen-size bed. Mazie clicked off the light and pointed the remote at the television, her thumb on the off button.

"Can we leave it on?" Ariel lay beside her, the covers at her chin.

"Won't it keep you awake?" Mazie stroked her daughter's hair.

"I just want a little light and sound. This room creeps me out."

"All right." Mazie turned the volume down low and set the sleep timer for one hour. She punched her pillow and slid down under the covers.

Ariel inched over until their arms touched.
~~~~~~~~

Mazie smiled. She slipped her arm under her daughter's shoulder and hugged her against her body, placed a gentle kiss against the thick hair on the top of her head. "Night, bug."

Mazie closed her eyes against the television's glow and tried to empty her thoughts, to steady her breath. Lost in the fog between asleep and awake, Cullen's hands tightened around her throat. She fought for air and gasped. The television flickered. The clock glared at her. They'd only been in bed for fifteen minutes.

Each time sleep beckoned, a leg spasmed, or her own snorts shook her awake. And guilt crushed her chest. She hadn't unloaded the dishwasher. Hadn't cleaned the bedroom or scrubbed the carpet.

Cullen would be furious.

Laughter bubbled to the surface. She'd gone through the daily motions like an obsessive compulsive zombie, dragging her dead limbs behind her, mindless and rote, scrubbing and washing and cooking and trying to avoid the inevitable punishment when nothing she did was good enough.

It was his turn to be the zombie in this relationship. His absence from the feeling world was permanent. Why was it taking so long for that to seep into her subconscious? And when it did, why was it so damn funny?

~~~~~~~~

A hundred kilometres into day two and Ariel was already moaning about how bored she was. "It's just flat and grass and kilometres of nothing. There aren't even mountains."

"We're in the heart of the prairie. Haven't you learned Canadian geography in school?"

"Yeah. But it's even more boring in real life."

"I think it has a quiet beauty about it. The way the wind makes
~~~~~~~~

the fields of wheat wave and undulate. Like a golden ocean that you can never drown in. And the endless horizon, the sky to infinity. Look how blue that is."

Ariel leaned forward and craned her neck to look up. "I suppose." She fiddled with the radio dials and grimaced when she was rewarded with nothing but static.

"When we stop for lunch, you can buy a book or some magazines."

"When's that?"

"A couple of hours."

"Two hours? I'll die of boredom by then."

Two rest stops and one lunch break later, they pulled into Winnipeg late in the afternoon. "We could stop here," Mazie said. "Or just gas up and keep on going. Get to Grandma's a day early."

"Yes, keep going. Can I get some chips and Coke?"

"That would ruin your dinner. Your fath…" Mazie clamped her lips shut and glanced at Ariel. "Sure. Why not?"

Just past Kenora, Mazie's chin dipped to her chest. Her head snapped up to find the van drifting to the left. She jerked the steering wheel to correct. Her body jerked along with it, and Ariel's sleeping head banged against the door where it rested.

"What was that?" She sat up.

"Sorry. Maybe it's time to pull over for the night. I'm getting tired."

"Mom, look out!"

At the apex of a curve fifty yards ahead, two deer strolled across the highway. Mazie pumped her brakes and honked her horn. The deer stopped in the middle of her lane. Their eyes gleamed golden fire, lit by the setting sun. Mazie pulled to the right onto the shallow shoulder and skidded to a halt not two feet from the smallest deer.

Adrenaline accelerated her heart and turned her legs to pudding.

She rested her head on her knuckles that had a death-grip on the steering wheel. "Fuck," she whispered.

"Shit, Mom. You nearly hit them."

Mazie smiled at her daughter's profanity.

Ariel bounced in her seat. "You almost killed them."

"Or they almost killed us."

"They're so pretty. I wish we had a camera."

Venison on hooves. That's what Cullen always called them. Damn it, why wouldn't he get out of her head?

The deer were frozen in place, like so many plastic lawn ornaments dotting the highway. One ear twitched on the largest, an apparent signal to the rest. They reanimated, cantered across the asphalt and disappeared down the embankment. A semi came at them from the other direction and honked the air horn. Mazie jumped. "Holy hell."

"Where should we stop?" Ariel's gaze darted side to side, scanning the edges of the highway.

"Well, I'm awake now." Mazie's heartbeat pounded in her ears, and her hands trembled on the wheel. She checked her mirrors and pulled back onto the highway. "You keep watch for wildlife and we'll go for another hour. We can make Dryden tonight."

"Can we find another Pizza Hut?"

"Oh, sweetheart. I can't do pizza again. Let's see if there's a steakhouse."

Saliva filled Mazie's mouth. A glass of wine and a giant steak was just what she needed. Maybe between the food and the alcohol, she could get a decent night's sleep.

~~~~~~~~~

Mazie lay in bed and stared at her reflection in the mirror on the
~~~~~~~~~

opposite wall. A deluge of thoughts flooded her brain. Visions of the future were streaked and marred by the failures of yesterday. When she allowed her mind to find a happy tomorrow, the sight of Cullen's body, sliced and diced and left to rot in the torture chamber of her past, intruded on a perfectly good fantasy.

Even in death, he still ruined everything.

She pressed her palm against the lump in her gut. Only two bites into her steak the night before and she'd pushed the plate away. The juice and blood that oozed from the T-bone brought visions of crimson stains on her best bed sheets. She'd set aside her red wine and asked for a vodka tonic instead. Nothing but beige food for a while. And beige drinks. Beige, beige, beige.

She glanced at the clock radio. Eight forty-two. They should have been on the road an hour ago.

The sun streamed in through the dusty drapes and laid a sliver of bright heat across the bedspread. Ariel squirmed beside her. Mazie stroked her hair and leaned over to kiss the top of her head. A good night's sleep had eluded Mazie again. Between the highway noise and the urine-meets-sweat-sock smell in the room, there was no comfort at the Comfort Inn. The few times she did find enough peace to nod off, she jolted awake, her body atremble, her mind filled with murder.

Where were they? She reached for the nightstand and grabbed a notepad. A pen skittered off the edge of the table and dropped onto the carpet.

She eyed the hotel address on the paper. Dryden. Right.

She slipped out of bed and took a quick shower, pulled her hair into a ponytail and daubed foundation onto the yellow-and-green bruises on her face.

She ripped open a pack of coffee and poked the encapsulated filter into the machine, poured water into the reservoir, dropped the cup under the spout, and gave the start button a hard poke.

A stream of caffeinated elixir poured into the cup. Even shitty hotel coffee was better than no coffee at all. She breathed the aroma deep into her nostrils and closed her eyes.

Before he'd ever said a word, she could smell his arrival — an intoxicating mix of cheap cologne and post-coital sweat. His arms circled her from behind, slipped around her waist, tugged the sash of her robe free and brushed against the soft skin of her naked belly. He buried his nose in the fine hair at the base of her neck.

"Good morning. I smell coffee."

Her breath caught in her throat and she laid the back of her head against his shoulder. His right hand wandered down the front of her body until he found her sweet spot. He slid his fingers inside, one stroke for every pounding heartbeat, licked and bit at her neck and ear lobe.

Her palms against the counter's edge, she pushed against him, his erection prodding her through her robe. She climaxed and called out, her legs jelly. He slid her to the floor and made love to her on the tile. They came together at the exact moment the coffee machine announced it was finished.

"Mom, coffee's ready."

Mazie opened her eyes and stared at the crappy one-cup brewer on the mini-fridge.

Ariel yawned. "Can we have pancakes?"

"Sure." Mazie wrapped her arms around Ariel, gave her a long hug and kissed her temple. "Go get dressed and brush your teeth."

Mazie packed their belongings and grabbed her phone from the dresser. Before she could slip it into the front pocket of her purse, it vibrated in her hand and sent a shrill chime through the room.

She stared at the glowing screen like it was a can of fake nuts and coiled up snakes were about to jump out at her.

How the hell? Only Cullen had that number. And Ariel.

"Is that Daddy?"

"No, bug. Not Daddy."

The ringing stopped. Ariel took it from Mazie's hand and pressed a couple of buttons. A broad smile overtook her face. "It was Polly!"

Polly. Of course.

"Can I call her back?"

"Not now. We have to get on the road. Maybe later."

Ariel sighed. "All right."

A few kilometres down the road, the bright neon sign of a diner caught Mazie's eye. She angle-parked the van between two pickup trucks, both caked with muck. A bell above the door announced their presence. They found an empty booth near the back with a window view of the parking lot and the highway. Mazie sat facing the door, Ariel across from her.

Two menus, laminated and sticky to the touch, were stacked behind a chrome rack which held bottles of sugar and ketchup and vinegar. Mazie scanned the list of basic diner fare.

"Look, bug." She pointed at Ariel's menu. "French toast."

"Nah, I want pancakes."

A fat waitress in a pink polyester tunic stained with all manner of sauces and grease sidled up to the table and pulled a pencil from behind her ear. *Norma*, her faded and food-crusted nametag proclaimed.

"Mornin', ladies. What can I get you?"

Ariel looked at Mazie.

"Go ahead, you can order your own."

"Really? Daddy never lets me."

"Well, Daddy isn't here. Let's make a pact to break as many rules as we can."

Ariel pursed her lips and nodded. She held up her hand, pinkie extended. Mazie locked pinkies with her. They pumped their hands once.

The waitress smirked. "So what'll it be, young lady?"

"Pancakes please. And sausage. And orange juice."

"And for you, Momma?"

"I'll have the same. Except coffee, please. Do you have real cream?"

"Yes, ma'am, none of that petroleum product crap in this joint." She flipped a coffee cup over and reached past the shoulder of a man sitting at the counter. "'Scuse me, love." She grabbed a coffee pot, spun around in the narrow aisle and filled the mug. She pulled three creamers from her pocket. "That enough?"

"For one cup." Mazie smiled. "I'll need a refill soon. The hotel coffee was awful."

"Say no more. I think I know the place." Norma winked. She turned her head. "Two stacks, zeppelins on the side," she yelled toward a man with an apron and a dirty white linen cap. He raised a spatula. "Two stacks, zeppelins on the side," he called.

Ariel giggled. "What did we order?"

"I have no idea." At least the coffee was good.

Norma delivered their breakfast in less than five minutes, along with real maple syrup and whipped butter. They ate every bite, even groaned once or twice, the pancakes were that good. Mazie drank three cups of coffee and Ariel got a refill on her juice.

Norma stopped at the table again. "Can I get you anything else?"

"No thanks. It was delicious."

"I'll pass it on to the chef." She slid a bill onto the table. "You all drive safe."

"Thank you." Mazie flipped the bill over. Nine seventy-five. She dropped a ten dollar bill on the table, and tossed a toonie on top. The bell over the door chimed.

Two officers entered the diner, their short-sleeved black shirts covered by the ever-present bullet-proof vest, a crest emblazoned with "OPP" on each sleeve. One slid onto a stool and tipped his hat to Norma, then set it on the counter at his elbow.

Norma filled two coffee cups and kibitzed with the man. The partner stood and glanced around the diner.

Mazie froze. She pressed against the window and slouched in her seat, picked up the empty coffee cup and shielded her face with it. Was he staring at her? She peeked over the rim of the cup. The second officer was already seated and drinking his coffee. She closed her eyes and shook her head, huffing air out of her nose.

Stupid, stupid, stupid. Even if they had found his body, why would two cops out in the backwoods of Ontario know or care?

Ariel twisted around in her seat. "Mom, are those Mounties?"

"No. Ontario Provincial Police."

"What's the difference?"

"Different uniforms?" She put the cup down and squeezed Ariel's hand. "Mounties are federal. OPP are provincial, just in Ontario. Now let's get out of here. We've got a lot of driving to do."

She slid her butt along the worn vinyl seat of the booth and took Ariel's hand. She straightened her spine, lifted her chin, and set her shoulders back. She walked past the officers, guiding Ariel ahead of her through the narrow passage.

One of the officers looked directly at her. He nodded and smiled.

"Good morning, officer." Despite her attempt at confidence, her voice cracked. At the van, she aimed for the unlock button on the key fob. Her quaking fingers missed the button, the fob and her keys tumbled to the gravel at her feet. "Shit." She stooped and retrieved them, opened the door and scrambled in. She put the van in gear and shoulder-checked behind her before easing out of the parking lot, her mind fully on her breath.

"Mom, your face is all red. You okay?"

"Just anxious to get on the road."

~~~~~~~~~

Mazie cranked up the air conditioning. The sun beat on her left arm and burned her cleavage.

"Squeeze out a bit of sunscreen onto my fingers." She held her right hand out, palm up.

Ariel pulled a plastic tube from the glove box. "Say when."

"When." Mazie rubbed the greasy lotion onto her chest and down her arm.

The sun filtered through the tops of fir and pine that lined the highway. The mountainside was dotted with waterfalls, each one drawing an oooh, or an aaaah out of Ariel. In long stretches where the mountains broke, lakes caught the sun's rays and bounced light into their eyes, the glassy surface broken only by the mild wind and the occasional floating loon.

Mazie caught just glimpses of the beauty that is highway seventeen. All those years ago, when she was the passenger and her father was stuck with driving duties, she'd roll down the window and take in every tiny sight she could. Commit to memory the shades of purple and steel and orange and red of the mountain rock, the sound of every drip and trickle and raging torrent of the waterfalls. Every scent of pine, of sap and wet earth. Even of pungent animal dung, putrid road kill, and the occasional proof that one or two of the bodies squashed under speeding tires had once been waddling skunks.

How she adored this province, especially the stretch of blacktop yet to come. The road that skirted the edge of Lake Superior and
~~~~~~~~~

spanned the hump between Thunder Bay and Marathon before slicing back into the maw of the mountains. She'd stare out the back window until she lost sight of that magnificent body of water, not to see it again until the car emerged on the other side of Wawa.

But she wasn't a sightseer on this trip. Instead she contended with the dipshits and the assholes, semi drivers whose sole purpose in life was to get from point A to point B in as short a time as possible, no matter whose ass they rode, whose nerves they jangled with their air horns and their tailgating and passing when there was no passing lane. Each time she heard the roar of an engine and found nothing but a truck's grill in her rear-view mirror, she slowed, pulled as far to the right as possible with virtually zero shoulder and a sheer mountain face to cushion the passenger side, her daughter's side, if something went horribly wrong. And each time, the van got sucked into the vortex created between truck and rock. She gripped the wheel to stay on the road, focused and took deep breaths.

No wonder her father drank during overnight stops on their long summer road trips.

Heading into Thunder Bay, Mazie veered onto Dawson Road, a shortcut her father made so he could grab a coffee before their ritual pit stop at the Terry Fox Memorial. She hit the drive through at Tim's on East Avenue for her beloved double-double, a couple of maple creams, and a lemonade for Ariel, then continued east on the Trans-Canada. She eased the van along the long leftward curve, the vastness of Lake Superior to their right.

"There it is!" She poked Ariel's arm and pointed. She turned left and followed the loop of road around to the parking area of the memorial. They gathered their snack and approached the memorial. Her mind flooded with memories of her father, of his British Sterling aftershave that no amount of salty wind could tame, of his scratchy five o'clock shadow that always showed up by two, and of their shared love of this exact spot.

They stood at the back side of the memorial and stared up at the curly-haired icon of hope and determination.

"Do you know who Terry Fox is?" Mazie put her arm around her daughter's shoulder.

"Duh, mother. We do the run every year."

"Of course. How silly of me."

"Do you remember it?" Ariel shrugged off Mazie's hand. "When he actually ran? When he died?"

"No, I was just little then, two or three. But every time we took a summer road trip, your grandfather insisted we stop. I didn't know at the time that he had cancer. Didn't understand what it meant to him." A breeze picked up and brought a cool wind off the lake. She turned to admire it, to take a deep inhale of the bitter sweet alkaline odour complemented by algae and fish undertones. Some might turn their nose up. Not her. This was the scent of her innocence. The smell of happiness. If only time machines were real, she'd jump right in, turn back the dial, and slam the door on the past fifteen years.

Ariel took the bag of doughnuts from Mazie's hand, sat on the bench with her back to the water, and took a big bite of maple cream.

Tears pooled in the corners of Mazie's eyes. How could she wish away any moment that brought this beautiful girl into her life? She would just wish away all the horrid Cullen times, and keep the rest for herself.

<center>~~~~~~~~~</center>

The last time Mazie set foot in North Bay, Ariel had been an infant. In all those years, not much had changed.

Her father, because he was stubborn, wouldn't tell anyone of his condition and refused the treatments his doctors offered, died of

119

prostate cancer before he'd ever had a chance to meet his granddaughter. Mazie had been furious with him. Still was. How dare he let disease suck his life dry one day at a time without a word? Without giving her a chance to say goodbye?

Her eyelids fluttered and she glanced at Ariel. The hollow pit of Mazie's stomach ached. Ariel hadn't had a chance to say goodbye to her father either. But he hadn't denied her that. Mazie had. Different kind of disease, all of their lives being sucked dry. At every turn, she'd failed as a mother.

She followed Main Street until it turned into Lakeshore Drive. A torrent of memories rushed at her the second she took a left onto Gertrude Street and passed the little clapboard house where her best friend, Ruthie, had lived. They spent the hottest days of summer on that front lawn, jumping through the sprinkler, gorging on sweet watermelon, spitting seeds at each other.

Ariel sat straighter in her seat. "There aren't any sidewalks."

"Nope."

"The houses are so small."

"In this part of town."

Mazie turned onto the road where she'd grown up, had lived until the day after she turned eighteen when she packed up and moved out in a huff over her mother's incessant need to know everything, share everything, be everywhere she was. She hadn't gone far, just into a crappy apartment in the Gateway, the oldest area of town. The only place she could afford to live on the paltry sum she made waiting tables at the diner. When she landed an executive assistant job downtown — just a glorified title for an old-fashioned secretary, the kind who makes coffee, takes dictation, and lets the boss slap her ass — she could have afforded to move. But she stayed. It had become home. The home she lived in when she'd met Cullen. Where she fell in love with him. Where he convinced her to move to

Calgary.

"Here we are. Grandma's house."

The thousand-square-foot bungalow sat back from the road, the yellow bricks filthy, the wooden window panes rotted and crumbling. Mother hadn't even painted, and it looked like she hadn't mowed the lawn since spring.

Mazie rolled to a stop in the driveway. She eased the gearshift into park, leaned back against the headrest, and stared at her childhood home.

She'd loved this house. Loved her tiny room, her pink and purple oasis, her safe haven. Eleven years ago, she came home to bury her father and discovered her parents had knocked the bedroom wall down, made the living room ninety square feet bigger, and bought a big-screen plasma television and two La-Z-Boy recliners. She had locked herself in the bathroom, sat on the edge of the tub, and bawled like a spoiled little girl who didn't get the biggest piece of cake. All for a bedroom that she hadn't stepped foot in for years. That wasn't hers at all.

She took Ariel's hand and made her way up the short walk, glanced behind the massive boulder on the front lawn where she'd had her first kiss. It was the boy across the street after their first day of grade one. He'd walked home with her, held her hand. What was his name? She closed her eyes but couldn't muster his face, couldn't recall any details about him — except that his breath smelled of Cheezies and Juicy Fruit.

Ariel went to poke the doorbell, but the door swung open before her finger touched the illuminated button.

Mother looked crazy. Her hair was full-on old-lady gray and looked like it hadn't seen a comb in days. The crow's feet around her eyes had become crevasses. Proof of her own fight with illness and disease, of aging at an unnaturally rapid pace.

Mazie's chest tightened. She should have come home more often. But Cullen would never allow it. She should have insisted, risked the repercussions. A lousy mother and a lousy daughter.

A spark of the vibrant woman her mother used to be flashed across her faded blue eyes. That twinkle she had when she'd held down a full-time job, did volunteer work on the weekends, cared for her daughter and her husband and the household, and still found time to play bridge with the girls. But with Dad's insurance payout, his government pensions and no mortgage, she had no need to work. Is that what was killing her? More than aging, more than failing kidneys and clogged arteries and gout. It was stagnancy. She was dying of boredom.

"Get inside!" Her mother grabbed her arm and yanked her through the door. "Come on Ariel, get in now."

"Hello to you too, mother."

"I'm sorry, darling." She hugged Mazie, but pulled away quickly. Tears glistened in her eyes. "Oh, my little Ariel." She brushed a strand of black hair from Ariel's face and pinched her cheek. "You're almost a grown woman."

Ariel blushed. "Hi, Grandma." She hesitated, then held her arms out. It was surreal to watch grandmother and granddaughter meet in an awkward embrace, Ariel now an inch taller than her Grandma. They'd not set eyes on each other since mother came out to visit one summer, four years ago. Cullen could never hide his contempt for his mother-in-law. Could never hold his tongue or show her an ounce of respect. She cut her visit short, unable to bear the weight of his oppressive presence in Mazie's life.

Ariel had tried to get her grandmother to use Skype, but she never did get a computer. Didn't want 'the internets' in her home, like it was some evil force intent on stealing her soul or some such crap. Yup, mother was definitely nuts.

"Ariel, darling, there's cookies in the kitchen. And soda in the fridge." She turned to Mazie. "Is that all right?"

Mazie nodded. "We're not playing by any rules this trip. She can have anything she likes."

Her mother's face lit up. "Down the hall, dear."

"Thanks, Grandma."

Mazie's mother watched Ariel until she was out of earshot then grasped Mazie's wrist and stomped into the living room, dragging her along. She pulled the drape back a bare inch and peered out the front window, her head bobbing side to side and back and forth like a hen on crack.

"Mother, what the hell is going on?" No matter what it was, Mazie couldn't rely on anything her mother told her. Her memory was spotty, she kept forgetting appointments. Granted, Mazie was failing to make their weekly phone calls, but when they did talk, her mother often forgot what she'd been told the last call, couldn't recall details about Ariel's school and friends. Maybe she'd lost it for real this time.

She turned to face Mazie, the puffy sacs under her eyes a lovely shade of mauve.

"The police have been to see me. Twice."

Mazie's chest hollowed. "What? Why?"

Mother stepped toward her, squinted and focused on her face. She touched Mazie's cheek under her left eye, licked her thumb and rubbed it against her daughter's skin.

Mazie was six years old again, getting ice cream drips spit-shined off her face.

"How bad was it this time?" her mother whispered.

"What?"

"The makeup doesn't work." Her face softened. "Oh, darling. I'm so sorry."

"Why are you sorry? You never beat the ever-loving crap out of me."

Her mother's hands trembled, her eyes red-rimmed and swollen. "Darling, what did you do?" Her voice broke.

Mazie looked over her shoulder then back to her mother. "I was leaving. Was going to come home. Then he started talking about Ariel. He was going to…" She swallowed hard and balled her fists. "I did what I had to. The only thing I could." A lump formed in her throat and tears bubbled to the surface. "It was him or me."

Her mother rubbed a hand on Mazie's arm. "It's about damn time."

"What?"

"He deserved it. Don't you think I knew what he was up to? The scarves, the makeup, the long sleeves. The way he looked at you, spoke to you. The way you jumped at the sound of his voice whenever he snapped at you. You never fought back. Not one damn word." She held Mazie's upper arms with her frail, age-spotted hands. "I know he would have killed you one day. I kept waiting for the phone call. But I didn't know what to do."

Mazie laid her head on her mother's shoulder and sobbed.

"I know he wasn't always like that." The stroke of her mother's hand over her hair was familiar comfort. "You loved him for good reason. Once." She stiffened and pulled away, peered out the window. "Look, you've got to go. The police might be watching. They're probably going to come back. They didn't believe me, that I'd not heard from you or that I didn't know where you were."

Mazie straightened and wiped her nose. "I'll turn myself in."

"No! Think of Ariel. I can't take care of her. I'm dying. I probably only have a few months."

"What? Since when?"

"Since they found cancer in my bones."

A wave of misery and guilt body-slammed Mazie. She buckled to the floor and sobbed. "Oh God, Mother. I'm so sorry."

"What for?" Her mother kneeled beside her, both hands on Mazie's shoulders.

"For not being here more, for abandoning you. Especially after Dad died."

"You did not abandon me. You had your own life to live, your own crosses to bear. I just wish *he* weren't ever a part of it."

Mazie pulled away and wiped tears from her face. "If he hadn't been part of it, I wouldn't have Ariel."

"Well, that's true. But what toll has it taken on you?"

Mazie gazed at a family picture on the wall, taken twenty-three years earlier when she was about Ariel's age. They were such a happy family. No violence, no abuse. How she longed to know that feeling again. "Where will I go? I can't go back west."

"Take my car. Put your van in the garage. I've got money for you." She scurried to the dining room and rifled through her purse, pulled out a wad of cash and pressed it into her daughter's palm. "My car is parked in the back alley. I'll go open the garage door." She turned toward the kitchen. "Ariel, we're just going outside. We'll be right back in. If anyone comes to the door, please don't answer it."

Ariel came out of the kitchen holding a Coke and an oatmeal raisin cookie. "Okay, Grandma. Why not?"

"It'll just be those pesky God people. I don't need any of their silly pamphlets. I have my own God."

Mazie ran out to the van, her gaze jerking in all directions, shoulders slouched and head down. She was right to have been afraid of those cops in Dryden. But why hadn't they noticed her? Seen the van? She raced around to the back alley and pulled into the garage. Her mother stood beside her car, the engine running, trunk open.

Mazie yanked luggage from the rear of the van and tossed each bag into the trunk.

Her mother was in the garage, wrestling with a huge, blue tarp. "Here, help me put this over your van. In case the nosy neighbours see it."

Mazie understood about nosy neighbours. She remembered the message from Polly the day before. Maybe it was Rachel? Had that stupid woman figured it out? Called the police?

"Mother, when did the police come see you?"

"Yesterday afternoon. And again this morning."

Her mother ran, as fast as she could run, more of a zombie trot — step drag wheeze, step drag wheeze — into the house to fetch Ariel. She came back carrying a grocery bag, Ariel had an armful of blankets and pillows.

"There's sandwiches and cookies and water and sodas." Words spilled from her mother's mouth. "And a big Thermos of coffee. Sugar and real cream, lots of it." She looked stricken. "You still like it that way, right?"

Mazie nodded. "Yes. Thanks."

Ariel stared at her grandmother, her black brows knit together, one arched high. A look Mazie was familiar with, one she was sure had graced her own face a thousand times in the past. But mother wasn't nuts. She was just mother.

"Mom?" Ariel turned to Mazie. "What's going on?"

"We have to go, bug. I'll tell you about it on the way."

Her mother hugged Ariel and kissed her cheek, ran both hands over the sides of her head and smoothed her hair. "Goodbye, sweet Ariel. You are so beautiful. You look just like your mother did at your age."

"Bye, Grandma. Love you."

Mazie hugged her mother. "Thank you," she whispered through the mane of curly, grey hair. "I'm so sorry."

"I love you, darling." Her mother pushed her away. "Here are my keys. Tank is full." She ran her hands down the front of her jeans. "Now go." She shooed them away with one hand.

Mazie climbed into the old Charger, yanked on the lever between her legs and pushed the seat back. The smell of her father's cigarettes still lingered in the upholstery. She closed her eyes, inhaled, and held onto his scent for a few seconds. She opened her eyes, emptied her lungs and glanced in the rear-view mirror.

In the passenger seat, Ariel twisted her entire body around and watched out the back window.

Her mother stood in the middle of the alley, her oversized sweater hanging almost to her knees, bundled against the heat of the day that no longer penetrated her fragile body.

Mazie turned right at the end of the alley and headed for Trout Lake Road. She had to stay off the Trans Canada, off the main streets.

Ariel stared out the passenger side window. "Mother?"

"Yes, bug?"

Ariel faced forward. "What's going on? Why are we running away?"

Mazie sighed. "I'll explain it all later, okay? Right now I have to figure out where we're going."

"Can't we go home?" Tears dripped down Ariel's cheeks.

"No, we can't."

"Is it Daddy? Are you running away from him?"

Mazie held the steering wheel with her left hand, reached out with her right, and squeezed Ariel's hand. "Yes. But I don't want to talk about it right now. Okay?"

Ariel sniffed and snatched her hand away.

Mazie drove northeast along highway sixty-three. Forty minutes passed before either spoke another word.

Ariel squirmed in her seat. "I need to pee."

"Next gas station."

"Where are we going?"

"Not sure yet." The route was unfamiliar. She'd never ventured north of North Bay and had no idea what lay ahead. Twenty minutes later they approached a small township. "Here, there has to be somewhere to stop."

The Charger lurched through the hamlet, the streets eerie and quiet. "There. A restaurant." Mazie pulled up to the front of the building, the parking lot abandoned. A faded sign hung from the door, its text barely visible through the filthy glass. "Damn it." She glanced at the clock. "Closed at supper time?"

They got back on the highway and were soon on a bridge over the Ottawa River. "Look, bug. We're in Quebec. I've never been to Quebec before."

"Does Quebec have bathrooms?"

The highway veered left and then right, went over another bridge then turned a sharp left.

"Tem-is-cam-ing-uh." Ariel shook her head. "Never heard of it."

"Me either. But there's a Shell station." Mazie checked the gas gauge. "May as well top up the tank. This old thing is a guzzler."

A bell jangled when she pushed the door open. The place reeked of dirt, motor oil, and burned coffee.

The woman behind the counter looked up and broke out into a huge smile. "*Bonjour madam et mademoiselle.*"

Mazie nodded. "*Bonjour.*" Her hard "j" gave her away as full-on Anglo.

"*Comment allez-vous aujourd'hui? Avez-vous besoin de gaz? Café?*"

All she got was 'coffee.' Mazie shook her head. "Sorry, do you speak English?"

"*Oui, madame.*"

"Is there a bathroom? And I need to top up the tank and grab a coffee."

The woman smiled. "How much dollars you want for gas?"

"Ten ought to do."

"The bathrooms, they are down the hall." She pointed behind Mazie.

"*Merci.*" She tugged on Ariel's sleeve. "You go first. I'll fill up and meet you back here. Pour me a coffee?"

Ariel was already on her way to the bathroom. She waved over her shoulder.

"Your daughter, she is teenage, no?"

"Not yet."

"Ah." The woman nodded. "She act like it."

Mazie paid for the gas, coffee, and a map of the area. She gave Ariel the keys to the car. "Don't start it, just turn the key part way for the radio."

Ariel rolled her eyes. "I know how."

Mazie sat on the toilet, sighed when the pressure in her full bladder started to ease. She dug the phone out of her purse and stared at the voice mail alert.

Damn that Rachel. Maybe she was apologizing for ratting her out to the cops. Or maybe it was just Polly dying to tell Ariel about the latest cute boy in school. It didn't matter now.

She popped the SIM card out of her phone and crushed it under the wooden heel of her sandal. She gathered up the remains and dropped them into the toilet. She'd seen enough cop shows to know that they could track her by that damn phone. She watched the bits of it swirl, swimming in a yellow eddy until gravity sucked it down the pipe and out into the Quebec sewer system.

She stared at her reflection while she scrubbed her hands. She should feel free. Should be happy to be rid of him. Instead she'd tightened her own shackles and thrown away the key.

~~~~~~~~~

After a modest dinner of tuna sandwiches and grandma's homemade cookies, they'd continued north until darkness swallowed the world around them. Ariel slipped into a fitful sleep, a pillow wedged between her head and the window pane.

She hadn't asked again about the drama whirling around her. Didn't mention her father or going home. Only asked if she could call Polly, spoke of the fun she had in the Simpson's home, how nice Rachel was, how she treated her with kindness. "Did you know she plays DDR with us, Mom? You should play next time."

"DDR?"

"Dance Dance Revolution."

Mazie laughed. "Well I do love to dance." Or she used to.

Lights of a roadside motel glowed ahead at the end of a long bend in the highway. She'd begun to think they'd be sleeping in the car.

Gravel crunched under the tires. Mazie parked in front of the office, a neon vacancy sign flickered above the door. She shook her daughter. "Wake up."

Ariel rubbed her eyes and looked around. "Where are we?"

"We're at a motel. Grab your bag."

They entered the office, empty except for a dim lamp, a smouldering cigarette, and a tiny television sitting on the desk, the volume low. A chrome bell sat on the counter. Ariel tapped it with her palm. A sharp clang rang through the silence.

"One sec!" The voice came from a back room.

A man, as wide as he was short, came through the entry. He eyed them over the top of wire-rimmed glasses that looked like they
~~~~~~~~~

may fall from the tip of his bulbous nose. The entire room reeked of whiskey.

Mazie's stomach lurched.

He waddled behind the counter, a beaming smile pinched the corners of his eyes. "What can I do for you ladies?"

"Do you have any vacancies?"

His laughter belched from deep inside his oversized belly. "Honey, all I got is vacancies." He dragged an open ledger closer and picked up a pencil. He licked the tip of the lead and perched it over the paper. "Name?"

Mazie froze. She couldn't give him her real name. The cops would find her in no time. "Let's play a game," she whispered in Ariel's ear. She turned to the man. "Charlotte. My name is Charlotte Smyth."

Ariel giggled. The man raised his eyebrow at her then printed the name in messy block letters.

Mazie grinned and watched him write. She pointed to the last name. "No, Smyth, with a y."

"Sorry." He turned the i into a y and eyeballed Ariel. "And what's your name, sweetheart?"

"Do you need her name for the register?"

"No, no. But a pretty little thing must have a pretty little name, right?"

Mazie's eyelids fluttered and she pressed her fingers against a growing pain in her gut.

"Clementine," Ariel said, her face alight with the fun of the game.

"See? A pretty name. My grandmomma's name was Clementine. Not many folks these days use those nice, old-fashioned names." He ducked his head down and rummaged beneath the counter top, his face scrunched in concentration. He smiled, his eyes lit. He handed a piece of paper to Ariel. "Here, a coupon for half off breakfast. Which way are you heading?"

"North," Mazie said.

"Perfect. Little place about twenty K up the road. Great coffee, and they'll fill your to-go cup for free too."

The tension in Mazie's shoulder's eased. "Thanks. That's very kind."

He handed her a key. "You're in cabin three. Follow the gravel road behind the office, take a left, then a right after cabin one. There should be a light on over the door so you don't trip in the dark. Check out is noon, but if you're a little after that, I don't mind."

"We should be on the road pretty early."

~~~~~~~~

Mazie picked up the receiver of the phone and stared at the dial pad. "Shit." She turned to Ariel. "What's Polly's number?"

Ariel reeled off the ten digits. "Why don't you use your cell phone?"

"It's broken."

"Can I talk to Polly?"

"We'll see. It's pretty late, even in Calgary. Crawl into bed and turn on the television. But keep it down."

Mazie poked the numbers on the pad and waited for one, two, three rings.

"Hello?" A tentative greeting in a near-whisper of a voice.

"Rachel?"

"Mazie? Is it you? Where are you? Are you safe?"

"Yes, we're fine."

"Did you get my message?"

"No. I broke my cell phone. What's going on?"
~~~~~~~~

"The cops are all over your place. Crime scene tape, body bag in the middle of the night. Sunday. Or I guess that's Monday morning. Hell, two days ago."

Mazie dropped onto a bench beside the table that held the phone and laid her head on her arms.

"Mazie?"

"I'm here."

"They wanted me to tell them where you are. Some stupid neighbour told them our daughters are best friends."

"What did you tell them?"

"That you took Ariel to Disneyland."

Mazie pressed the fingertips of her free hand against her closed lids. The nosy neighbour, bane of her daily existence, cause of so many issues with Cullen, was protecting her?

"Look, Mazie. I know what he's done to you. I say power to you. One day I'd like to hear what you did." There was rustling and muffled voices as if she had covered the receiver with her hand. "Honey, the cops are heading our way. George went out to meet them to slow them down. I'm going to hang up. Call me in a couple of hours, you hear?"

Mazie glanced at the bed. Drool dripped from Ariel's mouth, little snorts of sleep blowing through stray hairs that fell in front of her face.

"Yes. I'll call. And thank you. I... I don't know what to say."

"Just be safe. Tell Ariel we love her."

"I will." She hung up the phone and stared at it, tears stinging her eyes. She focused on the prints her fingers left behind on the grimy receiver. Her heart leapt. She wiped the receiver with the sleeve of her sweater, then wiped the number pad.

She shook her head and snorted.

What, was she going to wipe down the entire hotel room too?

The restaurant? She'd never been arrested, they didn't have her prints on file.

She closed her eyes and took some deep breaths. Reality took seconds to dawn on her. Her house. The blood. Her fingerprints in his blood. Everywhere. In the bedroom. On the scissors and the knife. On the pictures she left behind. On the notebook.

Not that it mattered. They knew who killed him. She'd told them in the letter. But they might be able to find her that way. Right? Is that how it worked?

She ran a bath and soaked in the steaming water for almost an hour, scouring the fold-out maps. Timmins. They'd head to Timmins.

She crawled into bed next to Ariel and pulled the blankets up high around her neck. She glanced at the clock and picked up the phone.

"Hello?" George's voice.

Mazie froze.

"Is there anyone there?"

She held her breath, her finger hovered over the disconnect button. "Mazie?" Rachel's voice, a sound that used to grate on Mazie's last nerve, had lost its irritating edge.

"Rachel, I'm sorry, I didn't know what to say to him."

"It's fine. Sweetheart, George knows all about it."

Mazie sank into the pillows. "What, exactly, does he know?"

"Honey, nobody wears turtlenecks and long sleeves in August. Not unless they're hiding something. We hear how he talks to you. And those walls are thinner than you think." Rachel sighed. "Sweetheart, the whole neighbourhood knows."

Mazie squeezed her eyes shut. Cullen's screaming face came into clear view, his wrists and ankles bound, the headboard slamming against the wall.

Creak, gasp, thud.

She opened her eyes and focused on a stain on the bedspread. "So the whole neighbourhood knows the hell I live with," she said, deadpan. Anger pinched at her chest. "But nobody did or said anything?"

"I been trying to catch him. Been watching him, you know? But lady, you are so damn guarded. You won't let anybody in. And that bastard keeps his snotty nose pretty clean in public."

Mazie covered her face with one hand, tears sprung to her eyes. "I had no idea. Honestly, Rachel, I just thought you were a nosy neighbour."

"Well, shit. I am. But only because I knew what was up. I can't tell you how many times George wanted to go over there and beat him to a pulp. But that wouldn't help you."

"No, it would have made it worse."

"And we didn't have good reason to call the police. But I am glad Ariel did."

Mazie sat up straight. "She told you?"

"Well the whole neighbourhood saw him get hauled away, saw the ambulance. Ariel just confided in Polly that it was her that called."

Mazie sighed. "I took him back."

"I know."

"I didn't know what else to do."

"I know."

"Oh, Rachel. What have I done?" Her voice cracked and faded into a breathy whine.

Ariel shifted in her sleep.

Mazie stroked her head, slipped from beneath the covers, and sat in a chair by the window.

"You did what you had to do, right? I mean, I'm assuming you killed the bastard, being as how there's a body bag and all." Rachel breathed into the phone for a few seconds. "But it was self-defence, right? He would have killed you first, right?"

"He would have. One day. He kept talking about Ariel. How he wanted to take her to the cabin alone. How she's pretty like I used to be."

Rachel gasped. "No. Oh, Mazie, I had no idea."

"I didn't plan it, Rachel. I was just going to hurt him. Leave him tied to the bed until somebody found him. I was just going to take Ariel and run away." She peeked at her daughter's silent form before cupping her hand over her mouth next to the receiver. "It just went terribly wrong. I knew if he ever found us I'd be dead. I just... lost it." Her heart beat a heavy rhythm. "Oh God, Rachel. I'm a murderer."

"You listen to me. You are a wonderful mother. You did what any good one would do to protect her child. You took his shit for years. But there's a breaking point. Don't matter what happened, don't matter that you planned to tie him up or even that you planned to hurt him a bit, give him a taste of his own damn medicine. It was still self-defence."

Mazie nodded. "Thank you," she whispered.

"You sound exhausted. Get some sleep. And keep in touch."

"I don't know where we're going. I'll try to call when I can."

"Go get yourself one of those burner cells."

"A what?"

"You know, like on those cop shows. Prepaid, when it runs out, throw it away and get another."

"Rachel. I had no idea you were such a bad-ass."

Rachel's laughter filled the phone. "Why, thank you. Now, don't you wish you'd talked to me before?"

Mazie began to cry again. "Lady, you have no idea."

~~~~~~~~

"Ding-dong, the psycho's gone."

Mazie blinked against the sunshine. Ariel sat on the end of the bed, remote in hand, still in her pyjamas. An old episode of *Friends* played on the television.

Mazie reached out and poked her daughter's back with one toe.

Ariel spun around and glared at her. "Don't."

"Jeez, sorry. What time is it?"

Ariel pointed the remote at the television and pushed a button. "Almost nine."

Mazie fell back into the pillow and covered her eyes with her palms. "Shit."

"What's wrong?"

"I wanted to be out of here by seven. I guess I fell asleep before I set the alarm." Maybe confession truly was good for the soul. She hadn't slept that well in years. "I'm going to grab a shower. Did you brush your teeth?"

"Not yet. Can I have a shower too?"

"Of course."

"Thanks, Charlotte."

Mazie raised one eyebrow. "You're welcome, Clementine."

Ariel giggled. "Can we always use those names?"

"It is kind of fun." And it wouldn't hurt to get used to some new identities.

Ariel clicked off the television. "Can I call you Charlie?"

"What about Mom?"

"Nah. You look like a Charlie."

"I like Mom. We're going to aim for Timmins today. When we get there, want to get some, oh I don't know…. some makeup?"

"What? You'll let me wear makeup?"
~~~~~~~~

"Just a bit."

Ariel bounded to her feet and crushed Mazie in a hug. "I love you, Charlie Smyth."

~~~~~~~~

Mazie poked at her overcooked egg, tore a piece of soggy bacon in half and held up its limp form. She tossed it on her plate and settled for just coffee. The tepid brew sat on her tongue like warm bathwater. Ariel shoved forkful after forkful of waffles into her mouth.

She wiped her lips and guzzled half a glass of milk, sat back and stared out the window. "Mom?"

"What, bug?"

"Are we ever going home?"

Mazie swallowed. No matter how many times she'd played out this conversation in her head, tried to prepare for the inevitable, she still had no idea what she was going to say.

"Not for a while."

"Because Daddy hits you?"

Mazie nodded.

Ariel dragged her finger across her plate and licked off the dregs of maple syrup. "How long has he been doing that?"

Mazie's eyes filled with tears. No point in lying to her now. "Years." She pulled a napkin from a chrome dispenser and wiped her nose. "Sweetheart, I'm so sorry."

"It's not your fault, you know. You do everything for him. He's hardly ever even nice to you."

"I didn't realize you noticed that."

"Yeah." She looked out the window. "Sometimes I'm not very nice to you either."
~~~~~~~~

"Don't say that."

"Polly and George never talk to Rachel like that." Ariel licked more syrup from her finger and stared out the window. "Why didn't you leave before?"

"I thought about it." Almost every day. Even packed a bag once. Then he brought home flowers and another cheap ring. Or was it earrings? She'd convinced herself he had changed again. But it was another lie piled on top of a mountain of lies. "But I'd never go without you. And I didn't want to take you away from your friends, from your school."

"I'd have come with you." Ariel wiped a tear from her cheek.

"Doesn't matter anymore. Now we're gone, right?"

Ariel nodded. "Right." She wiped more tears and looked out the window. "Will we ever see Daddy again?"

Mazie took a sip of her coffee, tried to rein in the choking sob that caught in her throat. "I don't think so."

"What about Grandma?"

"Probably not."

Ariel swallowed hard and sniffed. "Polly?" she whispered.

"I doubt it, bug. I don't think we can go home again."

"So, just you and me."

"Afraid so."

They sat in silence for a few minutes. Mazie dropped a ten and three toonies on the table, and they left.

Ariel popped a Bon Jovi CD into the player. The guitar riffs of the first song boomed out of the speakers, and soon Ariel was singing along to "Runaway." She stopped mid-song and turned to her mother. "Hey, this can be our theme song."

Mazie turned to look out the window, to shield Ariel from yet more tears. If running away was all she'd done, he'd have found them eventually and killed her. She was more certain of that every day. But at least then she'd be running for her life. Not from it.

They headed north, the thick forest on either side of the highway broken only when the road cut through granite and stone.

Mazie patted Ariel's leg. "Hey, you want to get haircuts? Maybe I'll colour mine."

"Why? Your hair is so pretty."

"I don't know. Another change. Something different."

"Can I get purple?"

Mazie laughed. "If you want to."

"I do. Short and purple."

"You want short hair? Really?"

"Yeah. Daddy won't see it, so he can't get mad at me. My hair, my choice, right?"

"Agreed. Your hair, your choice."

"But where would we get that done out here? There's nothing but trees and rock and old houses."

"Grab the map."

Mazie eased the car onto a narrow turnout, climbed out, arched her back and stretched her arms high above her head. Ariel unfolded the map and laid it across the hood of the car. She traced her finger from Ville Marie, past Notre Dame du Nord, and to the next town on the map. "This looks kind of small." She kept running her finger along until she found one that looked promising. "Maybe there?"

An hour later, they slowed down to sixty kilometres per hour on the outskirts of Englehart.

<center>~~~~~~~~</center>

"I want a pixie cut. And I want it all purple."

"Purple?" The stylist, Audra, looked aghast. "I don't think I have any purple." She turned to Mazie. "Not too many folks around here looking for any punk rock styles, you know?" She picked up a colour sample wheel and handed it to Ariel. "The closest I have is maroon. Maybe we could do some blonde highlights. Or blonde tips and spike it up?"

Ariel's face lit up. "Yes!"

The salon was nothing more than a couple of barber chairs and mirrors in the living room of a tiny house with one employee — the owner. Audra chopped and clipped at Ariel's long black locks. They fell from her head and dropped to the floor in thick chunks.

Mazie turned away when tears sprang to her eyes. It wasn't Ariel's first haircut, but this was no trim. Since spring, she'd transformed from a little girl playing tag on the front lawn to a young woman. A 'tween about to become a teen, fully formed and ready for anything.

Audra mixed the colour and painted it onto Ariel's hair. She set a timer and turned to Mazie. "How about you, love? We can cut while your girl's colour sets."

Mazie hadn't had short hair since elementary school. As a teen she loved it long. As a young woman, it doubled as a security blanket. And a man magnet. And the last man it attracted never let her cut it off.

Audra patted the back of the seat and grabbed a black cape. "Take off your scarf."

Mazie brought one hand up and fingered the silky protector of secrets. "I can keep it on."

"Honey, it'll be ruined. I'll put a towel around instead."

Mazie glanced at Ariel.

Ariel was distracted by her reflection in the mirror. She turned her head side to side and inspected her profile, batted her eyes, poked at the plastic bag on her head.

Mazie tugged the knot loose and let the scarf fall from her neck.

She balled it up and held it in both hands. Audra secured a towel around her neck without a word, without a flinch or a wince or a glance or a sideways comment, then floated the cape in front of Mazie's face and attached it with Velcro at the back.

She held her trembling hands in her lap, secreted by the cape that was like a vice around her throat. She swallowed and squirmed.

"You okay, honey?" Audra stood, scissors poised.

A bead of sweat trickled down Mazie's temple. "It's too tight."

"I'm sorry." Audra ripped the Velcro open, place two pudgy fingers between the cape and Mazie's skin and reattached the Velcro. "Better?"

"Yes. Thank you."

Audra took the first slice.

Mazie's eyes locked on the scissors, on the glints of light that caught the blade. A chunk of her hair fell in front of her face and landed in her lap. She shut her eyes, listened to the clip of metal on metal. Her shoulders dropped away from her ears and her spine sank into the leather chair. It was the same cathartic release she felt when that knife slid through Cullen's flesh.

She cast her eyes to Ariel in the other chair, brown goop in her hair, plastic bag over her head, pinned in the front. Ariel spun the chair round and round. It was one of those moments where the young woman faded and the child took centre stage.

Mazie smiled and sighed. She shot a split-second look at herself in the mirror, expecting to see a stranger staring back at her. But it was just her. With slightly shorter hair.

"So where are you all from?"

More nosy people. What did it matter? They'd never run into each other again.

"Toronto."

Ariel gave her a look, one eyebrow raised. She looked like her father in that moment.

"Well why you come all the way out here for a makeover?"

"We're taking a road trip. The haircuts were just a whim."

"Wow, that's quite the whim. I know women who agonize for months over a little change." She patted Mazie's shoulder. "Good for you. Now, how about blonde?"

"I'm sorry?"

Audra rolled her eyes. "Blonde. You know, dye it light."

Mazie stared at herself. With her blue eyes and pale skin, blonde would be just the thing. "Do it."

Two hours later, her scarf secured around her neck, Mazie stood beside Ariel in front of the mirror. Ariel looked years older, on the verge of high school. Not like a child who'd just finished grade seven.

Mazie barely recognized herself. She touched her lightened brow, turned her head and watched her hair bounce around her face. She smiled.

Ariel rested her forearm on her mother's shoulder. "Looks great, Charlie. You were born to be a blonde."

~~~~~~~~

The nauseating stink of gasoline swirled around Mazie. She waited in line to pay for gas while Ariel poured her a coffee and chose some snacks.

Mazie approached the counter and pointed to the car outside. "Number three."

Ariel put the coffee on the counter and piled a soda and two bags of chips next to it. "Mom, look. Can we get one?"

Prepaid cell phones. Just like on television. "And one of these phones, please."

Two hours later, the outskirts of Timmins came into view. For
~~~~~~~~

some reason she'd always envisioned it would be a big city, but it was more like a big town. With few exceptions, there was no building taller than three stories.

Ariel crossed her arms. "This is it? Where's downtown?"

"I think we're in downtown."

"Can't we go to Toronto or something?"

"Look." Mazie pointed to a five story building ahead. "At least that hotel looks decent."

They pulled luggage from the car, dragged it into the front entrance, and asked for a room. Before the door closed behind them, Ariel fell face first onto the bed. Mazie ran to the bathroom, the large coffee pressing on her bladder. She joined Ariel on the bed and pulled out the cell phone. "I'm going to call Grandma." She dialled her mother's number.

When the phone connected, there was no greeting, just muffled voices in the background.

"Hello?" Three interminable seconds passed before her mother spoke. The last time her voice sounded that strained was when she'd called Mazie to break the news about her father's death.

Mazie hung up without a word and tossed the phone on the nightstand. She lay back on the bedspread and imagined her mother, her house swarming with cops. They had probably tapped her phone. Or maybe were tracing her calls.

Ariel flipped onto her back. "No answer?"

Mazie shook her head. "She must be out."

Lying came easy. She'd been lying to Ariel for years. Protecting her from her father, from the horror of the truths that lived under their roof. Was she protecting Ariel now? Or only herself?

"I'll call her back later." Maybe in the middle of the night. Cops had to sleep sometime, right? "In the meantime, let's order in. Chinese?"

They sat on the bed, the extra pillows from the closet piled up behind them, and ate straight from the take-out containers while noise from the television filled the space. The room smelled of old grease and sticky ginger beef, overpowered by the musky, salty stench of overcooked squid.

Mazie raised her chopsticks to her mouth. The phone vibrated against the nightstand. The chopsticks jumped, noodles flew through the air and landed on her lap. "Damn it!"

"Mom. It's just the phone." Ariel looked at her like she'd lost her freaking mind.

Mazie snatched the cell phone from the table and squinted at it. Seven oh five area code. North Bay. But not a number she recognized. It had to be a mistake. No one had this number. Hell, she didn't even know what the number was.

She pressed talk and listened to dead air. "Hello?"

"Mazie? Oh my god, they were right in my house. They were going to trace that call, made me pick up. It was you, right? Maybe it wasn't even you."

"Mom, calm down."

"They're trying to use me to catch you. My own child!"

"It was me, Mom." She covered the phone with one hand and pointed to the door. "I'm just going to talk outside," she whispered.

"Is grandma okay?"

"Yeah, she's fine." She stepped out into the hall and clicked the door shut. "Mom?" Her voice ricocheted off the walls in the empty hall.

"I'm here."

Mazie sighed. "I figured something was up the way you sounded. I was going to call back after midnight."

"They've got my phone all rigged up to listen in on my calls."

"Where are you calling from?"

"I had a doctor's appointment. I'm at a pay phone. Damn it, Mazie, they wanted to escort me to the doctor, like I'm some kind of criminal. I told them to shove it."

Mazie smiled. "Good for you. How did you get this number?"

"I have call display. I'm not too much of an old lady you know."

"Of course you're not." Voices and footfalls in the medical facility echoed through the receiver.

"They took down the number. Tried to find out who owned it, but they couldn't."

"No, it's prepaid. My name isn't attached. But I don't know if they can tell where I bought it." She rubbed her forehead with her fingertips. "Damn it mother, this is not fair to you, having to cover for me. Lie for me."

"It's not a lie to tell them I don't know where you are."

Tears sprang to Mazie's eyes.

"Not a lie when I told them all the awful things that bastard did to you over the years."

Mazie wiped her nose on her sleeve.

"But they knew all about that. Tried to tell me they just wanted to talk to you, but they were just trying to trick a feeble old broad."

"What did they say?"

"That if you turned yourself in, they'd work something out. Because of the battery or some such thing. But you'd still be arrested. And Ariel would be put in foster care."

Mazie leaned her head against the wall and swallowed hard. "I can't let that happen."

"You just keep going. Keep that little girl with you. She needs you, darling."

"What about you, Mom?"

Silence was followed by muffled sobs. Her mother cleared her throat. "It's spread to my liver and my kidneys. They can't stop it now."

"Oh, Mother, no." Mazie's voice cracked.

"I've declined treatment. Chemo would buy me a couple of months at best, but damn it, those would be some shitty-ass months."

"How long?" All Mazie could muster was a whisper.

"A few weeks. Three months, tops. I've already made arrangements at a hospice."

"I'll come back. Take care of you."

"No, you won't. My life is done. Only thing left for me to do is to protect you. And I'll be damned if anyone is going to take that away from me. Now you go. Before they use that cell phone against you and find you through those towers or satellites or whatever the hell they do."

"Okay, Mom. I love you so much. Call me when you're near a pay phone, okay?"

"Of course I will. I love you and I love Ariel. Now get on with your life. Maybe go to one of those countries where they have some treaty or something and won't send you back home."

She ended the call, leaned her back against the wall and slid down until her butt hit the carpet. She laid her head on her knees and sobbed.

The door beside her clicked open. "Mom?"

She looked up at her daughter. Tears filled Ariel's eyes. "Is it Grandma?"

She nodded. "The cancer has spread. They can't stop it."

Ariel joined her on the floor, rested her head on Mazie's shoulder and wept.

~~~~~~~~
~~~~~~~~

The sun streamed in through a crack in the drapes and laid a slice of light across Mazie's closed eyelids. She blinked against the intrusion, groaned and rolled on her side to block it, and pulled the covers over her head.

Another day of running. Of not belonging anywhere. Of knowing that within weeks she would be an orphan of sorts. Why did that suddenly matter? She'd hardly ever visited her mother, but those weekly phone calls kept her grounded. Kept her sane while insanity swirled around her. She never should have stopped calling. Maybe she would have chosen a different path. Maybe just left him, without the violence. Without death.

She rolled onto her back and slid the covers away, allowing the full force of morning in. The sliver of sunlight was warm in the cool of the air-conditioned hotel room. It must be after nine. They should be on the move.

The thought pinned her to the bed.

Ariel stirred and rolled, a snort of sleep exploded from her nose. Mazie grinned. Just like her father.

She stood and pinched her thigh. No, not like her father. Nothing like her father.

She set the coffee pot to brew and stared at the stream of caffeine filling the cup. When the aroma hit her, she shut her eyes, blocked Cullen from her mind, shut out any good thoughts of those few years where good was their normal.

Fuck him. He didn't deserve to be remembered in a good light.

She sat at the window, steam curling in lazy swirls from the mug. She sipped the coffee and wrinkled her nose.

Damn. Why was hotel coffee always crap?

She pulled the dusty drape aside and peered out the window. The city had a small town look about it. A small town feel. Probably a small town mentality.

"What time is it?" Ariel sat up in bed, her new short 'do askew and matted from a good night's sleep.

"I'm not sure. Mid-morning maybe."

"Shouldn't we get going?"

Mazie glanced out the window. "How about we stick around here for a while?"

Ariel bounced out of bed and pulled the drapes wide open. She stood, hands on hips, and surveyed the scene. "Kind of small. This is the tallest building. Look, we can see all the rooftops."

"Does size matter?" Mazie put her coffee down and patted her lap.

Ariel sat on her mother's knee and put one arm around her shoulder.

Mazie breathed a deep inhale. Sweet coconut sunscreen, a hint of morning breath, and the lingering pungency of fresh hair dye.

"I suppose not." Ariel scratched her head. "It's just different."

"Everything will be different. We have to find our new normal."

Ariel nodded. "Just wish the new normal included Polly."

"I know. But you'll make new friends fast." As soon as the words left her mouth she wished she could take them back. New friends weren't Polly. Everything revolved around Polly.

Ariel glared at her, slid off her lap, disappeared into the bathroom, and slammed the door.

Mazie stared out the window. They had to stop, had to put down roots, find some sense of normal. The money would run out soon. She had to find a job. But how? All she had was her own government identification. She'd be arrested in no time. Wouldn't she? Did Canada have some kind of criminal database that all new hires were checked against? Or maybe they'd get her when she filed her taxes.

She was no criminal, had no criminal mind, no diabolical

thought process. She'd need a fake driver's license, fake social insurance card. How the hell do people get those things?

~~~~~~~~

The car crept along the narrow streets. Businesses dotted the crumbling sidewalks. A bowling alley, a pizzeria, a Laundromat. Did Calgary even have one of those? Mazie poked Ariel's side.

She flinched and pulled away.

"We should do some laundry. Let's go back after we eat."

"Whatever." Ariel stared out the window. She'd barely spoken since Mazie suggested Polly was replaceable.

They continued down Riverside Drive. "Look, a Wal-Mart!" Mazie pulled into the lot.

Ariel crossed her arms. "What do we need here?"

"Well, a newspaper for one."

"Why do you care about the news in this stupid town?"

"I know you're mad at me, but don't blame Timmins. I thought I'd look for a job. Maybe an apartment so we don't spend all our money on hotels." She eased into a parking spot, put the car in park, and took Ariel's hand. "Come on, it's an adventure, right?"

Ariel pulled her hand away and glared at her. She exited the car and headed for the store.

Mazie sighed, gathered her purse, and ran to catch up. A security camera above the entry was pointed right at her. "Ariel," she called out to her daughter's back.

Ariel turned. "Don't you mean Clementine?"

Mazie grinned. "My darling Clementine, it's kind of chilly. Maybe put your hood up?" She pulled her own hood over her hair and turned her back on the camera.

"Are you nuts? It's warm out. And we're twenty feet from the
~~~~~~~~

door." Ariel spun around and walked away, each step punctuated her growing frustration. She shoved her hands in the pockets of her hoodie and left the hood dangling down her back.

How could Mazie convince Ariel to cover herself and avoid cameras without telling her the real reason they'd run away? Not that anyone was looking for a blonde woman and a burgundy-haired girl with a pixie cut.

They picked out a few groceries. Mazie grabbed a box of tampons. She needed them for real this time, and wouldn't have to skulk into another store and return them just to squirrel away a few dollars ever again.

At the end of a long aisle with house wares on one side and toys and sporting goods on the other, they came to the electronics department. Ariel made a beeline for the computers. "Mom, look! Tablets are on sale. Can we get one, please?"

"What do you need that for?"

Ariel stared at her, her lower jaw slack. That eyebrow she inherited from Cullen shot straight up. "Facebook. Twitter. Skype. Any modern way to keep in touch with my friends."

"You're on all of those?"

"God, Mother. Of course I am." She rolled her eyes. "And we can get any map to anywhere anytime. Don't need those stupid old paper things that never fold up right."

Mazie sauntered past the row of tablet computers. She poked one price tag. "Is this a good price?"

Ariel peered at it. "It's okay. How about this one?" She pointed to a much smaller screen, not much bigger than the disposable cell, for just under a hundred dollars.

"Kind of tiny." Mazie continued down the row. "Here, ten-inch screen, forty bucks off. Only a hundred thirty nine." She turned to her daughter. "Is that good?"

"I don't know the brand, but eight gig of memory. And it's got Ice Cream Sandwich."

"It's got what now?"

"It's Android, Mom. It's not bad at all." She grinned and shook her head. "Don't you use the computer?"

She used to. Until Cullen started reading her private emails and hitting her for sharing her feelings with what few friends she had left. What was that, seven years ago? He started making daily records of her search history, accusing her of cheating on him, all while he frequented porn sites and wasted the money he begrudged her for groceries on internet poker.

"Mostly to search for recipes."

~~~~~~~~

Mazie slathered hot mustard on whole grain bread and layered Black Forest ham with slices of Swiss cheese and slivers of Granny Smith apple. "What I wouldn't give for the panini press right now. Would love to toast these and get the cheese all gooey."

Ariel lay on her stomach on the bed poking at the tablet screen. "Okay. I'm in."

"In where?"

Ariel glanced up at her. "The internet. Connected to Wi-Fi. Online."

"How do you know how to do that?"

Her daughter rolled her eyes and looked at her with that patented 'duh' look. "Everyone knows how to do that." She tossed a folded tent card across the bed toward Mazie. "Free Wi-Fi. There's the password. You want to see Google maps? See where we've been?"
~~~~~~~~

Mazie handed her a sandwich on a Kleenex and sat beside her on the bed. A blue squiggle snaked from the lower left of the screen up to the right, twisted left, and trailed off near the top.

Ariel rested her index finger on the screen. "That's Grandma's." She moved it to the top. "This is us. Timmins."

Mazie nodded.

"That's just the past couple of days. Check this out." A few taps of her fingers across the screen and up popped a map of most of Canada, a blue line meandering from Calgary eastward. "Thirty five hundred, eighteen kilometres."

"We've come a long way, baby."

Ariel rolled her eyes. "Lame."

"Yes I am." Mazie took a bite of her sandwich.

Ariel typed, her eyes skipping across the screen. "Can I call Polly?"

"I don't want to use up all the minutes. In case Grandma calls." Or Rachel has police updates.

"We can connect online, for free, no minutes. It's like a phone call but with video." She pointed to a little button on the screen. "Camera." She scrambled to her knees, gathered pillows against the headboard and leaned against them, the tablet resting against her bent legs. She patted the bed beside her, beckoning Mazie to sit.

"We can call Rachel on the computer?"

"Yup."

Mazie swallowed. "Can anyone trace it?" she whispered.

Ariel scrunched up her nose. "I don't know. Daddy sure wouldn't know how."

"Okay. How do we connect to them?"

She stabbed at the screen, typed in a user name and password, scrolled down a list, and poked one more time. A tiny picture of Polly's freckled face popped up.

"Well I'll be damned."

"Look, she's online." Ariel poked 'video call.' In two seconds, there was Polly, staring back at them.

"Ari? Is that you? Oh my God, what did you do to your hair?"

"Cut and colour. You like?"

"Love."

Mazie leaned her head next to Ariel's. "Hey, Polly."

"Mrs. Reynolds? Holy crap, you're blonde!"

Mazie winced at the sound of that name. "Honey, you can call me Mazie. Is your mother there?"

Polly twisted around in her chair. "Mom, it's Ariel and Mrs. Reynolds! I mean, Mazie."

Rachel's voice was tinny through the tablet. "What are you talking about?" Her large shadow loomed behind Polly. She bent down, her head over Polly's shoulder, their faces squished together. Mazie had never noticed before how much alike they were.

"Oh my God, Mazie, Ariel! Look at you two!" She turned to look behind her. "George, they're safe." She spun back around. "Where are you?" She held her palm out to the screen. "No! Don't tell me. I don't want to know. Just tell me, are you all right?"

"We're okay. Thought we might stay where we are for a while."

Polly leaned closer to her screen. "Dude, what's with the cops at your —"

"Polly!" Rachel barked her daughter's name and jabbed her arm with one finger. "Let me talk to Mazie."

"Mom! It's my Skype, my computer!"

Rachel forced herself into Polly's chair. Polly disappeared from the screen and a thud came through the speaker. "Mom!"

"Just go. Get some ice cream or something." Rachel looked to her right. Polly mumbled and a door slammed. Rachel turned back to the screen. "Ariel, honey, can you let me and your mom talk in private?"

Ariel turned to her mother. "Mom, what's going on?"

"I just need to speak to Rachel. In private."

"What am I supposed to do, go wander the streets alone?"

"Turn on the TV. I can take this into the bathroom."

"Fine. But don't disconnect. I want to talk to Polly."

Mazie clicked the bathroom door shut, put down the toilet lid and sat on the cool plastic. "Rachel, what's happening? Are the cops still around?"

"Not as much. Yesterday a few of them were in your back yard. I snuck out and listened through the fence."

"You eavesdropped on the police?"

"Hey, nosy neighbour, remember?" She winked. "My thighs may rub together when I walk, but I can be stealthy when I need to be."

"How did they find him so soon? I told everyone he'd be gone for ten days."

"Some guy he works with. He came by a couple of times. I caught him pounding on the back door. Told him no one was home. He said he was supposed to go fishing with Cullen. Said he'd been trying to get him on the phone." Rachel finished off her cigarette and butted it out of camera range. "I told him Cullen had already gone, but he could see the truck right there. Next thing I know, there's a cop car parked out front and two uniforms knocking on doors and shining flashlights in the windows."

Mazie was certain Ariel could hear her heartbeat through the door. She wiped a dewy line of sweat from her cheeks. "Damn it."

Rachel nodded. "Yeah. I know." She lit another cigarette, leaned back and blew smoke at the ceiling. "Anyway, damned if the police didn't set up a ladder and peer into all the windows on the second floor. I guess there was a crack in the drape. Apparently they could see enough because all hell broke loose."

"You lied for me." Mazie let tears drip down her face.

"Hell yeah I did. But I'm worried."

"Why?"

"Look, hon, I don't know how to tell you this except to just up and say it." She took another long drag and blew the smoke at the screen. She crossed her free arm across her chest and rubbed her forehead with the hand holding the smoke. "Mazie, it's your mom."

Mazie swallowed, her chest vibrated. "I talked to her yesterday. I know about the cancer spreading."

"Sorry, I didn't know about that. Cops found your van in her garage. They know you have her car. They've been hounding me no end, but I keep telling them the same bullshit story about Disneyland." Rachel wiped tears from her face with one shaking hand. "Honey, they put a lot of pressure on her. And shame on them, harassing a frail old lady like that."

"Rachel, is she all right? She doesn't know where we are."

"I think they told me this to try to get me to tell them wherever it is you're hiding." She put her lips to the cigarette and took a long drag. "She overdosed on sleeping pills and scotch last night."

Mazie's focus narrowed. The small screen blurred and the rest of the room faded to black. She gripped the counter with one hand, but her legs came out from under her and she slid off the toilet seat and landed on the floor. "She. She's —"

"I'm so sorry."

Mazie let the tablet slip out of her fingers. Waves of sobs overtook her body. She wrapped both arms around herself, rocked, and wailed.

Ariel knocked on the door. "Mom? Mom are you all right?"

Mazie couldn't form any words.

Ariel pushed the door open until it met the resistance of her mother's feet, then squeezed herself through the small open space it offered. "Mom, what the hell?"

Mazie grabbed Ariel's hand and pulled her to the floor, hugged her hard and put her lips next to her daughter's ear. "Grandma died."

Ariel pulled away, her eyes wide, mouth agape. "What? But we just saw her!" She melted to the floor and curled into her mother's embrace.

"I'm gonna disconnect." Rachel's voice on the tablet seemed a million miles from reality. "Call me back. Tonight."

They lay on the bathroom floor until the tears receded and Ariel's shoulders stopped shaking. Mazie sat up, her back against the cupboard, the knob poking into her spine.

"We need to tell Daddy about Grandma."

"Your father didn't like my mother. He wouldn't care."

Ariel pushed away from her mother's arms. "He still deserves to know." She wiped her splotchy cheeks with the sleeve of her shirt. "You have to tell me what's going on. What did Polly mean by police?" She swallowed hard. "Is Daddy all right?"

Nausea welled up in Mazie's stomach and saliva filled her mouth. She rolled to her knees, lifted the toilet lid, and vomited. Second-hand mustard burned her throat.

When she sat back down, Ariel handed her a fistful of toilet paper, reached over her head and flushed the toilet. Tears filled her eyes. "Mother, tell me. Now."

Ariel helped Mazie to her feet. She led Ariel out of the bathroom and sat beside her on the bed. She held her daughter's hands, took two deep breaths, and closed her eyes — like that would make confessing this sin go down any easier. "Sweetheart." She opened her eyes and tucked a stray lock of Ariel's hair behind her ear. With the new cut, that years-old habit no longer worked and the strand popped back onto her temple. She cupped her daughter's chin. "Your father." She blinked one long blink and swallowed. "He's dead."

Ariel's face contorted, her chin dimpled, her cheeks and eyes blossomed with red patches.

"What?" she whispered.

Mazie hung her head. "I didn't mean to. I just wanted him to know how I felt. I was just going to leave him, take you with me, before —"

Ariel jumped away from Mazie like she'd burst into flames. "You killed him?" she screamed. Both her hands flew up and grabbed the sides of her face, she buckled over and fell to her knees on the carpet. "No, no, no, no."

Mazie slid onto the floor and put her arms around Ariel.

She shoved Mazie away, clamoured to her feet and ran to the door. She spun around, one hand on the doorknob. "I hate you!" She ran from the room, the door left open behind her.

"Ariel, stop!" Mazie stumbled to her feet, snatched the key card from the dresser, and fled out the door. By the time she got out of the hotel, Ariel was nowhere.

Mazie raced back into the room and grabbed her keys, ran to the car in the underground parkade. Her trembling fingers fumbled the keys and they landed on the floor mat. "Damn it." She fished them from the floor and managed to get the car started. By the time she pulled out onto the street, her vision was blurred by unstoppable tears. Her eyes darted in all directions searching for any sign of long black flowing hair and purple polka dotted denim capris.

No. Short hair. Maroon hair. Damn it! She pounded on the steering wheel with her open palms. "Fuck, fuck, fuck."

The alleys darkened in the increasing dusk, every shadow sinister, every doorway a potential hiding place.

A police car crossed the intersection ahead of her. She slammed on the brakes, turned a hard right and slipped into a narrow laneway a few blocks from the hotel. She slapped the gearshift into park and draped her arms over the steering wheel, laid her head on her arms, and gulped for air.

She'd murdered her husband. Her mother was dead. And now she'd driven the only person who mattered out of her life. She should just kill herself. Should have done that right off the bat, as soon as he was dead. Then maybe Ariel could have forgiven her. Found a happy life in a home without anger and violence. A life devoid of lies.

She leaned back in the seat. Time to call the cops. Turn herself in. Find Ariel and send her — where? She had no home left. No relatives left. Just a murderous mother doomed to spend eternity behind bars.

Maybe Rachel would adopt her.

She sped back to the hotel and parked the car out front. Three people hovered around the elevator. Mazie yanked open the door to the stairwell and took the steps two at a time to the third floor. Her jogging footfalls thudded in the dim hallway. When she rounded the end of the hall, she stopped short. Her knees weakened and she began to cry. "Ariel?" she whispered.

Ariel sat next to the door to their room, her forearms on her bent knees. At the sound of her mother's voice, she looked up. Her face was swollen from grief, her eyes bloodshot. "I didn't know where to go."

Mazie sat beside her and took her hand. "I am so sorry. I can't even start to tell you how truly, truly sorry."

Ariel rested her head on Mazie's shoulder. "Why? I mean, I know he was mean to you and hit you. A lot. But why?"

"I didn't plan to. It just happened. I was afraid he would kill me."

"Daddy would never do that."

Mazie sighed. "I used to think that. But he threatened to. And he'd nearly done it before."

Fresh tears pooled in Ariel's eyes. She sniffed and wiped them away. "You never told me."

"How could I?" She rested her head against the wall. "I can show you now if you like."

"Show me? What do you mean?"

Mazie stood and offered Ariel her hand.

Ariel hesitated, then slipped her soft palm into her mother's and allowed Mazie to pull her to her feet.

Mazie opened her suitcase and unzipped the removable lining from the hard outer shell. She slipped her hand in and felt around until her fingers found the envelope. The paper that contained evidence of his cruelty shot tiny tendrils of pain through her fingers. Negative energy. Bad juju. Ariel needed to see it. To understand. Or Mazie would never be forgiven.

She held the envelope, heavy with the weight of the duplicate set of Polaroids and her second diary, in both hands. "I kept a journal. Not feelings or anything. Just dates. Times." She swallowed. "And pictures. Of what he did."

She sat on the edge of the bed. Ariel sat cross-legged at the edge of her peripheral vision. "I never planned to share this with you." She turned to face her daughter. "I didn't want you to know. Didn't want you to see who he really was."

Ariel held out her hand.

Mazie shook her head. "Just a sec." She cleared her throat. "You have to know that he wasn't always like this. It was good in the beginning. But things changed. It was years after he first hit me before I took the pictures or wrote it down."

"Why'd you start?"

"I'd fooled myself into thinking he didn't mean it. He'd stop. But he never did. And I knew it would never end. I was certain that he would kill me one day. He'd come close before."

"Like when I called the cops."

"Yeah, like that. And other times."

"Why didn't I know?"

"You weren't usually there. That's another reason I knew it was time to leave. He didn't care if you saw anymore." She licked her lips. "He started to treat you the same way," she whispered.

Ariel nodded. "Do you still love him?"

"I don't think so. Not for a while." She smiled. "But I used to. Oh boy, did I love him." She closed her eyes and let a picture of Cullen, young, handsome, long chocolate hair, strumming his guitar and singing to her in their bedroom, fill her mind. "I miss him." Her voice cracked.

"Really?"

She opened her eyes. "The old him. The original him. Not the him I'm going to show you." She took a deep breath and bent the flap of the envelope open.

The pictures had shifted. They were out of order, in total chaos. Where to start? She stared at the one on top, a hand print on her neck. She touched her scarf, found the knot, loosened the noose, and let the scarf fall away.

Tears sprung to Ariel's eyes and she gasped. She touched one finger to the bruises and red marks, like blood that never washes off.

Mazie sifted through the photos and flipped the ones of her freshly choked neck upside down on the bed. It was like dealing a tarot deck where every card was the death card. She gathered them and tapped them until they were in a neat pile. The first one was the last time he'd choked her, just days before she'd done the same to him. She handed it to Ariel. "That is what happens when you get choked over and over again." She rubbed her neck just below the jaw line. "I don't think it's ever going away."

Ariel held the picture but looked at her mother's face. She swallowed hard, closed her eyes, turned to face the Polaroid, and then opened her eyes. She squeezed her lips together, her chin atremble. "He did that?"

"Just last week." She handed Ariel the stack, about fifteen pictures in all. "And these too. The dates are on the back."

Ariel looked at each picture, tossed one after another on the bed. With four left in her hand, she flung them all away. Two teetered on the edge of the bed. Two sailed off and drifted to the carpet. "I just thought you liked scarves."

"Oh, sweetheart. I fucking hate them."

Ariel's eyes bugged out. "You said fuck." She giggled, then clamped her hand over her mouth. "Sorry. I don't know why I laughed."

"It's okay. Laughter is good." Mazie put one arm around her daughter's shoulder and squeezed. "I'll put the other pictures away."

"No." Her eyes pleaded, but a tinge of fear and apprehension pinched at the corners. "I want to know."

"Are you sure?"

Ariel nodded.

Mazie pulled a random picture from the pile. "This is the second time he broke my wrist. I wasn't documenting things the first time."

Ariel took the picture and ran her finger over the image of Mazie's left arm, black and swollen, bent slightly at an awkward angle. "Is that when you had the purple cast?"

"Yup."

"You said you fell down the stairs." She looked up at Mazie. "You fell down the stairs a lot."

"I've never really fallen down the stairs. Tripped on a laundry basket once or twice, but never hurt myself." She sifted through the stack and pulled out a shot of her broken ribs. "This was another 'fall down the stairs.' Three broken ribs and a bruised kidney." She shuffled the deck. "Concussion and broken collar bone." Underneath that picture was one of her face, cut and broken, purple and black. She sighed. "This was the accident that never happened. The one time he broke my nose."

Ariel stared at each picture in silence.

"Most of the black eyes I just covered with makeup, but that time it was impossible. So he told people how I'd been hit by a car in a crosswalk." She shook her head. "I'm amazed everyone bought the lies for so long."

Ariel sniffed. "I'm sorry, Mom." She wiped her eyes. "I should have seen it."

"No, no, no." She turned her daughter to face her. "You were a child. Still are a child." She stroked Ariel's cropped hair. "None of this is your fault."

"How long had you been taking the pictures?"

"The last four years."

"And you were going to leave him?"

"Yes. Planning to for the last year. Saving money. Waiting for the right time. I knew it was time when he hurt you. When he said — " She bit her lip. "It was just the right time."

Ariel squinted. "Said what?"

"You don't need to know everything."

Ariel turned her head and stared at the window. "How did he die?"

"Like that. You don't need to know that." Mazie gathered the pictures from the bed and picked up the ones that landed on the floor. She turned to find Ariel reading the diary, her fingers gripping the gold chain Cullen had given her. "You don't need to read that."

"I do. Please?"

Mazie shifted her feet and looked to the ceiling. Had she written anything about what he said he'd do to Ariel? No, not in the journal. Just in the note she left for the police. "All right. But you don't have to."

"I know."

"Are you hungry? It's getting dark out."

"No."

"Me neither. I have to call Rachel back."

"Does she know?"

Mazie nodded. "She's trying to give me a heads up on what the police know. But I think I might turn myself in."

Ariel looked up from the diary. "No! You can't. What would happen to me?"

Mazie sat on the bed and engulfed Ariel in her arms, kissed the side of her head. "I'm not sure. But I either have to turn myself in, or we have to get out of here."

"Why?"

"The police know I have Grandma's car. They'll be looking for it." A chill ran through her. "Damn, I have to go get the car into the parkade. Then we'll call Rachel and figure out what to do next."

~~~~~~~~

"Oh, thank God. What took you so long?" Rachel had connected within two seconds of starting Skype. She shoved a mouthful of mashed potatoes in her mouth and washed it down with a slug of beer. "I been sitting here playing solitaire waiting for you to call back. Got George to bring me my dinner so I didn't miss you. Sorry for the mouthful."

Ariel smiled.

A vision of Ariel in a wedding gown passed through Mazie's mind. George walking her down the aisle, Rachel in the front pew
~~~~~~~~

crying, Polly all pretty in lavender and pearls standing next to the bride. And Mazie rotting in a jail cell.

"Can I talk to Polly?"

"Sorry, love. She's having a bath." Rachel took a bite from a chicken leg. "Can I talk with your mom for a bit?"

Mazie squeezed in beside Ariel. "It's okay, Rachel."

Rachel pursed her lips and stopped chewing. "She knows?"

Mazie nodded.

"Everything?"

"Enough."

Rachel put down the chicken and leaned her elbows on Polly's desk. "How you doing, honey?"

Ariel's eyes filled with tears. "I'm not sure." She scratched at her cheek. "Did you know what he was doing?"

"Not for sure. But I knew something was happening. I could see it in your mother's face. In his too. Seen it before, with Polly's father."

Mazie gasped. "George hit you?"

"Not George. He's my second husband. First one is in jail for attempted murder." She leaned toward the screen. "Mine."

Mazie covered her mouth with one hand. "Rachel, I had no idea."

"Yup. Polly was just an infant. Met George a year later. Took a whole lot of wooing before he got past first base, let me tell you." She laughed. "But it was worth the wait. He's a sweetheart." She pointed a finger at the screen and wagged it back and forth. "You remember this, Ariel. A good man will never, and I mean ever, raise a hand to you. And never force you to do things you don't want. *Capisce?*"

"Yes ma'am. I understand."

"Good. Now how are you going to ditch that car and get out of

Dodge? They know you passed through Temiscaming. Something about a gas station and security cameras.”

“Rachel, you ought to be a spy.”

~~~~~~~~

Mazie knocked on the bathroom door. “Are you ready, bug? We’ve only got a couple of hours before daylight.”

“Mother?”

“What’s wrong? Are you crying?”

“Mom, I’m bleeding.”

Mazie jiggled the door handle. “Unlock the door.”

The knob clicked. Mazie opened the door.

Ariel sat on the toilet, tissue smeared with pink and dotted with red spots in one hand.

Mazie sighed. “Oh, sweetheart. You’ve got your period.”

“Already?”

“Well, twelve isn’t unusual.” She pulled two feet of toilet paper from the roll, folded it into a makeshift pad, and handed it to her daughter. “Just tuck this into your underpants. We’ll make a quick stop at a drugstore and then you can use the bathroom when we stop for gas.”

“What do I do?”

“Don’t worry, it’s all normal. You’ll get used to it in no time. We just need pads.”

“Don’t you have any?”

“Only tampons, but you’re too young for those.”

“Turn around?”

“Yes, sorry.” Mazie left the bathroom and closed the door behind her.

The whole privacy thing was new this past year. Before she
~~~~~~~~

turned twelve, Ariel pranced around her room naked, only covered herself when her father was around, and even then, not always. When her breasts started to bud and pubic hair sprouted, everything changed. Like it had between Mazie and her mother all those years before.

They checked out of the hotel and inched the car into the dark streets. The first gas station they came across was attached to a small market. Mazie parked in back and they entered with hoodies up and heads down. Mazie guided her daughter through the sparse array of feminine hygiene products the market carried and dropped them on the checkout counter along with a blue Sharpie, some sweet snacks for breakfast, and an extra-large, extra-strong coffee with extra cream and twice the normal sugar.

Ariel went into the bathroom to start hew new life filled with pain and discomfort. And blood. Mazie returned to the car, tore the marker from its cardboard packaging and crouched in the dark lot. On the front and back license plates, she changed the C into an O, a three into an eight, and the F into an E. She stepped back to appreciate her work. Not perfect, the blue was a bit darker than the plate colour, but flying by on the highway at a hundred and ten kilometres per hour, it could pass for authentic.

Once on the highway they headed west. They'd scoured maps on the tablet the night before, finally settled on a final destination — Cornwall. A hop and skip into the States if it came to that. And a city Mazie had never visited. Never even passed through. Somewhere that no one knew her name. Or her face.

Every car they passed, that came up behind them, that sped along the highway in the opposite direction, was a threat. She held her breath each time, waiting for the inevitable police cruiser.

When a sign announced that highway one-forty-four loomed ahead, Mazie slowed, and turned toward south toward Sudbury. At five twenty-three by the dashboard clock, the sun crested the horizon to the left. A few kilometres down the narrow two-lane highway, a gravel road came into view ahead. She checked the rear-view mirror. No one behind them, no cars coming the other direction. She slowed and pulled onto the shoulder, then cranked the wheel to make a sharp right. The road narrowed, the gravel soon disappeared and they were bouncing between thick copses of fir and pine.

The axle groaned against deep ruts of dried muck. "It must be an old logging road." She slowed and swerved until the path disappeared altogether and they were surrounded by nothing but wilderness.

"Look at those trees. You think I can manoeuvre the car in there?"

"Maybe."

Mazie eased the gas pedal and sandwiched the car between the firs. Branches screeched across the metal body, one side-view mirror snapped off. No more than ten yards in, the tires caught on something and the wheels spun. She turned to Ariel. "This is it. The car's final resting place."

Ariel opened the door. It clunked against a tree. "Mom, I can't get out."

Mazie opened the windows. "Crawl out." She popped the trunk. "Grab everything you can.

Ariel took her CDs and put them in the bag with their remaining snacks. Mazie gathered up loose change and anything usable. She ran her hands over the steering wheel. "Sorry, Dad. I know how much you loved this old beast."

She reached one arm out and rested her purse on the roof of the car, slid her head and shoulders through the window, and shimmied out of the vehicle.

She dodged branches and fought her way to the rear of the car, pulled luggage from the trunk and turned to see where they'd come from. "Bit of a hike back to the highway."

Ariel rubbed her arms against the cool of the dawn. "Then what?"

"Hope for the kindness of a passing motorist?" She flashed a fake smile and bounced her eyebrows up and down.

"Yeah, one that's not a serial killer." Ariel pulled the handle of her suitcase up.

"Or a cop."

A loud snap echoed through the forest. Mazie and Ariel froze and stared at one another. Mazie scanned the area and hesitated at the motionless form of a deer not twenty feet away. It stared back at her, flicked one ear and blinked.

"Well, at least it's not a bear. Let's get out of here."

They jogged down the road, their luggage bouncing in the ruts. When they got to the gravel, they slowed to a walk and dragged their bags across the small rocks.

They walked along the shoulder of the highway until engine sounds echoed between the banks of trees. If it looked like there were lights on the roof, they'd hide in the thick trees at the edge of the road. But every time, it was only a car with a roof rack.

Twenty minutes later a van crested the hill and headed toward them. Mazie put out her thumb. Ariel sat on the blacktop and rubbed her shins. The van slowed and pulled to the side. An older man sat behind the wheel, a grey-haired woman in the passenger seat. The woman rolled down her window. "Now what are you young ladies doing hitchhiking in the middle of nowhere? Do you know how dangerous that is?" Liniment and cinnamon wafted from the open window.

"Yes, ma'am, we know." She motioned to Ariel. "Would you be able to give me and my daughter a ride to the next town? We just need to find a bus station."

"We're heading home to Sudbury. That work for you?"

"That would be wonderful. Thank you."

The man leaned over his wife's lap. "You hop in back." His door clicked open. "I'll get your bags."

"That's okay, sir!" Ariel grabbed her suitcase. "We can do it."

The man smiled and saluted her. "Yes, ma'am."

Mazie and Ariel piled their luggage into the back of the van and climbed in through the sliding side door.

The woman twisted around in her seat. "I'm Effie, and this is my husband, Edward."

"Pleasure to meet you." Mazie reached forward and shook Effie's hand. "I'm Charlotte. This is my daughter, Clementine."

"Clementine?" Edward called, and looked at her in the rear-view mirror. "Like the song?" He broke into a gravelly rendition of *My Darling Clementine*, his wife joined in near the end and they shared a laugh.

"Our son is OPP," Effie said. "We hear all kinds of stories about what happens to girls who hitchhike. You're lucky we came along."

Mazie swallowed and nodded. "Yes ma'am, we certainly are."

Effie opened the centre console. "You look thirsty." She handed Ariel a juice box and opened a plastic container of cookies. "Homemade."

Ariel took a big bite of a ginger snap. "Thank you," she said with her mouth full.

Effie flashed a sweet and genuine smile at her. "You remind me of my granddaughter. Though she's only five, and her hair is longer. But it's the eyes. Beautiful green eyes."

Mazie glanced out the window.

Cullen's eyes.

~~~~~~~~

"Charlotte, dear. Wake up."

Mazie started at the hand on her arm and bolted upright. Ariel snoozed beside her in the back of a strange minivan.

Right. Edward and Effie.

She rubbed crud from the corner of one eye. "Are we in Sudbury?"

"At the bus station. Eddie is getting your bags. You girls must have had a rough night, you both conked out almost two hours ago. I didn't have the heart to wake you."

"That's very kind of you." Mazie turned and grazed Ariel's cheek with the back of her fingers. "Bug, time to go."

"What?" Ariel jerked awake. "Where are we?"

"Sudbury. Let's get our things and thank these nice people for the ride."

Mazie climbed out of the van and stretched.

Effie handed Ariel two more cookies, turned, and gave Mazie a hug. "Where are you headed?"

Mazie hesitated. "We're on our way home. Regina."

Effie's eyes grew big. "That's a long bus trip!"

"Yes ma'am."

Ariel slipped her hand into her mother's.

That simple gesture said more than words could ever convey. It meant Ariel still loved her, still trusted her. If only she could believe it meant forgiveness.

Mazie squeezed Ariel's hand.

They thanked Effie and Edward and made their way into the bus station. Within the hour, they boarded a Greyhound bus and headed for the back row. "You want the window seat?"

Ariel nodded. She sat, retrieved the tablet from her backpack
~~~~~~~~

and pressed the power button.

"It works without a plug?" Mazie looked over her shoulder.

"As long as there's a Wi-Fi hot-spot. And until the battery dies." She pulled up a map of their route. "About an hour and forty minutes to North Bay."

"How long did she say the bus stops there?" The thought of passing through her home town again brought Mazie's heart into her throat.

"An hour." Ariel took Mazie's hand. "You look freaked out. We could get off now. Change the route?"

"No. We'd have to be nuts to travel back through North Bay."

Ariel grinned. "So, we're nuts?"

~~~~~~~~~

The bus rolled to a stop at the North Bay Greyhound station. Mazie scanned the area. No police cars, no foot patrol. She rested her forehead against Ariel's temple. "Let's grab a bite inside. Keep your head down and don't look at any cameras," she whispered.

"That's why you keep telling me to put my hood up?"

"Yeah."

"And that's why the haircuts and the makeup and the fake names? Not a game, not breaking Daddy's rules? To hide?"

"Afraid so."

"And I thought you were just being cool. And weird."

They put their hoods up, exited the bus and headed for a small café in the station.

Ariel picked at a roast beef sandwich. "This sucks."

"We'll try to find a place with a kitchen in Cornwall. Make our own food." Mazie sipped at her coffee. At least that didn't suck.

Ten minutes before the bus was scheduled to leave, they
~~~~~~~~~

gathered their things and approached the exit. Mazie pushed the door open. It hit the back of a police officer who stood just outside.

Maze grasped Ariel's sleeve. "Shit." She shook her head. "I mean, I'm so sorry."

"That's okay ma'am." He looked her up and down, tipped his hat to Ariel. "You in a rush?"

Ariel took her hand.

"Our bus is leaving soon."

"Where you all headed?"

Before Mazie could reply, Ariel blurted out, "Regina."

"Regina? Well you've got plenty of time. The westbound doesn't leave for a good half hour." He squinted at Mazie. "Ma'am are you feeling all right? You're kind of flushed and sweaty."

She swallowed. "I think it's something I ate."

"Well, no surprise if you ate here."

The radio clipped to his shoulder stuttered to life. He clicked a button. "Ten-four." He tipped his hat again. "Have a safe trip." He jogged to his car and sped out of the parking lot, lights flashing.

When he was out of sight, Mazie's knees gave out and she fell to the ground. The bus driver lumbered over.

"You okay? It's Charlotte, right?" He hitched his pants up under his belly and held his hand out.

"I'm fine. Just a little faint." She took his hand and he pulled her to her feet.

"Can I get you some water? I have to run in for a coffee."

"That would be nice, thanks."

He checked his watch. "You folks get on board. We head out in two minutes."

<p align="center">~~~~~~~~</p>

Fluffs of high cloud glowed tangerine against the darkening sky. Teal streaked with purple graduated to a bright blue glow at the horizon. At first blush, Cornwall was beautiful. As long as you kept your gaze skyward.

Modest houses of beige brick on acre-plus sized lots lined the east side of the road, Canadian flags proclaimed many an owner's patriotism. Businesses, mostly housed in Quonset huts and double-wides, lined the west. Antiques, a garden centre, a row of yellow bull dozers, graders and front loaders, like so many giant Tonka toys lined up in an adult sandbox.

The deeper into town the bus drove, the closer together the houses grew and the smaller the lots shrank. Industry slipped away, and a peaceful neighbourhood — with a highway slicing it down the middle — took its place.

The rush of airbrakes shook Mazie from her thoughts. She sat up, a flutter in her chest. Could this be their new home?

The bus slowed and veered right into the parking lot of a gas station and pulled to a jerky stop. The driver stood and called out "Cornwall!"

Ariel jolted awake. "Are we here?"

Mazie stared out the window. "I guess so."

The driver made his way down the aisle toward them. "I think you're the only ones getting off here. I'll grab your bags."

Ariel peered out the window. "This is a gas station."

"Yup. Doubles as the Greyhound bus station."

Mazie retrieved her purse from the floor at her feet. "Are we anywhere near a hotel? A hostel or something?"

"Sorry, Charlotte. I just drive through." He pointed out the window. "There's a pay phone over there." He shifted his finger toward the gas station. "And MacEwen has a decent café. I bet Loretta'd be happy to give you some ideas."

"Thanks."

He lumbered down the aisle. The bus rocked side to side with each step and lifted with relief when he disembarked.

"Well, bug. Let's get out of here and check out our new home."

"There's more to it right? Like a downtown and real restaurants and stuff?"

"Here's hoping." Mazie grabbed the backs of empty seats on her way to the front of the bus and stepped out onto the asphalt. She took a deep breath of bus fumes, dirt, and grease from the greasy spoon. It had to get better than this. "You stay here, I'll go see if there's a hotel nearby."

The phone booth was old-fashioned, the kind that turned Clark Kent into Superman. But this one had seen better days. A broken cord dangled where the phone book used to be. Mazie peered out the Plexiglas, milky with age and smudged with filth.

At the pumps, Ariel spoke with a man who was filling his gas tank. Who the hell? She jogged to her daughter's side, her eyes locked on the stranger who had no business chatting up a young girl.

He'd watched Mazie approach, grinned at her when she neared. She touched her hand to the side of her face, shielding it from his stare, and took Ariel by the arm. "We'll have to go talk to Loretta. There's no phone book." She pulled up the handle of her suitcase and glanced back at the man. He set the pump back on its cradle, paying not one whit of attention to them. "What did he say to you?"

"He asked where we were going. I told him I had no idea."

A bell over the door announced their entrance into the café. A woman stood behind the till, engrossed in a worn paperback.

"Excuse me, are you Loretta?"

"I certainly am." Loretta dog-eared the page and tossed the book on the counter. "Did Bill send you my way?"

Mazie smiled. "Yes, he sure did. Said you'd know where there was a decent place to stay." She did a mental calculation of her resources. "A cheap one."

"Well, you want decent, or cheap?" Loretta let out a huge laugh. "Just kidding, honey. I know just the place." She scrawled an address on a piece of scrap paper. "It's not too far, you can grab the bus just down the road a bit, take you right to it. Should come in…" she glanced at her watch, "forty minutes or so. You could take a cab, be quicker. But that's not as cheap, right?" She winked. She looked at Ariel. "Love your hair, sweetheart."

Ariel touched her hair. Her cheeks pinked.

"Where are you coming from? What brings you to our sleepy little city?"

Back story. Why hadn't she thought of that?

"Just a change of pace. Divorce. You know how it is."

"Ah yes. Yes I do. Damn bastards."

"Hey, Loretta, I gotta jet. Can we move it along?"

Mazie turned around to face a truck driver, a wad of chewing tobacco lumped inside one cheek, credit card at the ready.

"Sorry," Mazie said. "We're done." She turned back to Loretta. "Thanks for everything."

"Any time, honey. Good luck."

Mazie skirted around the trucker dragging her luggage, battered and beaten, behind her. She bumped right into the man from the gas pumps. He stood a good eight inches taller than her, his reedy body drowned by his corduroy pants and tweed jacket.

"Pardon me, miss." He glanced at his feet before lifting his eyes to meet her gaze. "I overheard you at the till. I know you have no idea who I am, but I'd like to offer you a ride. Looks like you've been travelling a while," he looked away and scratched the back of his head, "and it's almost dark."

"Thanks, but we're fine."

"I know, kind of crazy, right? Complete stranger. Offers a ride." He held his hand out. "I'm Norman Day."

"Nice to meet you, Mr. Day. But we do all right on our own."

He held up his hands. "Didn't mean to suggest otherwise. Just thought I could save you a long wait. I could have you to the hotel in ten minutes flat."

"Norm, you're up!" Loretta's voice boomed across the shop.

"Just let me pay my bill and we can talk?"

"Thanks, but no." Mazie grabbed Ariel's hand. "Come on Ar —" She pressed her lips together. "Just come on."

"Take the ride, honey."

Mazie spun around.

Loretta was ringing up Norman's gas purchase. "He's a straight arrow. He'll just drop you off, get you in safely before dark. Known him for twenty years. He's above board."

Norman blushed and shrugged his shoulders.

Mazie looked at Ariel. "What do you think?"

"I think I'm tired. Take the ride, Mom."

Mazie nodded. "All right, then."

Norman had paid his bill and held the door open for them. His eyes were kind, his smile genuine. And he smelled familiar. Like vanilla. Or cookies. Oatmeal cookies.

"I'm Charlotte. This is my daughter, Clementine."

"Nice to meet you, Charlotte."

"She likes to be called Charlie." Ariel's face was alight with mischief.

"And what do you like to be called?"

"Clem is fine."

"Clem it is. What does the 'A' stand for?" Norman pointed to her necklace.

Ariel touched one finger to the gold pendant that rested in the hollow of her collarbone. Her cheeks paled. "Uh, it means … Awesome."

"Ah, of course it does." He smiled and piled their luggage into the trunk of his rusty old Buick LeSabre. He opened the back door and gestured to Ariel. "Mademoiselle." He gave a slight bow then turned to Mazie. "And the front of the carriage for madame."

Mazie squinted.

He clicked the door closed and walked around the front of the car.

"He's got a crush on you," Ariel said in a sing-song voice.

"Yeah, right. That's just what I need." Another bloody man to mess up her life even more.

Norman pulled out onto the highway. His headlights cut through the growing darkness. He cleared his throat. "So, where are you coming from?"

Mazie stared straight ahead.

"Sorry. Didn't mean to pry." He slowed at a red light and tapped the steering wheel with his fingertips. "Are you just passing through?"

Mazie glanced sideways at him. "No. We're planning to stay for a while."

"So, you have a place?" He turned to look at her, his cheeks pinked and he looked ahead again. "No, of course not. That's why I'm driving you to a hotel."

Ariel snickered.

"I'll have to look for something. And a job." Mazie rubbed one palm down the front of her pants. How long was this quick drive going to take?

"A job?" He made a quick left and pulled into the parking lot of a small hotel in the middle of nowhere. "I could help with that." He parked the car and turned in his seat. "The company that cleans my office building is hiring. It's not glamorous, but it would be a start."

Mazie looked back at Ariel who shrugged her shoulders. "What office building?"

"A small group of businesses, marketing and the head office of a trucking firm. I have a law practice."

Mazie's chest hollowed. Law practice. She'd be working in the belly of the beast, in plain sight right inside the system. That wasn't hiding. It was suicide. She shook her head. "I … I don't know."

"Come on, let me set you up with them. It's decent pay."

She stared at him. Was this guy for real?

"And a fellow I know owns an apartment building downtown. Kind of run down, but passable. He owes me a favour."

She furrowed her brow. "Why are you doing this?"

He straightened in his seat. "You look like you could use a leg up. That's all."

She eyed this man who looked like he spent more time behind a desk than in a gym, his hands callous free and his nails clean and trimmed. He reminded her of Allan, the accountant she'd dumped for Cullen. They could use the money and a place to call home. If he wasn't who he appeared, she could cut and run.

Cut and run.

She was getting good at that.

She nodded her head. "I'll take you up on the job offer."

His face lit up. "Great." He drew his wallet from the inside pocket of his tweed jacket pulled out a business card. "Call me tomorrow. I'll get you their number." He handed her the card.

She took the card between her thumb and index finger. Norman Day. Criminal Defence Attorney.

Son of a bitch. He was on her side.

~~~~~~~~
~~~~~~~~

Mazie and Ariel settled into an uneasy calm. The musty apartment was liveable, despite the body odour and exotic spices that clung to the walls. Norman fixed a leaky tap and hired someone to change the locks. Ariel dotted the rooms with air fresheners and scented candles in the hopes that fake cinnamon and orange blossoms would over-perfume the stink.

Mazie worked evenings and Saturdays, dusting and vacuuming when the offices were closed and the normal people had gone home to their normal families. Except Norman. He was there most of the time, working well into the night and through the weekend. He was dedicated. Or he had no other life.

The cleaning company paid her cash under the table. No tax returns to worry about, no bank accounts required. And no need to show identification.

She used her old trick, a false back in a drawer — just enough room for a stack of cash, the photos, and her journal — to keep the money she'd drained from the bank accounts hidden and safe. With the money she made scrubbing strangers toilets, she could afford to let that sit. An emergency fund. Her stay out of jail not-so-free stash.

The work was menial, grimy, and so familiar. But she was damn good at it. It kept her body busy and her mind at peace. She hadn't earned her own money since Ariel was born, and didn't have to account to anyone for one cent she spent. In an unsettling way, life was sort of good.

But the peace that manual labour brought only lasted while she dusted shelves and emptied trash bins, vacuumed behind desks, and polished a myriad of DNA and fingerprints from door handles and telephones and windows. Outside the relative sanctuary of that office building, she spent every moment with her eyes cast down, casting furtive glances to assess if strangers on the bus, in the grocery store, walking the sidewalks, were in fact evil enemies waiting for the opportunity to out her.

In early August, Ariel turned thirteen. She was letting her hair grow, and dying it regularly. Purple first, like she'd always wanted. Then blonde like Mazie. But the home dye jobs were nothing like the professional ones, and the result was never what she expected. The latest, back to the deep maroon that started it all, had turned a muddied pink.

As the stifling summer wore on, an ever-growing sense of panic set in. Ariel would have to go to school. Mazie had to enrol her. Without identification. With a fake name. How the hell would she do that? Two months of dodging the law had done nothing to turn her into a savvy crime maven.

She dusted the shelves next to Norman's desk for the third time since she'd entered his office just twenty minutes before. He glanced over his shoulder at her, returned to his computer screen, glanced at her again.

"Charlie, are you okay?"

She plastered a casual smile on her face. "Me? Sure. I'm good."

"Really? Because I think the dust is not only gone, but future dust is afraid to land."

She flopped into the chair across from his desk. "Sorry. I do have a problem."

He pushed aside a folder and rested his forearms on his desk, his fingers entwined. "Let me help."

"You've done nothing but help. I don't want to bother you."

"Nothing you do bothers me."

She tried to contain an affectionate smile. He'd become her closest friend next to Rachel, and her fondness for him grew each day.

"I have to enrol Clem in school."

He raised his eyebrows and spread his hands out, palms up. "And?"

"I left all her identification behind. I have nothing, no birth certificate, no immunization record."

"Well the birth certificate is easy." He typed on his keyboard and clicked his mouse. "We can just ask for a replacement. You can enrol her without it. Just get the school a copy when it comes in." He wrote on a pad of paper and tore a piece off. "Here's the website."

She leaned forward. "Right. Of course." Tears threatened and she bit her lip.

He pushed back in his chair, tented his fingers and rested them against his lips. "Why are you here, Charlie?"

"Excuse me?"

"In Cornwall. I'm curious. Why here? You never speak of your ex. You have a daughter, there had to be a father." He leaned forward, his elbows on the desk. "You can trust me, Charlie. Honest you can."

"What about you? You have an ex?"

"I'm a widower."

She swallowed. "I'm sorry. You seem too young for that."

"Yeah, well, drunk drivers don't give a good God damn how old the person they mow down in a crosswalk is." Red blotches blossomed on his face. He took a gulp of cold coffee.

"How long ago?"

"Twelve years. She was four months pregnant."

"Oh, Norman. I am so sorry."

He cleared his throat. "Your turn."

She pulled the cloth through her closed fist, her eyes trained on the cloud of dust that wafted from it. "I'm divorced. He didn't take it well. I wanted to get as far away as I could."

He stood and stretched. "Can you type?"

"Can I what?"

"Type. On the computer."

"It's been a while. I'm not that good anymore. But I used to be, back in the day."

"I'm in a jam. I have to finish going through this discovery, but I need something typed up for first thing Monday morning. I was going to break down and call Dory, but she hates it when I do that after hours. Especially on a Friday night."

"Sure, I can do it. Nice break from dust and dirt. You won't tell on me, right?"

"Your secret is safe with me. They must be happy with you. You clean better than anyone they've ever had. Like the magic feather duster woman. She'd come in the office, smile at me, wave her duster in the air and leave."

"Cullen would have killed me —" She put her hand to her mouth.

He nodded. "Ah. One of those guys."

She nodded and stared at her lap. They sat in silence, the weight of her outburst like a thick fog between them.

"Well, let's do this, shall we?" Norman's voice shattered the tension. He showed her to Dory's desk in the front of the office, booted up the computer, and pulled pages from a manila folder. "These are the questions I need transcribed."

She sat in Dory's chair, seat of the infamous receptionist. Or secretary. Assistant? Whatever she was, Mazie had heard her name many times but not set eyes on her. Dory didn't do overtime.

Mazie stared at the monitor. She placed her right hand over the mouse, the silver paint worn through where Dory's thumb and index finger spent many hours a day clicking and dragging. She moved the cursor to the right spot, clicked it into place, and poised her fingers over the keyboard. With a deep breath, she set her eyes on the document to her left and began to type.

"See? You got this."

"I'm rusty, but it's like riding a bike, right? Never forget?" She twisted around and smiled up at him.

He nodded. "Yeah. Never forget." He put one hand on each of her shoulders and squeezed.

A jolt of energy shot through her shoulders, and not the static electricity kind from shuffling across the old polyester carpet. No, no, no, she couldn't be attracted to him. There was too much at stake. And sex remained twisted together in a ball of pain and horror and pending death. No, her relationship with Norman had to remain as it was. Comfortable. Like a faded pair of old Levis.

"Coffee?" He let his hands fall to his sides.

"Sure." She pushed her chair back and stood. "How do you take it?"

"You sit and get started. I'll make it."

She put one hand on the back of the chair and hesitated before sitting down and facing the computer.

Her fingers found the keys and she focused her mind on the task, blocked out stupid thoughts of romance with a kind, sweet man. In no time, she was typing like in the old days, with speed and accuracy. It really was like riding a bike. Would love be like that? Sex?

No. Stop it. Focus.

At first it was just anonymous words, meaningless letters strung together. Soon some of them started to jump from the page.

Struck. Broken. Beaten.

When *choked* popped out of her fingertips she froze. The cursor blinked to the right of that word, like a flashing light on a movie theatre marquis advertising the horror show within.

She picked up the paper, scanned through his loose, neat cursive. She swivelled the chair around. "What is this?"

He looked at her through the doorway. "It's for a case." He took something from his desk drawer, came out and stood beside her. "It's a woman who killed her husband. Took a shotgun to him." He flashed a pack of cigarettes at her. "You mind?"

She shook her head.

"She's charged with murder." He lit the cigarette and took a long drag, blowing the smoke straight up. "Don't tell Dory. She hates it when I smoke in here."

"So, you're her lawyer?"

"Yup. There's no question she shot him. But the bastard had it coming. Maybe killing him wasn't the right way to go, but he'd brutalized her for years." He shook his head and sucked on the smoke. "Can you imagine?"

Her eyelids fluttered out a slow blink. "What will happen to her?"

"Not sure yet. We're in discovery. Our defence will be battered woman syndrome. There came a point when it was just too much and she snapped."

Mazie nodded.

Snapped.

"She's in a psychiatric hospital in Kingston. I asked that she be put there. Better than jail. She really couldn't function, and her kids, grown fucking adults, pardon my French, abandoned her. They blame her." He shook his head. "Idiots."

Mazie turned back to the screen. The cursor blinked at her.

Battered woman syndrome.

"This client never speaks to me, but she does write. That's why I'm going to send the questions. I'm hoping this gets some answers so I can defend her properly." He stepped behind Mazie's chair. "I don't think she trusts men at all. Even if they are on her side."

He touched her hair, an almost imperceptible brush of his

fingertips. The nape of her neck broke out in gooseflesh and a shiver ran up into her scalp.

"I'm sorry, Charlie. I shouldn't have told you all that. Dory just ignores the words and what they mean. Just types and files and answers the phone. Maybe she's bored. Or jaded. Or she just doesn't give a shit anymore." He kneeled down beside the chair and rested his forearms on the armrest. "You give a shit, don't you, Charlie?"

She nodded, her gaze fixed on the monitor, his gentle grey eyes tugging at her peripheral vision. She resumed typing.

He butted the cigarette on the bottom of his shoe and returned to his desk.

An hour later she came to the end of the document. Fifteen years ago she would have had it typed, proofread, printed in triplicate, filed, and been out the door in half that time. She glanced over her shoulder. "I'm done," she called out.

The castors on his oversized leather chair squeaked. He leaned over her shoulder. "Great. I'll get Dory to send it to the hospital administrator on Monday. They'll try to get her to answer the questions." He grabbed the armrest and spun the chair around. "Can I buy you dinner in return?"

"No need. I'm getting paid to clean your office, remember?" She grinned. "And I have to get home."

"Of course. I'm sure Clementine is much better company anyway." He smiled. "Look, if you'd rather have a day job, there might be an opening here. I need an assistant."

"What about Dory?"

"Yeah, Dory. She's fine as a secretary, but she's got one toe dipped in the retirement pool. She won't do anything if she doesn't like it and never works a minute past office hours. I need someone with a bit more energy."

"I'm not really qualified. I have no legal training."

"I can teach you the legal stuff. Dory can give you some word processing training. For now it'd be filing briefs, doing research, typing, and maybe making some phone calls."

No more toilets to scrub or carpets to vacuum. That sounded good. "Okay. I'll do it."

"Great!" His eyes twinkled. "Why don't you quit the cleaning firm tomorrow and take the weekend off. I'll see you Monday morning." He closed his laptop and pointed a finger at her. "After you get Clementine all signed up for school."

~~~~~~~~

"How about this one?" Ariel held up an eggplant blouse with too much frill in the boob region.

"Love the colour, but too much going on." Mazie gestured at her chest. "I need something plain"

"I like the frills."

"Yeah, wait until you're in a D-cup and see if you change your mind. Just makes everything look even bigger."

Ariel looked down at her chest. "I doubt I'll ever have to worry about it."

"You're only twelve!"

"Thirteen."

"Sorry. I'll get used to having a teenager soon." Or never. "Besides, you need a bra. You may not think so, but you're looking just like me at that age."

"Should we go look for one?"

Mazie wrinkled her nose. "Not here. I can live with used tops and skirts. Can even get my mind around wearing someone else's shoes. But I draw the line at underwear." She leaned into Ariel. "Besides, this place smells like pee and dirty feet," she whispered. She
~~~~~~~~

took the blouse from Ariel and put it back in the rack. "We'll go to Wal-Mart." Hanger after hanger of used skirts got pushed aside. Too outdated. Too pink. Tear in the seam. She pulled a black one from the rack and held it out, scratched at a stain on the front. It flaked off in white dust. "Gross. Maybe next year we can afford to shop for something new."

"Can I get some jeans for school?"

"Sure. You've grown at least two inches this summer. Get some tops too." At two bucks a pop, they could almost go on a shopping spree.

Mazie wriggled into her choices in the confined change room. "Can you give me your opinion?" she called to Ariel in the next cubicle.

She stepped out and examined herself in the full-length mirror. Hands on her hips, she turned and craned her neck to check out her backside. If only she wasn't so fat. She shouldn't have eaten all those burgers and pancakes on their road trip.

Ariel whistled. "Wow, I've never seen you dress like that. You look beautiful."

"Really?" Mazie turned back to the mirror. "It doesn't make my gut look huge?"

"Mother, you're a stick."

She raised an eyebrow at her daughter. "That's sweet. But it's crap."

Ariel stood beside her in tight skinny jeans and a black V-neck T-shirt emblazoned with a glittery skull, her own curvy body screaming to be looked at. She took her mother by the waist and turned her sideways. "See? Thin. No gut. Big boobs, but you can't help that. It doesn't make you fat."

Mazie scrutinized her reflection. How many times had she been told how fat she was? Gross, disgusting, piggish. No amount of dieting or exercise made the insults stop. She turned side to side, closed her eyes and opened them again.

Not fat. Not fat. Not fat.

Under the green glow of the fluorescent lights, a thin line of black jumped from the part in her hair. "Damn."

"What?"

"I have to stop for hair dye again." Mazie neared the mirror and inspected her roots. Flecks of grey salted her natural black. That was new.

"I'm going to grow mine out."

Mazie eyed her daughter in the mirror. Her hair would be black again. Just the colour the cops were looking for. "Will you keep it short?"

"Yeah, I love it like this. Can I frost the tips?"

Mazie smiled. "Of course."

<div align="center">~~~~~~~~</div>

Mazie tugged her skirt down and shifted her feet. When the line moved, she shuffled forward. The sound of her heels on the waxed gym floor ricocheted off the walls like gunfire. Very slow gunfire.

Three women sat at a row of portable tables. The one on the right motioned for them to come forward. Mazie took Ariel's hand and tugged on it.

Ariel pulled her hand away. "Don't."

"Sorry for being your mother."

Ariel was focused on something across the gym. Mazie followed her gaze and landed on a tall young man, football in hand. He stood at the edge of the room by the folded bleachers, his broad smile aimed directly at her daughter. Ariel smiled right back at him.

The woman at the table had to be ninety — tight grey bun

sitting on the collar of an ivory cardigan, cat's eye half-glasses on the tip of her nose. She peered over the top of them.

"Name?"

Ariel ignored her.

Mazie sighed. "Clementine Smyth, with a Y."

"New this year?"

"Yes."

"Grade?"

"Eight."

"Fill this out." She slid a piece of paper toward Mazie and put a pencil on top. "We'll need a copy of her birth certificate. And immunization records."

Mazie filled in the form, glanced between the page, her daughter, and the too-old-for-her boy who seemed smitten with her thirteen year-old child. "We lost those in the move."

"Her ID?"

"Among a whole bunch of other stuff, yes."

The woman gave her a scathing look and flipped through a file at her elbow. "Okay then, Mrs. Smyth."

"It's Ms."

The woman shot her a look. "*Mizz* Smyth." She rolled her eyes. "Here's where you can get a new certificate."

"I have the website address already, thanks. They said it would take a few weeks."

"Yes. Well as soon as you have it, we need a copy."

Mazie nodded. "So you said."

"Now, about the immunization records."

"She's had all her shots."

"I need something on file."

Of course she did. "I work for a lawyer. How about a sworn affidavit?"

"Oh. Well yes, that would be fine. Clementine?"

Mazie poked her daughter in the ribs. "Clem, pay attention."

Ariel turned. "What?"

"Take this over there," the woman pointed to a line of kids, "and get your photo taken. They'll give you a school identification card. Then we'll see you on Thursday."

Mazie took Ariel by the elbow. "That boy is too old for you."

"He's cute. And he was smiling at me."

"No dating."

"Charlie, come on! I'm thirteen."

"So you keep reminding me. And don't call me Charlie."

With Ariel's new school ID in hand, they walked to the nearest bus stop two blocks away. "Can you walk home on your own? I'm going to grab the bus here and try to be at the office before ten."

"Yeah. I'm good."

"See you later. Wish me luck."

"Luck."

"Can I have a hug?"

Ariel looked in all directions then gave her a quick hug.

Mazie watched Ariel walk away. Was that swing of the hips new?

Enrolled her daughter in a new school. Without official paperwork. Maybe she should become a spy.

<div align="center">~~~~~~~~</div>

Mazie stood at the threshold to the office, her hand on the brass knob.

Just turn the damn thing and walk through, already. Dive into the deep end of a whole new life.

She let go of the knob. She was letting too much ride on this. It was just a job, that's all. Just another job.

She buttoned the top two buttons of her blouse, ran one finger between the collar and her scarf, undid one button, took a deep breath, and turned the knob.

A greying woman of ample proportions sat at the reception desk.

Mazie smiled and approached her. "Hi. You must be Dory. I'm Charlotte Smyth." She held out her hand.

"Right. Mr. Day told me he'd hired a paralegal." Dory crossed her arms over her massive bosom and eyed Mazie up and down. "What's your background? Where you work before?"

Mazie drew her hand away and smoothed her skirt with it. Beyond the fortress of Dory, Norman sat at his desk, the phone to his ear. He glanced up, did a double take and smiled broadly. He waved her in.

She smiled, looked down at Dory, and tilted her head to one side. "Maybe we can talk later." She refrained from adding "bitch" under her breath and instead stuck her chin in the air and glided past. She hovered just inside his door, straightened a stack of files sitting askew on the filing cabinet next to her.

Norman hung up the phone, pushed his chair away from the desk and swivelled toward her. "Well, look at you."

Her gaze shifted to her feet, her cheeks hot. She straightened her skirt. "Is it all right?"

"All right? You're the loveliest thing to ever walk in this office."

Dory let out a snort.

"Come on in. Close the door and have a seat so we can chat."

Mazie did as she was told. She pulled her skirt down as far over her knees as it would go. Why hadn't she bought a longer one?

He flipped through a file on his desk and pulled out two pieces of paper. "You'll have to fill these out, so we can be sure to pay you on time."

She took the forms and swallowed. Social insurance number. Damn, why hadn't she thought of that? She handed the pages back. "Maybe this was a bad idea." She went to stand but he held up one hand.

"Have a seat for a second." He leaned forward, his elbows on the desk, his head tilted. His eyebrows were furrowed, but not in anger. Concern perhaps. Affection even. He'd never shown her any hint of aggression. "What spooked you?"

She took a deep breath. "Look, it's complicated. The cleaning company, they just pay me cash."

He sat back, his eyes never leaving her face. "I see. Under the table. No tax. No questions."

She turned away, her eyes burned with the threat of tears. "I'm going to go." She stood and put her hand on the door handle. "I'm sorry to waste your time."

"Charlie, wait."

She shot him a quick look over her shoulder.

"I can pay you cash. No questions asked."

"Isn't that illegal? Some kind of ethical conflict?"

"You let me worry about that."

"I don't want to cause you any trouble."

He stood and joined her next to the cabinet and took one of her hands. "Charlie, the last thing you are, is trouble."

He walked her to a small desk in the front office and motioned to a chair. He leaned over her shoulder, one hand on the back of the chair, and showed her how to log on with her own user name and password, where to find the files she'd be working on. A stack of documents waiting to be typed sat next to the computer.

Each time he reached over her shoulder to poke at the monitor or sift through one of the files, the scent of a spring meadow filled her head. Or maybe an ocean breeze. Whatever it was, it wasn't cologne. Only laundry detergent or soap, and the faintest hint of vanilla she'd first noticed when he drove her and Ariel to the hotel their first day in Cornwall.

"All right, you're good to go." He straightened and patted her shoulder. "Coffee's in the back room. Would you like some?"

"I can get it."

"Nonsense, let me. Dory, how about you, refill?"

Dory glared at him and handed him her cup. He smiled at her and turned to Mazie. "Double cream and two sugars, right?"

She nodded.

"Coming up."

~~~~~~~~

Mazie's fingers soon shredded the keyboard. The speed and accuracy of her younger years improved with each passing day. Smiling came easier, and she could barely contain herself when she got home. She had to tell Ariel of her daily accomplishments, the stories spilling from Mazie's lips and onto her daughter's increasingly bored ears.

Dory continued to freeze her out, didn't acknowledged Mazie's presence, walked right by on her way for coffee without so much as a smile, let alone offering to fill her cup.

Within a week, Norman had asked Mazie to assist with research for the case of the battered woman. The case that got her this job. The case of perfect irony.

The woman, with the sweet-old-lady name of Betty Wardell, still wouldn't speak to him. Wouldn't speak to anyone, except one particular nurse. Just sat in the sunroom in the loony bin, staring out the window.

Mazie searched for precedent on law websites and pored over
~~~~~~~~

dusty old books in the library. She read of a woman in Hamilton who'd killed her husband and faced murder charges. Was found not guilty. She had entered a plea of self-defence. Her lawyers brought forward mounds of evidence proving years of the severe abuse she'd suffered at the bastard's hands.

Not guilty. Of murder. Not in jail. But confined to the mental ward of a local hospital all the same. She'd never recovered. Not from the abuse. Not from the broken heart. She missed her husband, regretted her actions. Despite the regular beatings, the near-death traumas he inflicted, she still loved him. Looking in life's rear-view mirror, the woman had come to believe the abuse was his way of showing affection. That he really did love her and she'd killed him for it.

Mazie stared at the screen, at the words that seemed so ridiculous, so unbelievable. So familiar.

In the last month, glimpses of happy Cullen popped up unexpectedly amidst nightmares of the hell he'd wrought. The Cullen she'd longed for. The handsome, young, fun Cullen. Those moments were like the first bloom of spring breaking through the weight of a May snowstorm. He was the Canadian prairie weather. Stormy, with just a hint of sunshine. Ice cold for weeks, with brief Chinook winds bringing warmth and relief. Oppressive like the heat of a late August day, cooled by the lovely evening chill of the looming autumn.

She missed him. The truth of it was a punch in the head.

Was he affected by weather? Could he have been cured, fixed — normal — if they'd moved to a temperate climate?

She shook her head. That was absurd. He was just as abusive in winter as summer. Just as thoughtless and violent in spring as in fall. Red flags had slapped her upside the head almost as hard as he did. But in the beginning she'd missed them all. Or chose to ignore them.

"Charlie? You all right?"

She looked up into Norman's face, all scrunched up in that endearing, inquisitive way he had.

She straightened her spine and rolled her neck. "Fine. Just taking a typing break." She rubbed her wrists and placed her fingertips back on the keyboard, searched the faux-mahogany desktop for her work. But she hadn't been typing. She'd been doing research. She slouched back in her chair. "Sorry. This is just a bit overwhelming."

He put his hands on her shoulders and dug his thumbs into her aching muscles.

She groaned and rolled her head forward.

"You're tense as hell. Why don't you take a real break. Get out into the sunshine." He dug his wallet out of his pocket and peeled a twenty and a ten from the fold. "Maybe grab us some lunch?"

~~~~~~~~

"Things have really chilled. I haven't seen a cop in two weeks." Rachel raised a glass of white wine toward the webcam. "Cheers to this being well on the way to the cold case files."

Mazie raised her plastic tumbler of five ninety-nine shiraz. "Do you really think so?"

"Well, can't guarantee it, but it's been quiet. No more interviews, no more showing up on our doorstep at all hours. I'm sure the file's still open, but shit, there was a murder this week, two shootings last Saturday and a knifing downtown just last night."

"In Calgary? What are we becoming, Toronto or something?"

Rachel snorted. "Christ, I hope not. But they've got fresh meat to worry about."

Mazie took a long gulp of wine, then swirled it in the glass. A flash of Cullen's mutilated skin skipped through her head.

"You getting enough sleep? You look tired."
~~~~~~~~

"Not really. Can't shut off my brain." Mazie rubbed under her eye with one finger. "But I get these nice bags as a reward." And a few extra crow's feet.

The weekly Skype-and-wine date with Rachel had become a lifeline to home. She always knew the latest news, the juiciest gossip. And was always easy with her laughter and her friendship.

"How's your cutie-pie lawyer man?" Rachel flashed her eyebrows up and down.

Mazie rolled her eyes. "Oh, please. Like that's what I need." She wiped dust from the tablet with her index finger. "I mean, he's sweet and all. But shit, how would that work? I haven't even figured out how to get fake ID. The school is after me constantly to get them Ariel's birth certificate. Or Clementine's. How could I have a relationship? You're supposed to be honest and be able to trust each other. I can't do either." She slouched down in her seat. "I just want to come home," she whispered.

"I get that. But you can't. So get your shit together, woman."

She could always count on Rachel to tell it like it is.

"Surely your lawyer dude knows some shady characters. Don't you ever get to meet his clients?"

Mazie laughed. "No. Not yet. I'll keep your sneaky idea in mind though."

"Look, I need to tell you something. We've been opening some of your mail."

"Oh?"

"Paying the utilities and all."

"What? You don't have to do that. I don't know when I can pay you back."

"You don't have to pay it back." Rachel sipped her wine. "But there was another letter from the bank today. Final notice. I bet it's your mortgage. It has been a few months. Should I open it?"

"Yes. I have no secrets from you, Rach. Like, not a single one."

Rachel tore into an envelope and unfolded the paper inside. "Yup. They want payment *tout suite* or they're threatening to foreclose."

"Shit." Mazie drank the rest of her wine and poured another glass. "Let 'em. I don't ever want to set foot in that house again. They can have it."

"Are you sure you want to do that? There's gotta be equity in there. You could sell."

"How? I don't exist, remember?"

Rachel pursed her lips. "Right. Sorry."

"Mom, can I talk to Polly yet?" Ariel yawned.

"Rach, gotta give the computer up for the girls. Talk to you next week."

"Keep your head down. Love from George."

~~~~~~~~

The office sat in pure and eerie silence. No ticking of fingers on keyboards, no huffing and snorting from Dory's jealous nose. No reassuring timbre of Norman's gentle voice on the phone or over Mazie's shoulder.

Dory had taken the afternoon off — thank God for small mercies — and Norman was at a client meeting.

The phone receiver was cool in Mazie's hand. She put it to her ear and cradled it against her shoulder. Fresh pain in her knotted muscles coursed down her arm. The mouthpiece smelled of cabbage and coffee, a scent that wafted through the office each time hurricane Dory rolled through.

Mazie took a deep breath and punched ten digits on the number pad. "Saint Lawrence Psych." The woman's clipped voice reeked of
~~~~~~~~

efficiency.

Mazie cleared her throat. "I'm looking for a patient."

"We have patients. Lots of 'em. Do you have a name?"

"Elizabeth Wardell."

The woman put her through to a nurse's station and Mazie repeated her request.

"Betty Wardell?" The nurse snickered. "She doesn't talk much. You a relative?"

"No ma'am. I work for her lawyer."

"Ah. Mr. Day. He's trying a new tack? Didn't the written answer thing work?"

"He — he told you about that?"

"Told me? It was my idea. I see her scrawling notes and thoughts all over the place. Sometimes it's gibberish, sometimes it's just her husband's name. Once she did permanent marker on the sunroom wall. A heart with BW plus TW. I think all those beatings he gave her knocked the sense right out of her."

Mazie winced. "Well, in your line of work, you ought to know how devastating the lasting effects of long-term abuse are. Maybe a bit more kindness and understanding are in order." She put her hand over her eyes. Did she just scold a mental health professional?

"Look, lady, if you saw the shit I deal with every day, maybe you'd throw me a little kindness and understanding, eh?"

"I'm very sorry." Mazie took a deep breath. "Can I please speak with her?"

"Hold the line."

She was going to have to practice the fine art of drawing information out of the unwilling. Without pissing them off.

Mazie rifled through Dory's drawer. Seven pencils with broken leads later she found one with just enough tip to write with. The pencil stood poised above the yellow lined pad of paper, ready to record every word Betty spoke.

The phone clicked, something rustled on the other end. And then breathing. Just breathing.

"Elizabeth Wardell?" No response. "Betty, is that you?" Mazie cleared her throat. "Betty my name is Charlotte Smyth. Charlie if you like."

Betty remained silent.

"I work for Norman Day."

Betty's breath became heavy.

This wasn't working. She didn't need a lawyer, she needed a friend. A confidante. Someone who got it. Someone just like her.

Mazie twisted her head to one side until a loud crack relieved some pressure in her sore neck. "Look, Betty. I just want you to know that I understand. I'm sure a lot of people say that to you, right?"

No response.

"My husband beat the shit out of me for years."

A huff of air was her reward for that confession.

"He choked me too. Usually during sex. Until I passed out. I thought he would kill me."

A whimper. A sniff.

"So you see, I really do understand. Everything. I broke free too, Betty. Completely free. I get it. I understand."

The phone went dead.

Mazie slammed the phone on its cradle. "Damn it." She tapped the pencil against the paper, then pitched the yellow stick across the desk and covered her eyes with the heels of both hands.

The phone's shrill ring sliced through the silence. She jumped and stared at the ancient handset. When Norman got back, she would insist he upgrade and get caller display.

She picked up the receiver like it might morph into a snake and bite her. "Hello?"

"Is this Norman Day's office?" The gruff voice of the angry nurse bit her ear.

"Yes. This is Charlotte Smyth."

"Well, Charlotte Smyth, I don't know what the hell you said to her, but Betty, here, wants to meet you."

"What, in person?"

"She hates phones. Must say, I'm impressed. She didn't even write it down, whispered it right in my ear."

Mazie reclined in the chair and pumped her fist in the air. "I'll have to discuss it with Mr. Day and get back to you."

"Shit, you don't have to make an appointment with her or anything. She's always available. Just drop in. Visiting hours are nine until four."

Mazie hung up the phone, crossed her arms in front of her chest, grinned and nodded. Now how would she tell Norman she'd done something so bold and stupid?

~~~~~~~~

"So, that case in Kingston." Mazie stood in the doorway to Norman's office, her shoulder against the jamb, arms crossed.

He pulled his attention from whatever case he was enrapt with. Or maybe it was a porn site and he was into bondage. A flash of him slapping her face darted through her mind.

"What about it?" The arch of his eyebrow seemed familiar. Yet not at all.

"I spoke to her."

He cocked his head. It was a habit, maybe a tick. It made her smile. He looked like a puppy trying to decipher its master's words. "To Betty Wardell?"
~~~~~~~~

"Yes."

He pushed away from this desk. His chair rolled until the back of it hit the credenza. "Did she speak back?"

"No. Just a lot of breathing. But the nurse said that she wants a meeting."

He inched his laptop cover shut, his eyes never leaving hers. "When?"

"It's already after four. What is it, a two hour drive? So I was thinking first thing tomorrow morning?"

He leaned back in his chair, the ergonomic lumbar support squeaking as it accepted his thin frame. "I've been trying to get a meeting for weeks, but she keeps refusing." He opened his calendar, flipped a couple of sheets, and ran his finger down the page. "I'd have to shift some meetings, but I can swing tomorrow." He sat back, swivelled her direction and eyed her, stroking his chin with the tips of his fingers. "I should be pissed at you for making that call."

"I know. I'm sorry."

"Don't be. That's the kind of gumption this practice needs. I'm impressed."

She looked at her feet. "What if I went?"

"You?" His eyebrows squished together. "Charlie, you're not a lawyer. You don't know what to ask, what to look for."

"I know. But she said she wanted to talk to me. Maybe you've never been able to get a meeting because the last thing she wants is to speak to another man in authority." She shifted her eyes back to her feet and waited for him to scold her, tell her she's stupid to even consider it. That she's not qualified and never would be.

"That could work."

She jerked her head up to see if he was joking, but he wore his serious face, had reopened his laptop, and his fingers flew across the keyboard.

"Really, I can do it?"

He glanced up. "Yeah, I believe you can do it." He pointed at his screen. "Let's review her file, find parallels with the case you found in Hamilton." He pulled a notepad from the top drawer of his desk and snatched a pencil from a cup overflowing with erect yellow sticks, all sharp and ready for action. "I'll draft the questions so you have a guideline." He glanced at his watch. "We might be here a while if you're leaving early in the morning. Do you have a sitter for Clementine?"

"She's thirteen. She'd be pissed at me if I got her a babysitter. I'll just call and let her know. There's leftovers in the fridge. She'll be fine."

"Perfect. You can take my car." He stood, turned his chair, and swept his hand over it like a magician about to say abracadabra and pull a rabbit out of a hat. "Have a seat and start reading and making notes. I'll order in Chinese and make a pot of coffee."

She sat at his desk and looked at the huge monitor. Three different law websites, two depositions, email, and a spreadsheet. No porn.

Mazie scanned the files and scratched notes on the long, lined pad. Her life had some eerie parallels with Betty's. They'd both married young. Both packed up and moved across the country — in opposite directions — to be with the men they loved. Men who would evolve from caring husbands to evil fiends, who'd turn their hate and anger and disappointment in themselves on their wives until they were forced to make a life-or-death decision.

The big difference was documentation. Betty's abuse was all over the police files. Restraining orders, nine-one-one calls, hospital reports. Betty didn't lie about it when it happened. Hell, she told everybody what the bastard did to her. She just wouldn't talk about it now.

Mazie sat back and crossed her arms, tilted her head and stared at the ceiling. Brown water spots stained the tiles. Gobs of greasy dust hung from the air-conditioning vent. She grinned. Just who cleaned this place anyway?

She sat up, her elbows on the desk. She'd kept her own abuse private. Hid it under makeup and clothing. Lied to the whole damn world. To Ariel. To herself.

Why hadn't she done more to protect herself? Told the doctors the truth about her bruises and broken bones? Why hadn't she spoken up the one and only time the police were involved and let him rot in jail? Maybe he'd still be there. Maybe she wouldn't have sliced him to bits. Maybe her daughter could be home, in school with her friends.

Maybe they could quit being Charlie and Clementine.

Norman placed a cup of coffee at her elbow. "I ordered my usual. Hope you like Kung Pao chicken, dumplings, garlic veggies, and chow mein noodles?"

"I love all of it."

He rested his hand on her shoulder. "Perfect."

A palpable tension hung thick in the air. He didn't move his hand. She held her breath.

She wasn't ready for this.

She cleared her throat, swivelled the chair, and his hand dropped away. "So there are some similarities. A lot of documented abuse. Neither of these women hid their torment."

He nodded. "Right." He put his cup on the desk and pulled a monitor from the top of a filing cabinet. "Let's plug into this, then we can see both cases side by side." He connected the second monitor to the laptop, clicked the mouse with practiced confidence. The second screen flickered to life. He dragged one of the cases to the second monitor so they were side by side, then rolled the spare chair over and sat beside her.

They pore d over the two files, made notes and devised questions until the jarring clang of the night bell announced that their dinner had arrived.

Mazie unwrapped chopsticks from their paper covers and pulled them apart to split the wood where they were connected. An old habit, she ran the two sides together as if she were about to start a fire.

He took lids off of aluminum containers and dug paper plates and soy sauce packets from a second bag. All the while, he watched her out of the corner of his eye "Why'd you do that? You a girl scout from way back?" His amused half-grin gave him a youthful appearance, despite the flecks of grey at his temples.

"It smooths the rough edges. Just need one splinter in your lip and you'll never forget to do that again."

He nodded. "Got it. No slivers."

She focused her attention on the monitors, but Norman focused his on her. After years with Cullen, her peripheral vision had become her ninja power. She could see an entire room while looking at just one point too far from her real focus for him — or anyone — to notice. She'd learned to sense him beyond sight, to pick up on the subtleties between him simply moving across the kitchen and moving with the intent to slam her into the fridge.

Norman didn't have malicious intent in his bones. He was gentle in his words, in his actions. There were no red flags. He never got angry. Not even when she'd deleted a file she'd spent two days working on. When she got up the nerve to tell him, braced herself for punishment, he told her not to worry about it and found the file in the desktop recycle bin. Even made a joke that they were lucky they weren't on some big server set up or he'd have to restore from back up. Laughed and said maybe he should back up this week. Thanked her for the reminder.

"So, Charlie." He chewed and swallowed, stared at the next bite of noodles dangling from his chopsticks. "Why am I paying you cash?" He shoved the food in his mouth.

She closed her eyes and listened to her heart beat in her ears. "Why do you need to know?"

"I'm putting myself out there. It is pretty unethical. And as a lawyer, I've got a high ethical standard to uphold."

She opened her eyes and looked at him. Most lawyers she knew where pretty damn unethical. They'd sell out their own mother just to make a case.

He reclined in his chair, chewed, and stared at her, that half-grin betraying his joke.

Damn, he was cute.

"Right. High ethical standard."

"I am curious though. You just looking to avoid tax?"

"No, nothing like that."

"You seem to know a lot about these cases. Not these particular cases, but the way they feel, why they did what they did." He popped half a dumpling in his mouth. "Your ex," he said through the food. "He hit you, didn't he?"

She shoved as much chicken in her mouth as would fit and chewed. Can't talk with your mouth full, that's what mother always told her. She shrugged.

"Come on, he either did or he didn't." He sighed and tossed his empty plate into the trash can, the chopsticks clanged against the metal. "You can trust me. You really can."

She pitched her chopsticks on top of her plate. She still had a pile of chow mein and Kung Pao, but her stomach had turned on her.

"Why do you need to know?"

"Well, for one thing, I can help."

"Yeah? You can make a man stop being an alcoholic, stop punching me, throwing me into walls and furniture, nearly drowning me, choking me, raping me? You can do that?" She covered her mouth with one hand and squeezed her eyes shut. Tears dripped from the corners. "Oh, God. I'm so sorry."

He leaned forward, took her other hand and stroked her knuckles. "Don't be. I'm sorry, on behalf of all men, that you endured that. The bastard doesn't deserve you."

Tears streamed down her cheeks. She snatched a tissue from the box on his desk and pulled her hand away, wiped her eyes, and blew her nose. She scrunched the tissue into a ball, squeezed it in her fist, and stared at her hands.

He pulled her hands apart and took her snotty tissue from her, tossed it in the garbage. He leaned his elbows on his knees and lifted her face with one finger under her chin. "You're not divorced, are you? You ran away."

She stared at him but no words came.

"He must be looking for you."

Anything she said would be a damn lie and she had already lied to him enough. To Ariel. To everyone.

"Is Charlotte Smyth your real name?"

She shook her head.

"I see. I bet all your identification is in your real name, right?"

She nodded.

"And you never ordered another birth certificate for Clementine."

He wasn't asking. He knew the answer.

"Charlie, you're not a criminal. I know you don't want him to find you, but you have done nothing wrong. You shouldn't be the one hiding. Or running."

She bit her bottom lip and looked up to the stained ceiling, willed the tears to dry up.

"I could represent you. We could make the divorce legal, get you full custody of Clementine. And he would be charged. Do you have witnesses? Proof?"

Air huffed from her nostrils. "Scars. Photos. A journal. And Ari —" She clamped her lips closed. "Clementine. She called the police, they arrested him. Just a couple of months before we left. He was good for a few weeks. He didn't get angry. At least not on the outside. He drank himself silly of course, but I think all that did was make it build up inside." She slumped in her chair and stared at the lines on her knuckles. "When his court date came, I went too. Told them I'd take him back."

"Wait, he was home with you before his sentencing? That violates standard conditions of release."

"I let him. For Clem. And he really was trying. But after court, everything he was bottling up came out. And it was the worst. He said he wanted our daughter." She shifted her gaze to the monitor. She couldn't look him in the eye.

"Wanted her for what?"

"He was bored with me." Her voice was barely a whisper. "Kept talking about her hair and her figure." She dropped her head and wept. "I just couldn't let him. I had to do it, I had to."

"All right, all right." He scooted his chair closer until her knees were between his, and took her into a gentle hug. "Let's just forget we had this conversation. But I'm coming with you tomorrow." He stroked her hair and let his fingers trail down her spine. "And maybe in a few months you can go back to your regular hair colour."

She pulled away, ran a palm over her fake blonde locks. "You can tell?"

He smiled. "Everyone can tell. You have black eyebrows."

Her hand darted to her forehead and she touched the tips of her fingers to her brow. She pressed her lips together. "I've got to get home."

She was a lousy fugitive.

"Busses are only running every hour at this time. Let me drive you."

"No, that's okay. I have to run an errand."

"I can take you for your errand then drop you at home. Save you an hour at least."

She relented and let him drive her home with a quick stop at Wal-Mart.

He rolled to a stop in front of the apartment building. She fished her keys from her purse and stared at them gripped in one hand. "Thank you."

"For what?"

"I don't know. For seeing through me perhaps? Except if you can, then maybe others do too. That scares me."

He put a hand over hers. "I don't see through you, Charlie. I just see you." He lifted her hand and kissed her knuckles. "Now go see that daughter of yours and I'll pick you up right here in the morning. Eight o'clock?"

"Eight o'clock." She ran up the walk and punched in the access code. The door buzzed and the lock released with a loud click. Once inside, she turned back. He was leaning over the passenger seat, watching her to be sure she got in safely. She smiled and waved. He waved back before pulling away from the curb.

Inside the apartment she kicked her shoes off, draped her coat over the armrest of the couch. "Clementine? Oh my darling, Clementine!"

Her daughter came from her room, a bowl of ice cream in her hand. "What's up, Charlie Brown? Er, Smyth."

A glint of light sparkled on Ariel's nose. Mazie took Ariel's chin in one hand and turned her head sideways. A tiny crystal stud nestled in the crevasse of one nostril. "Where did you get this?"

"Jen's mom has a tattoo and piercing shop. She did it for free."

"Without my permission?"

"Mom, I'm thirteen."

"Who is Jen?"

"She's in my homeroom. And we have math together. She's a whiz at it. Said she'd help me."

She was still compelled to get good grades in math. Would they ever truly be free?

"You didn't get a tattoo did you?"

"Of course not. You have to be sixteen for that."

Mazie pursed her lips and sucked on her front teeth. In the short months since they'd left home, Ariel had become a woman before her very eyes. "I like it. It suits you." She tossed the Wal-Mart bag at Ariel. "Now help me dye these damn eyebrows."

<p style="text-align: center;">~~~~~~~~~</p>

Mazie split the blind with one hand and peered out. Norman's car pulled up to the curb. Eight o'clock on the dot.

"I'm going now."

Ariel came out of the bathroom, toothbrush in her mouth. She waved her fingers.

Mazie kissed her cheek. "Straight home after school. And do your homework. There's a plate of spaghetti in the fridge in case I'm late."

Ariel rolled her eyes. "I'll be fine, Charlie." Toothpaste sputtered from her mouth. She walked into the bathroom and spat in the sink.

Mazie grabbed her purse, ran down the three flights of stairs and out into the sunshine of a late summer morning.

Norman leaned against the car, an extra-large Tim Horton's cup in one hand. "Double-double?"

"Oh, bless you." She took the cup.

He held the door open and she climbed in.

An open box of Timbits balanced on the console between the bucket seats. She plucked a sour cream glazed from the box and popped it into her mouth.

She should feel awkward sitting next to him, so soon after she almost allowed confessions of murder to slip from her loose lips. Self-conscious. Something. What she shouldn't feel is so damned calm. So perfectly at home.

"Clem off to school?" He turned left and eased onto the on-ramp of the four-oh-one westbound.

"Not yet." She fished a dutchie from the box and bit into it. She covered her mouth with the other hand. "She got her nose pierced," she said through the sweet dough.

He gave her a sideways glance. "You okay with that?"

"Too late now." She dug a raisin from between her front teeth and sucked it off her fingernail. "It looks nice." Trees flew by her window, streaks of fall colours dotted the mass of green leaves. The highway was arrow-straight, almost as dull as driving through Saskatchewan. "She's not the same kid that I dragged away from home three months ago."

"How so?"

"Became a teenager, got her period, dyed and cut her hair. Makeup. Piercing. And attitude to spare." She sipped at her coffee. "Keeps calling me Charlie instead of Mom."

"Her whole life did change in an instant. Does she want to go home?"

"Sometimes. She misses her friends."

"What about her father? Does she miss him too?"

Mazie looked at her lap. "Sometimes."

"What the hell?" The car slowed behind a long line of red taillights that loomed ahead. In the distance, red and blue flashes bounced off the cement of an overpass. Norman tsked. "Accident."

Mazie craned her neck, but could see nothing but the tops of cars. The left lane merged into the right, the line of traffic inched forward. When they neared the scene, an officer guided traffic through a narrow laneway. They squeezed past a car that had slammed into the abutment head first. An ambulance waited on the west side of the overpass, fire and rescue pried the car open with the Jaws of Life. As they inched past, the cop stared straight at her.

She held his gaze, her breath shallow, her heartbeat heavy.

He nodded at her and waved them through.

When they were clear of the wreckage, Norman picked up speed. "Hey, you okay?" He patted her hand. "You're a little flushed."

"Yeah, fine. Just a nasty accident is all. Maybe slow down a bit."

~~~~~~~~

Bright lights assaulted her eyes, the blinding wattage reflecting off the white walls. Mazie brought her scarf to her nose, shielded herself against the mingling of piss and vomit and pine-scented cleanser.

Norman seemed immune. He rested his forearm on the high green countertop of a nurses' station. "We're here to see Elizabeth Wardell, please."

A large woman, her bubblegum scrubs in stark contrast to her short-cropped hair and full tattoo sleeve on her left arm, looked past him to Mazie. "You Charlotte Smyth?"
~~~~~~~~

"Yes."

"I'm Jess. We talked on the phone." She pulled a pen from behind her ear. "Betty won't shut up about you. She's been writing your name everywhere. Asked me last night when you'd be coming. Never seen her like this." She put her fingertips on a piece of paper held firmly to a clipboard, spun it around on the counter and dropped the pen beside it. "Sign in. I'll get her into an exam room for you."

The room faced east. The sun, high in the late morning sky, streamed through the large windows and lit the space like a thousand-watt bulb. It was stark and sanitized, white and beige, plastic and steel.

Perched on a hard chair near the window, Betty stared out into the world she was no longer allowed to be a part of. She didn't turn when they entered. Didn't appear to notice them at all. Unkempt hair fell past her shoulders, faded copper witness to an old home-dye habit. Eight inches of mousy grey roots was evidence of years of not giving a rat's ass.

An oversized sweater engulfed the slight woman, the loose knit of its orange yarn pilled at the elbows and clashed with cornflower blue hospital pants.

"Betty." Jess's voice boomed in the tiny room.

Betty's shoulders jerked. She turned and met Mazie's gaze. A glint flashed across her eyes.

Excitement? Mischievousness? Or perhaps uncertainty and mistrust.

She slipped a glance at Norman, pointed to Jess and jerked her head.

Jess approached and Betty whispered in her ear. The nurse patted Betty's shoulder and straightened. "Sorry, Mr. Day. You're out. Just Charlotte."

Norman nodded. "I understand, Betty." He touched two fingers to Mazie's arm. "I'll wait in the lobby. Take your time."

Jess let Norman out of the room and winked at Mazie before clicking the door shut behind her.

Mazie wandered to the window and looked out. The third floor vantage point offered a spectacular view of Lake Ontario. "It's a beautiful day." She turned to Betty. "Don't you think?"

Betty nodded.

Mazie sat in an identical chair and pulled it toward Betty. "My name is Charlotte, but please, call me Charlie" She held out her hand. "It's a pleasure to meet you."

The woman hesitated, then held her hand out as if Charlie were a man about to kiss the back of it. Charlie took her fingers. The woman's skin was like rice paper, soft from months of doing nothing — no dishes to wash, no toilets to scrub, no garden to weed. No life to live.

Betty pulled her sweater closer around her body and gripped it shut at her collar bone. Above her tight fist, red marks marred the delicate flesh of her neck.

Mazie undid the knot of her scarf with one hand and allowed the satiny keeper of secrets to fall from her neck. She lifted her chin and ran a finger along her own evidence.

Tears welled up in the corner of Betty's eyes and dripped onto the lap of her hospital pants. "Choked?" Her shallow voice croaked from her throat.

Mazie nodded. "The red marks. They're never going away, are they?"

Betty shook her head.

Mazie reached up and ran a finger along a C-shaped scar that ran from Betty's forehead, around her right eye, to the middle of her cheek. "Did your husband do this?"

Betty nodded. She reached out and took Mazie's hand, guided it to the back of her neck and along her upper spine. She turned slightly and lifted her hair. "And this." Her voice was as reedy and thin as her bony fingers.

Mazie felt the length of a long scar that began under Betty's hairline and continued past the neckline of the sweater. "How?"

"Kitchen window. Pushed me through, flipped me over, dragged me back." She let go of Mazie and bonked her forehead with the heel of her hand. "Hit my head on the counter. Nearly died that day."

Mazie nodded and allowed her own tears to flow. "Not the only day you nearly died, I bet."

Betty shook her head and stared at her lap. "One week in jail. They let him out. I was in the hospital longer than that. When I came home, I had to clean the dried blood."

"Oh, Betty. I am so sorry."

Betty cocked her head and peered at Mazie. "What else did your bastard do to you?"

"Broken ribs, countless bruises, usually where no one else could see. Broken arm." Mazie glanced out the window. "He used fists, feet, stairs. He liked stairs a lot. Sometimes he tried to drown me." She pointed to her neck. "This was his favourite."

"How'd you get free?"

Mazie pressed her lips into a thin line and furrowed her brow. "Are we ever free?"

Betty sighed. "No."

Mazie leaned her elbows on her knees and held the woman's hands. "How did it start for you?"

"I'm not sure. He wasn't like that when I met him." With every word spoken, Betty's voice gained strength. "I fell for him so hard. He was such a bad boy." She grinned. "My mother hated him." She laughed and shook her head. "God, I could use a smoke and a beer."

She turned to Mazie. "You got any cigarettes?"

"Sorry. I don't smoke."

"How'd you cope? You drink?"

"Not much. Mostly it was my daughter. She kept me sane."

Betty sat back. "My kids think it's my fault. I drank." She put her fingers to her lips. "They hate me for killing him."

Mazie covered Betty's other hand with both of hers. "How many years?"

"Twenty-three. It was never going to end, right?" Her eyes pleaded with Mazie. "Right?"

"It was never going to end."

Betty squeezed her eyes shut, put her head back against the wall and wept. "You know what's stupid?"

"You miss him? And you still love him?"

Betty opened her eyes and gawked at Mazie. "You do know."

Mazie nodded. "I told you. I understand."

Betty raised one eyebrow. "Everything?"

"Everything."

"Does that lawyer know?"

Mazie shook her head.

Betty leaned close. "I won't tell him," she whispered.

"He only wants to help you, you know. You should let him."

Betty turned her attention to the view outside the window. "They can put me in jail forever. I don't care."

"Bullshit."

Betty turned to Mazie, her eyes narrowed.

"If you go to jail, then he wins. He's been in charge of you all these years. It's time you got to live life your way. Trust me, it's worth it." She took her hands again. "Now let me get Norman, and let him help you. He knows what to do. And he thinks you're innocent."

"But I killed him. I said so."

"It was self-defence, not murder. You are the victim." She squeezed Betty's hands. "You're innocent, Betty."

~~~~~~~~

Norman turned the volume of the radio down. He bounced in his seat like a toddler who needed to pee. "I just can't believe it. How did you get her to talk to me?" His focus ping-ponged between her and the road. "Those police reports might have been enough for a jury, and the hospital records. But her testimony, that'll seal it. We'll get her off for sure." He turned to face her, reached out and squeezed her hand. "Thank you, Charlie. Thank you."

"Norman, watch the road."

"Sorry." He put his hands back on the wheel. "How did you break through?"

Mazie stared at her lap. "We shared war stories. She needs someone who understands her. Not another man in charge."

"I see." He drove in silence. "Charlie, just how much of Betty's story can you relate to?"

Mazie cracked her neck. "What do you mean, how much?"

"You told me he abused you. Did he try to kill you? Are you worried he'll try that again? I assume that's why you ran away. Otherwise you'd have just divorced the prick."

She stared at the green and yellow blur the trees made as they winged by her window. "I'll never be free of him. No matter what happens."

He tapped the steering wheel with his fingertips and pursed his lips. "He can't find you, can he?"

She grit her teeth and pushed her tongue into the back of them to prevent the flood of her confession. How could she admit guilt to a lawyer? Didn't he have an ethical obligation to turn her in? Or at
~~~~~~~~

least a moral one.

"Charlie, haven't you figured it out yet?"

She turned her head. "What?"

He pulled over to the shoulder and eased the car to a stop. The engine cut and the radio silenced. There was nothing but the whiz of cars speeding past and her heavy heartbeat thrumming in her ears.

"You can trust me. That's what." He took her hand. "I care for you, Charlie."

A tear sprung from one eye and she slapped it away. "Norman, I can't." She turned away and stared out the window.

"Charlie, talk to me."

She sat up and whipped the scarf from her neck. "See?" She pointed to the red marks. "I'll never be free of him. He's always right here." She jabbed at her neck with one finger.

Norman wrapped his hand around hers and guided it away from her neck. "So, he had tried to kill you. His violence was escalating."

"He said he'd kill me. I believed him. It's not like he hadn't come close before."

Norman leaned over the console and put his arms around her.

She flinched at his touch.

"I won't hurt you, Charlie," he whispered in her ear. "I would never hurt you."

She dissolved into his embrace and let waves of convulsing sobs wrack her body.

~~~~~~~~~

"Mom?" The door slammed against the wall. Ariel's book-laden backpack hit the floor with a familiar and comforting thud.

Her daughter was home. All was well. And she was calling her Mom again.
~~~~~~~~~

Mazie glanced at the clock and peeled carrots. "You're late. Where've you been?"

Ariel kissed her on the cheek and snatched a piece of raw carrot. She crunched it between her teeth. "Sorry. At the library with Jen."

Mazie nodded. "Just text me next time, please?"

Ariel nodded and leaned against the counter. She chewed on the carrot and hovered.

"If you're going to stand there, the least you could do is toss the salad."

"I could." She poured the dressing on the salad and stirred it, her mind obviously elsewhere.

Mazie put the peeler down and faced her daughter. "Okay, what's up?"

Ariel stared at the salad bowl. "Can I ask you something?"

"Anything."

"When did you start dating?"

Mazie could lie. Say she was eighteen. Or even sixteen. She sighed. They'd promised to stop lying. At least to each other "Why do you want to know?" Obfuscation. Good strategy. She sliced another carrot.

"I met a boy. He's really cute and nice and he gets good grades and plays football."

"Whoa, take a breath."

"I just don't want you to say no before you have all the facts."

"He already asked you out?"

Ariel nodded.

Mazie's grip tightened on the handle of the knife. "I don't know. You're only thirteen. How old is he?"

"Sixteen."

"Ariel, that's too old for you. Wait, is this the boy from registration day?"

Ariel's cheeks pinked. She nodded and grinned at the salad.

"What grade is he in, ten? Eleven?"

"Eleven, but so what? It's only a three year difference. When I'm eighteen he'll be twenty-one. It's not a big deal."

"But you're not eighteen. You're thirteen." Not legal. Not ready.

"Did you date at thirteen?"

"Yes. But…"

"Oh my God, you are such a hypocrite!" Ariel's raised voice rang in her ears.

"Not a hypocrite, young lady." Did she just turn into her mother? "The boy I dated was also thirteen. Hand holding and the occasional kiss. No chance of sex. A sixteen year-old is looking for way more than holding your hand. And you're too young for it."

Ariel tossed the salad tongs onto the counter. Oil and vinegar smeared the fake wood surface. "I'm not stupid, mother. I won't go and get pregnant or anything." She balled her fists and took a step back. "You just think he'll be like Daddy. Just because you got hit doesn't mean I will. I won't do anything to deserve it."

Mazie reeled back. Her cheeks ached from held-back tears, the knife crashed to the countertop. She turned to face her accuser and poked one finger at the air between them. "I didn't deserve what he did to me."

Ariel paled. One hand flew to her mouth. "Oh, God. I'm so sorry. I didn't mean it." She threw herself into Mazie's arms. "It wasn't your fault. I'm sorry." She pulled away, her eyes pleading. "But Adam's not like that. He's so sweet and kind. He opens doors for me. At lunch he picked a dandelion, said he knew it was just a weed, but if we went out he'd bring me real flowers. Roses or something."

Sweet and kind. Romantic and filled with promises. Just like Cullen before the abuse started. Poor, sweet, naïve Ariel. But damn it, not every charming man would turn into an abuser. This was just a high school kid smitten with her beautiful daughter. He wasn't Cullen. Wasn't even a man.

"Have you kissed him?"

Ariel blushed and cast her eyes to the salad. "Just once."

"Your first kiss," Mazie whispered. She picked up the knife and lopped the top off a carrot.

"Well, second really."

Mazie dropped the knife. "Who? When?"

"Aaron Johnson. On the swings at school. It wasn't a big deal. He smelled like cheese and his lips were dry."

Mazie stifled a laugh.

"Mom, please? Just one date. Just a movie. Nothing else, I promise."

How had her baby girl become a woman in one short summer? She could impose strict curfews, keep tabs on Ariel's every move. Risk alienating her and losing her altogether. And suck all the fun out of her life in the process.

"Fine. One date. Then we'll see."

Ariel squealed and hugged her. "Thank you. I promise you, he is *so* not a bad guy."

Mazie turned away, snatched the knife from the counter, and hacked celery hearts to bits.

~~~~~~~~

"Good evening, Ms. Smyth. I'm Adam. Is Clementine here?"

Tall and handsome. Clean cut, short blond hair, and well dressed in high-end jeans, a clean golf shirt, and brand-spanking new runners. He held a bouquet of half-a-dozen red roses in one hand. His green eyes twinkled just a bit too much for her taste. Nothing but mischief and high expectations in those eyes.
~~~~~~~~

And so it begins. She sighed. "Come on in."

"Don't be lame," Ariel had demanded earlier. "And don't embarrass me."

Mazie had countered with what every parent in history had likely said. "But it's my job to embarrass you."

She knocked on Ariel's bedroom door. "Adam is here."

Ariel swept the door open — a grand entrance. She wore the best jeans Mazie could get at Goodwill, one of her own best shirts, and black pumps. Her little girl, sharing her clothes and shoes. She'd beg for time to turn back if she weren't painfully aware of the shit storm the past had in store for them.

"Hi, Adam." Ariel's cheeks pinked at the sight of him.

"Hi, Clem. You look pretty." He held out the flowers. "Real flowers, as promised." His smile was disarming, his teeth polished and straight.

Ariel accepted the flowers and put them to her nose, inhaled with a dainty sniff. "Thank you."

He tugged one rose free from the bunch and turned to Mazie. "For you, Ms. Smyth."

She smirked. He was a sly one. But he didn't fool her for one second. "Let me put them in water." She took the single rose from him and the bouquet from Ariel. "Wanna help me, bug?"

She set the flowers on the kitchen table, held her daughter's hands and leaned her forehead against Ariel's temple. "Be home by ten," she whispered, "like we agreed. Be safe. And please, please, honey." She forced back tears. "Just a goodnight kiss, okay?"

Ariel rolled her eyes. "Mother, seriously? Stop worrying."

May as well ask her not to breathe.

Mazie watched them stroll down the hall. He took her daughter's hand before opening the door to the staircase and guiding Ariel ahead of him. He turned back and nodded at Mazie.

Her gut lurched. She could follow them. Keep an eye on him. Make sure he was the prince charming Ariel believed him to be.

She stepped into the apartment clicked the door shut, leaned her back against it, and sank to the floor. What was she going to do, bubble-wrap Ariel and keep her under the bed until she was old enough to know who to trust? Would she ever be that old? Hell, Mazie hadn't even figured it out yet.

~~~~~~~~

The cell phone vibrated against the coffee table and jolted her awake. Her arm spasmed. The wine glass in her hand jerked and sent dots of cabernet into the air and onto her jeans. The darkened room was illuminated by the flickering glow of the television.

Mazie grabbed her phone and peered at the screen through blurry eyes. Ten-thirty?

"Ariel?"

"Is this Mrs. Charlotte Smyth?" A man's voice, clipped and authoritative.

"Ms. Who is this?"

"Ma'am, this is Constable Elders of the Cornwall Police."

The room became fuzzy, her hands numbed.

"Your daughter, Clementine, has been arrested for assault."

She shook her head. "What? Assault?"

"Yes ma'am. She assaulted a teenage boy."

"Adam?"

"Yes."

"Is she all right?"

"She's fine, but we need you to come to the station." He reeled off the address. She scratched it out, her hands trembling, her normally neat and upright cursive a jumbled mess of
~~~~~~~~

incomprehensible loops.

She ended the call and dialled Norman. "Clementine's been arrested. Can I borrow your car?"

"I'm on my way. I'll drive you."

Mazie rushed into the brick and concrete building and raced to a counter. "My daughter, she's been arrested. Where is my daughter?" She slapped the desk with an open palm.

Norman caught up with her and put a hand on her shoulder. "It's Clementine Smyth, with a Y."

The officer at the desk gave them directions and Mazie ran down the hall. Ariel sat on a chair against the wall, one hand covering her face, her shoulders slouched. Mazie dropped to her knees at Ariel's feet.

Black mascara streaked across her cheeks, her alabaster skin stark in comparison. "Mom, I'm so sorry." She burst into tears and threw her arms around Mazie's neck.

"It's okay, bug. Everything is going to be fine."

Norman approached the cop standing beside Ariel. "What is the charge, Officer?"

"Assault. She hit her boyfriend."

"He's not my boyfriend," Ariel snapped.

The officer grinned. "Well whoever he is, you did a damn fine job of it."

Adam came around the corner, his left eye swollen and bruised, his lip cut. He walked with his shoulders down, hands in the front pocket of his jeans. A man who looked like an older, balding version of him walked beside him, his hand on the scruff of Adam's neck. The boy glanced at Ariel as he neared. "Crazy bitch," he said, loud enough for all to hear.

Ariel stood and lunged at him. "Asshole!"

Mazie grabbed her and pulled her away.

Ariel turned to the constable. "Attempted rape, isn't that what it's called? Aren't you gonna arrest him for that?" She turned to Mazie. "It was self-defence, Mom. You were right. They're all pricks."

"Clementine, hush. That's not what I said."

Adam wiped his bloody lip with his sleeve. "You're just a fucking tease."

His father swatted the back of his head. "Shut your prissy mouth. You should be ashamed."

Mazie nodded. "Thank you."

"Not talking about your slut daughter, lady. He let some girl beat the ever-loving crap out of him. Fucking pussy."

Mazie took a step toward him, her heartbeat in her ears. "What did you say?"

The constable stepped between them. "All right, enough of this bullshit." He motioned to another officer. "Put Mr. Langley and his father in another interview room."

Mazie stroked Ariel's hair and watched the father and son retreat down the hall. She turned to the constable. "Can I take her home now?"

"Not yet." Constable Elders showed them into a small room. A single table sat in the middle, four hard plastic chairs circled it. "Have a seat, Mr. and Mrs, Smyth. I need to ask Clementine some questions."

"I'm not Clementine's father," Norman said. He glanced at Mazie. "I'm her lawyer."

The constable looked from Norman to Mazie and back. "I see." He moved the chairs so that he was on one side of the table facing the three of them. "So, tell me what happened."

Ariel glanced at Norman. He nodded. "It's okay, Clem. Tell him what happened."

"We were at the movie. He kissed me." She blushed, her gaze focused on the table top. "It was nice, so I kissed him back." Her face drained of colour and she squirmed in her seat. "Then he touched me. I said no. He tried again, and I pushed him away, told him to back off." Tears dripped down her cheeks. "He called me a tease. So I walked out."

Mazie shouldn't have let her go on this damn date. She was too young. And neither of them were ready. She brushed hair out of Ariel's eyes. "Why didn't you call me?"

"That's what I was going to do when I got outside. But he followed me and grabbed my arms, pulled me into the parking lot, and pushed me up against a Dumpster." Her shoulders quivered. "Mom, he put his hand up my shirt and asked if I liked it." She threw both hands in the air. "I freaked. I just started punching." She dropped her hands to the table, rubbed her swollen knuckles. "Someone called the cops." She looked at Mazie. "He just took it. Why didn't he try to stop me?"

"I don't know, bug. Maybe he's not the hitting kind."

Ariel snorted. "Yeah, just the date rape kind."

The constable scratched in his notebook. "That's not quite what Adam said happened. He left out the part about him forcing himself on you."

Norman cleared his throat. "Are you saying you don't believe her?"

"I'm just letting her know what he said. Did anyone else witness what happened between you two?"

"No."

"That's a shame. I'd like to pop the little bastard for sexual assault. I can press charges if you want. But I'm afraid with his injuries and no other proof, it might not stick."

Mazie whispered in Ariel's ear.

She looked at her hands. "I won't press charges."

Constable Elders eyed Mazie. "Are you sure?"

Ariel nodded.

"If he bothers you at school, or at all, you call me, understand?" He handed her a business card.

"I understand."

He slid a clipboard across the table to Mazie. "This is the Notice to Parent. Just a record of the offence and acknowledgement of your understanding of her rights and responsibilities. Once you sign it, I can release her into your custody."

Mazie scanned the form, scratched her Charlotte Smyth signature at the bottom. "Now can I take her home?"

"Yes ma'am." He handed her another slip of paper. Promise to Appear. "Just be sure your daughter doesn't miss her court date." He held his hand out to Ariel and she shook it. "I know you're getting the crappy end of this deal, Clementine. But you did the right thing. Always fight back."

~~~~~~~~

Mazie slammed the phone down and swivelled her chair. "Norman, can I borrow your car?" She snatched her purse from under the desk and brushed past Dory.

"Sure." He tossed her the keys. "What's up?"

"Clementine. Adam's been making her life hell this past week. I'm going to pick her up. Might look into moving schools."

"Let me come with you. Maybe I can have a chat with the little prick."

She smiled. "No, please don't. We don't need more trouble." Or more attention. "I'll get her to call Constable Elders." Would lying
~~~~~~~~

ever be difficult again?

She stepped out of the building, pointed the key fob at Norman's sedan parked on the curb halfway up the block, and pressed the unlock button. The car chirped in response.

Across the street a police cruiser sat, its engine idling. The cop in the passenger seat tracked her movements. She fingered her scarf and glanced down the block. Another cruiser was parked on her side of the street.

She hastened her pace but felt like she was getting nowhere, her feet lumps of lead dragging through quicksand. She hunched her shoulders and focused on Norman's car. When she got within ten feet of it, another cruiser approached from the front, flashed its lights and whooped its siren, pulled in front of the car, and blocked her way. Footfalls echoed behind her. She spun around to find four officers approaching, two with their hands on the guns still holstered in their belts.

A young officer, a baby-faced boy of a man, stopped a few feet from her. "Mazie Reynolds?"

She should be fleeing. Shaking. Freaking out. But instead she felt nothing.

It was over. It was finally over.

Her shoulders slumped and she gave the officer a blank stare. "Yes," she said, her voice monotone. "That's me."

"Ma'am, we have to place you under arrest for the murder of your husband, Cullen Reynolds."

"What the hell is this?" Norman jogged toward her, his nostrils flared.

Another officer blocked his path. "Step back, sir."

"I'm her lawyer." Norman bobbed around him. "Charlie, don't say one word, you hear me? Not one damn word."

"Sir, you can meet up with her at the station. Officers from

Calgary are waiting for her there."

The baby-faced cop pulled out handcuffs, turned her around, and clicked them onto her wrists.

"Must you cuff her?" Norman sounded like he might burst into tears.

"Yes, sir." The officer reeled off her rights and asked if she understood. She nodded. He opened the cruiser door and guided her in.

"What about my daughter?"

"Another unit picked her up from school. She'll be at the station. Child Protective Services in Calgary is expecting her."

"No." Norman stepped forward. "I'll bring Clementine to Calgary."

"Rachel." Mazie could barely speak.

Norman squinted. "Her name is Rachel?"

Mazie shook her head. "Rachel Simpson is my neighbour. Place Ariel with Rachel. She'll be happy there."

"Ariel." Norman nodded. "I'll make sure she's safe."

She smiled. "I know."

"Not another word, Charlie. Not until I'm in the room with you."

"It's Mazie. My name is Mazie." It was good to have it back.

~~~~~~~~~

Norman stood by Mazie's side during her first court appearance. With each motion of his arm, each shrug of his shoulders, his black barrister's robe and waistcoat swished. He ran his fingers under the white collar and wiped beads of sweat from his brow.

"How did they find us?" she'd asked him once she'd invoked her right to counsel and they were alone in the Cornwall police station.
~~~~~~~~~

"Was it Ariel's arrest?"

Norman nodded. "Fingerprints. AFIS matched her exemplars to latents from the crime sce— from your house."

Mazie squeezed her eyes shut. "She didn't tell me they'd printed her. I should have known that. We should have run when we had the chance."

Now here she stood, in the same building where Cullen had pled guilty to assaulting her. But in a much bigger courtroom.

When the clerk read the charge against her, murder in the first degree, the peace that had permeated her body since her arrest melted into a puddle at her feet, like so much pee on the gym floor during a grade four game of dodge ball.

Murder. In the first degree. Intentional. Premeditated.

At the preliminary hearing, the judge read the charge again. She sat up on her judgey throne, in her black tunic with the silly white collar under her second chin, and the blue sash that rested on her shoulders and hung over her breasts like some kind of gender-camouflage.

She'd reviewed the evidence, she said. Determined there was plenty to move ahead to trial. To put Mazie away for life.

Didn't they realize she was already serving a life sentence? Wasn't time served with a future filled with self-loathing and regret sufficient?

The woman peered over her reading glasses and trained her laser-eyes on Mazie. "How do you plead?"

Guilty. She'd done it. She'd killed the bastard. And she'd do it again to save Ariel from years of rape and abuse.

Norman cleared his throat. "Your honour, on behalf of my client, the plea is..."

Mazie straightened her shoulders. "Not guilty." Her voice bounced off the judge's bench and echoed in her own ears.

"Not guilty," she whispered.

~~~~~~~~

"I've got an apartment downtown." Norman tossed his jacket over the back of a chair.

The guard pulled the door closed and locked them inside the cramped interview room — the only bastion of free-speech in the entire institution. No one recording Mazie's every whispered word. No one spying on her through surveillance cameras or flashing beams of light in her eyes.

"How can you afford it?"

"Don't you worry about that. I'm here until the trial is over and you are finally free."

She stared at her hands. "What about your other clients?" She drew a sharp intake of breath. "What about Betty?"

"All taken care of. A colleague has taken my cases. I'll consult about Betty. Might have to fly back to Cornwall now and again. She'll get off. They'll probably stick her in a facility though. Not sure she can cope in the real world. But she won't be in jail."

Mazie shook her head. "That's not freedom." No, Betty would never be free.

He reached across the table and took Mazie's hand.

She flinched at his touch.

He pulled away and leaned back. "Remember, Char-" He clenched his lips and balled his fists. "Mazie." His cheeks pinked. "Just remember, you can trust me. You truly can."

She crossed her arms in front of her chest. "I think I do."

"Good. Then let's talk out your case. I'm going to file a motion to dismiss all charges."

"What? You can do that?"
~~~~~~~~

"I always do that. Never works. Just part of the process. Maybe a motion for a change of venue." He clicked open the briefcase and pulled out a stack of files and a pen. "I have the Crown's witness list. You ready?"

She nodded.

He reeled off the name of two of Cullen's friends. Men she didn't know, had never met. Probably cigar bar buddies. Or maybe fishing pals. People from the half of her husband's life he'd never let her in on. The happy half.

"Then there's an Edgar Applebaum." Norman eyed her over his reading glasses.

"Next door neighbour." She scratched at a scab on her arm.

"He says he heard screaming the night of the murder."

Whenever they talked about the case, Norman was all business. He didn't coddle her, didn't take the edge off the realities of what she'd done. She appreciated that.

"Well if he did, he didn't bother to check in on us. Just like he never checked in when it was me doing the screaming. But in the past few years, I learned how to take it without making much noise. If I screamed, he just hit me harder."

Norman leaned back in his chair. "Mazie, I have to ask. How did Ariel not know what was going on?"

Tears brimmed in her eyes. "Apparently she did. Not everything, but she'd seen bruises, cuts. And of course my arm cast. She says she heard us fighting and him yelling. But the worst of it? He'd do that when she was at school or at a friend's. When she was anywhere but right there in the house. He always had an excuse ready. Mommy fell down the stairs. Mommy was in a car accident. Mommy is a klutz. Mommy broke a glass and cut herself." She covered her eyes with both palms. "Mommy never did any such thing."

"Hazel McClellan."

Mazie dropped her hands into her lap. "Who?"

Norman scanned the page. "Cullen's aunt."

"I only know of one aunt, the one that raised him after his parents were killed in a car accident. Total piece of work, too. Would let her husband, her third I think he said, beat the crap out of him. Yardsticks, belts, fists." It all sounded so familiar. Maybe Cullen couldn't help it. Maybe violence was all he knew. "But she's dead and buried. Died when he was eighteen."

"According to the Crown, she's alive and well and living in Saskatchewan. And they're putting her on the stand." He scratched his pen across a yellow legal pad. "I'll file a motion to exclude her."

~~~~~~~~

The chill in the interview room soaked into Mazie's flesh and cut her to the bone. She rubbed her hands over her arms. She must look oh-so fetching with black roots to her ears and blonde ends, dried and frizzy from shitty shampoo and no conditioner, her face naked and exposed, her scarred neck bare. Not to mention the navy prison-issue sweat suit, droopy in the ass and armpits, that never quite kept her warm. She must look like the frumpy housewives at the grocery store on shopping day. The ones who'd given up. Or who had husbands who loved them no matter what they looked like.

The buzzer sounded and the squeak of crepe soles on concrete neared.

Her heart flipped. She smiled and sat straighter, ran one hand over her hair in a vain attempt to tame the mess.

Keys clicked in the lock, the guard opened the door, and there was Norman and his huge grin. He dropped his briefcase on the table and held out his hand. Mazie took it and stood.

It had become their custom to greet with a hug. A gesture of
~~~~~~~~

friendship, a sign of faith in each other. But for her, the brief connection had become an anchor. He prevented her from drifting into a sea of infinite pessimism.

She sank into his kind and gentle arms, inhaled the vanilla of his cookie scent. When he began to pull away, she tightened her grip on his waist and held on for a few more seconds. He needed no encouragement to return the long embrace.

When they finally released, he brushed hair from her eyes. "You okay?"

She smiled. "Yeah. As okay as possible." Goosebumps broke out on her arms.

He took off his suit jacket and placed it over her shoulders.

She was certain he cared for her as much as she did for him. Was she ready to call it love? No, not yet. That scared the hell out of her. Love was dangerous. Love hurt like hell. And what was the point? All she could offer him were shackles and prying eyes, iron bars and no future. He'd be better off without her.

"We've got a date."

Mazie squinted. "A date?"

"Trial date. September eighteenth."

She wrapped his jacket around her body and hugged it. "What day is this?"

"July twenty-third."

<div style="text-align:center">~~~~~~~~</div>

"How are final exams?" Mazie rested her palm against the grimy Plexiglas wall that kept her from touching her little girl. Though little or girl could hardly describe the Ariel who'd strolled into the remand centre for their regular Saturday visit. Every week brought changes, a new level of maturity. She was too damn young to be so damn adult.

"Not bad." Ariel held the receiver of the phone on the visitor's side in one hand, her other hand against the glass where Mazie's palm rested. The closest they could get to actual contact. "Eighty-seven in English. Seventy-nine in social. Math mark sucks, but I passed."

Mazie smiled. "Well, just don't be an accountant, then."

Ariel laughed. "Definitely not."

Other than the obvious, something about her was different. Mazie scanned her face and hair and blouse. "Where's your necklace?"

Ariel touched a finger to her bare neck. "I — I lost it." She focused on the table top and traced a random pattern with one finger.

Mazie swallowed. "Lost it how?"

Ariel sat back. "Fine, I threw it away."

"Oh, bug. Why?"

"I've tried to just think of the good parts of Daddy. The fun stuff. But every time I look at that necklace, all I see is your blood on his fists, that angry vein throbbing in his forehead. All I hear is him yelling." She sniffed. "So I tossed it in the toilet and flushed it. Except it just sat at the bottom and didn't go anywhere."

"Oh, dear. What did you do?"

"George reached in and grabbed it. Then Rachel took me to a pawn shop. It wasn't worth much. I gave the money to a homeless guy."

"I'm so sorry. I never wanted you to lose the best parts of him."

"Mom, how long are you going to be in here? It's been months already. When is the trial?"

"September eighteenth."

Ariel nodded. She dug a hand into her purse. "Want to see pictures from the lake trip last weekend?"

Mazie swallowed hard and plastered a smile on her face to

camouflage the wave of jealousy that rolled over her. The Simpson's cabin at Sylvan Lake. A place Mazie would never see. A trip she'd never make. "Did you take Nick?" Ariel's new boyfriend, according to the snapshots on the iPhone Norman had bought her, was a skinny fellow with warm eyes and a sheepish grin. Mazie didn't voice her constant concerns, didn't remind Ariel of the warning signs of control and abuse. She knew them by heart.

"Nah. Too soon for that. Maybe at the end of the summer. And don't worry, Rachel already told me he'd be sleeping on the couch. And George would be sleeping with one eye open." Ariel held the phone up to the glass and shared pictures of a bright June weekend, Ariel and Polly up to their knees in the shallow waters of the lake, both of them winter-pale but smiling and happy, each photo marred by the fingerprints and filth past offenders and visitors had smudged on the glass cage.

Ariel glanced over her shoulder. "Mom, can we cut this week a bit short? Rachel has to talk to you."

"What? No. Why?"

But Ariel was already standing.

"Love you, Mom. See you next week." She blew a kiss and retreated, a door buzzed, and Rachel's face poked around the partition that gave the inmates privacy from each another. When every visit, audio and video, was recorded, privacy was a relative concept.

Rachel plopped into the chair and snatched the phone receiver from the wall. "Whoa. Serious roots, Batman."

Mazie touched the crown of her head.

"Don't they let you dye it?"

"I haven't asked. I figure a couple more weeks and I'll just get it all cut off. Start over. With my real hair."

Rachel nodded. "Good plan." She dropped a stack of papers on the table. "So, look. George and I, we kind of kept something from you."

One eyebrow crept up Mazie's forehead. "Kept what?"

"We sort of saved your house from foreclosure."

"You did what?" Mazie sat straighter.

"Look, I know you said to let it go, but shit, honey, there's money in that house. So we took those final notice letters to the bank and we've been making the payments. We got it cleaned up, too. Had to replace the carpet in your room and repaint."

Heat rose in Mazie's cheeks. "Rachel, I told you I couldn't afford to repay you. What if I'm convicted? You'll never get that money back."

"Well, first off, we don't care. Second, yes you will. Sell the damn house of horrors. Neither you or Ariel want to live there. Hell, the darling girl can't even look that direction. It's always right there, every day. She even keeps Polly's blinds drawn since her room overlooks your back yard."

"Shit." Mazie rested one elbow on the table and dropped her forehead into her palm. She looked back to Rachel. "Can I do that from here, sell a house?"

"I don't know the ins and outs. But I bet your cute lawyer dude does. Or he can find out." She leaned toward the glass. "When it sells, if you want to, you can pay us back out of the equity. Then you'll have money for Ariel for university. Or for a down-payment on a house of your own when you're exonerated. Which you will be. I just know it."

Mazie wiped tears from her cheeks. "Damn it, Rachel. What would I do without you?"

"I don't know, be bored? My time is up, sorry. Talk to Norman. He'll figure this out."

~~~~~~~~

Time had marched on outside the halls of Canadian justice. Ariel was in her first semester of grade nine. She'd grown a good three inches, was taller still with her new high-heeled shoes of choice. The nose piercing wasn't alone anymore. Gold earrings gleamed from the lobes of each ear, and she begged to get a ring through her eyebrow. But none of her friends in Calgary had mothers who stabbed holes in young girls' flesh for free. She needed parental permission until she turned sixteen. And Mazie wasn't ready for that much maturity.

She witnessed the morphing of her child into a woman from behind a wall of glass, only heard her daughter's voice through the receiver of a tinny phone line. She was right there, inches away. But utterly untouchable.

Inside the judicial system, time stood still. Three-hundred-eighty-nine days had passed between Mazie's incarceration and trial. Another year spent in a different prison.

Murmured voices bounced around the courtroom. Onlookers dotted the public seats, rubberneckers there to steal a peek at her car-wreck of a life. Scattered among the curious, the occasional reporter, tablets and recording devices at the ready. No one she recognized. Not one sign of familiarity to support her. Her daughter and friends were all witnesses for the defence, and they weren't allowed to watch the trial until after they testified, Norman had made sure of that. Their testimony could be tainted, influenced by others. He only wanted the truth. The truth would set her free, he said.

He was corny and lame like that, and she loved him for it. Yes, she loved him. And it didn't scare her anymore.

She sat motionless and alone in the prisoner's dock, a touch of makeup daubed on her face, air conditioning cooling her bare neck. She'd left her scarves behind. Left her long, blonde hair on the
~~~~~~~~

concrete floor, victim to the prison barber's honed blade. All her camouflage fell away. Charlie was gone for good. She was Mazie. Just plain Mazie.

She glanced up at the sheriff. He smiled at her and winked, a human chink in his stiff, at-attention stance. He'd stand guard every moment of the trial, would watch over her with his eagle eyes. Just in case she broke free of her shackles and made a run for it.

Been there. Done that. Epic fail.

The crown prosecutor stood to deliver his opening argument, pointed his finger at her, sliced his hand through the air to prove to the jury just how many times she had stabbed her bastard husband until he died. Twenty-three he said.

She hadn't kept count.

"Now, you'll hear evidence that Mr. Reynolds hit his wife. We won't try to disprove it. There are pictures. There is his arrest for spousal abuse on the record. But being hit now and again, though vile behaviour, does not give Mrs. Reynolds the right to kill. Does not give her the right to strap him down, torture him for hours, and slice his body to pieces until he dies. You may think she's the victim in all of this, but she stole a father from an innocent child. That shows a level of heartlessness that belies her victim façade."

Mazie rubbed her hands to steady the tremors, but nothing stopped the shaking. Not closing her eyes, not blocking out the sound of that man's accusatory voice, not taking deep breaths like Norman suggested. All that did was fill her nostrils with the stink of stranger's sweat mingled with dozens of perfumes and colognes battling for attention amid the stale, cooled air.

The drama of the prosecutor's murderous mime during his opening argument was the climax of his emotional outbursts. Facts of her guilt were presented with cool detachment. The confession in her handwriting, left with callous disregard atop his dead body, was exhibit A. Her fingerprints in Cullen's blood all over the house. Crime scene pictures of the damage she'd done, to her husband, to her home, were handed around like so many family snapshots. Some jurors turned grey. More than one turned away. A few glared at her from across the courtroom.

Through it all, Mazie sat mute. She knew what she'd done. She'd seen it first hand, live and in three-D with smellovision and surround sound.

Cullen's friends took turns testifying to what a good ol' boy he was. On cross-examination, Norman confronted each of them about the drinking, about the other women. Had them relay all of the awful things, all the lies, he'd told them about his frigid bitch of a wife.

Pete told the prosecutor what a nice guy Cullen was, first to offer help when Pete's own wife kicked him out, first to lend him money. Norman made him confess to Cullen's constant references to Mazie as a fat slob who was totally unfuckable, how he'd hit on the waitresses at the cigar bar and had more than one backroom tryst.

Mazie dropped her head. Tears dripped onto her lap and left dark drops on her simple, gray pencil-skirt. Onlookers might think she was sad to learn her abusive husband had been unfaithful. The truth was she was sickened to finally know what she'd suspected for so long. That she'd been just another backroom fuck. That she'd allowed that moment, that lapse in judgement, to define her future. Define her daughter's future.

Next up was Jerry, a.k.a. J-Dawg. The guy Cullen preferred to take to football games over his own daughter. The one who texted him while Mazie stood over Cullen's dead body. He regaled the court with stories of fishing and football and friendship. Then Norman stood, cleared his throat, and made him admit that the cabin trips were just parties and affairs with chicks who were good to go. Jerry's glance flitted around the courtroom, but never once landed on Mazie.

Chicken shit.

Next day, the prosecutor stood. "Your Honour, I call Mrs. Hazel McClellan."

Mazie craned her neck for a look at Cullen's dead aunt. The witness Norman tried to have excluded. But that motion, like all of his pre-trial motions, was rejected.

An elderly woman, as wide as she was tall, waddled to the stand, held up her hand and swore on a bible to tell the truth.

"Mrs. McClellan," the prosecutor said. "Please tell us your relation to the deceased, Mr. Cullen Reynolds."

"He was my nephew. I raised him after my brother and his wife were killed in a car accident when he was just a boy." She put a Kleenex to her dry eyes. "I loved him like a son."

The hair on the nape of Mazie's neck bristled. She gawked at the lying bitch, wanted to scream, *Don't believe her. She's as big a faker as her nephew.* But all she could manage was a squeak and a furrowed brow.

"And what did your nephew tell you about his wife?" The prosecutor gestured toward the prisoners dock.

"That she cheated on him. Probably had a big life insurance policy out on him. He knew she was planning to kill him." Hazel glared at Mazie.

She struggled for breath, as if a scarf were being pulled tight against her throat. One hand flew to her neck, but all she found was her exposed skin. She dropped her hand and returned Hazel's glare.

"And how did he know this?"

Hazel crossed her arms and smirked. "Internet search history. She'd been Googling how to kill your husband."

Mazie's cheeks burned. She wasn't even allowed to use the internet. Where did this woman get this bullshit? Mazie looked at Norman, cocked her head and raised an eyebrow.

He winked at her.

"No further questions."

Norman stood and referred to a page of notes. "Mrs. McClellan, you currently reside in Saskatchewan?"

"Yes."

"You are living off social assistance, correct?"

She turned to the judge. "Is that any of his damn business?"

"Answer the question, please."

Hazel grunted. "Yeah, that's right."

"So, to obtain your testimony, the court is paying your travel and hotel costs, plus a reasonable allowance for meals. Is that right?"

"Yeah. So? I'm entitled."

"You've been married how many times?"

"Five."

"And your third husband was Jacob Hunter?"

Hazel counted on her fingers. "That's right."

"You were married to Hunter when your nephew, Cullen, lived with you as a teenager?"

"Yes."

"And was Hunter abusive to Cullen?"

Hazel scanned the courtroom. "Well, I'm not sure about that."

"He beat Cullen on a regular basis?"

"I said I'm not sure."

"And when Cullen was eighteen, Hunter beat him so severely he ended up in the hospital with his jaw wired shut?"

Hazel slumped in her seat. "Yeah. That happened."

"Mrs. McClellan," Norman said. "When was the last time you were in contact with your nephew?"

"Oh, I don't know. A year ago I suppose."

"I see." He raised one eyebrow. "Isn't it true, Mrs. McClellan, that you haven't seen nor heard from him since he was released from that hospital?"

Hazel squirmed. "I. I … I can't remember."

"So you remember him telling you lies about my client, but you don't remember whether or not he visited, called, or wrote to you? Which is it Mrs. McClellan?"

Hazel turned three shades of red and broke out into a sweat.

"And the only reason you agreed to testify today is to get a free trip to Calgary to visit a specialist about," he flipped a page, "a possible tumour in your left kidney?" Norman looked up at Hazel. "A trip you could not otherwise afford to make?"

"Well what am I supposed to do?" She leaned forward, spittle flying from her mouth with each word. "Stupid doctor in butt-fuck Saskatchewan can't get his head of out of his ass long enough to treat me. I need a real cancer doctor."

"Mrs. McClellan," the judge said. "Are you admitting to falsifying your testimony for a few hundred dollars in travel expenses?"

Real tears dripped down Hazel's cheeks. She stared up at the judge but didn't say a word.

The judge rolled her eyes. "Mrs. McClellan, step down." The judge turned to the jury. "Ladies and gentlemen, given that the witness has admitted her testimony is false, you are advised to be cautious on what, if any, of it you use in your deliberations. I'd suggest none."

~~~~~~~~~

"Ms. Bailey, is there an insurance policy on Mr. Reynolds' life?" The prosecutor gripped both sides of the podium.

"Yes."

"And who is the beneficiary of that policy?"

"Mazie Louise Reynolds."
~~~~~~~~~

"How much is Mrs. Reynolds entitled to claim?"

"Well, she murdered him, so nothing."

Norman stood.

The judge nodded at him. "Do you have an objection?"

"Yes, your honour. Mrs. Reynolds guilt has not been established."

"Sustained." The judge turned to the jury. "Please disregard Ms. Bailey's last statement."

The prosecutor cleared his throat. "What, Ms. Bailey, is the value of the insurance?"

"Two hundred thousand dollars."

"Thank you. No more questions."

Norman stood and tugged on his robe. "Ms. Bailey, did Mrs. Reynolds purchase this insurance? Is she the owner of the policy?"

"No. It's a standard group insurance policy through Mr. Reynolds' employer."

"And who determines the value?"

"It's a formula, a multiplier of annual salary."

"Are all employees entitled to the same coverage?"

"All permanent, full-time employees, yes."

"I see. Has Mrs. Reynolds made any attempt to claim against the insurance policy?"

"No. There is no record of a claim."

"Thank you. No further questions."

Norman picked at the testimony of every witness the prosecution brought to the stand. Scratched at the wounds of their words until the scabs bled. Then it was his turn to tell the other half of the story. The one the prosecution failed to mention. Tales of the abuse. Of a life lived in fear. A life not really lived at all.

He stepped up to the podium between the defence and

prosecution table, shifted his robe, and cleared his throat. He turned toward the jury. Eye contact, that was the key.

"There is no dispute that Mazie Reynolds killed her husband. It's all right there," he gestured to the evidence table, "in the pictures, in the confession. But guilt isn't always about deeds and actions. Sometimes innocent people pay a price for the brutality of others. The brutality of those who'd promised to love and cherish them. Sometimes innocent people must defend themselves. For Mazie Reynolds, it was kill or be killed. Classic self-defence. Mazie's act of self-preservation came after years of torment. Daily abuse, physical and emotional. Manipulation and control. He choked her during sex. It was the only way he could get," Norman eyed the jury, "satisfaction. The evidence is right there on her neck." He pointed at Mazie. "A permanent reminder. And worse yet, he threatened to move on to their daughter. Bored with Mazie, he'd told her. Time for someone younger, someone prettier, he'd said. His own child, that's who he wanted, in a way no man should want any young girl. Let alone his own flesh and blood."

His gaze was a laser focused on each juror in turn. He'd burn the truth into them. He wouldn't let Mazie take the stand to testify. He'd let her journal and the pictures testify for her.

"This is a case of provocation. A moment of passion. Of justifiable homicide. I ask you to open your minds to what Mazie has endured. What would you do to escape? What would you do to save your own daughter from the same fate?" He nodded and made eye contact with each juror. "The same thing, I'd bet."

Her life was under a microscope, being examined by a courtroom full of strangers. They dissected her motives for staying silent, for hiding her truth. Not of the murder, but of the abuse. Why she didn't confide in one living soul all those years.

How could she? He'd have killed her. Was that so hard to

understand?

She sat through it all, a spectator in the audience at the blockbuster hit that was her life. The prosecution had shared the confession she'd left on Cullen's body. Norman shared her journal. He showed the pictures she'd taken of the bruises, the hand prints, the physical damage, each snapshot imprisoned in plastic, each still stained with her fingerprints in his blood, all projected on a large screen at the front of the courtroom and on private screens in the jury box. The look on their faces when they witnessed those photos foretold her potential fate. Recoil. Disgust. Alarm. And maybe, just maybe, a tinge of understanding and sympathy.

Norman saved the most damning of those shots for last. The series of raw handprints on her choked neck. The black eyes. The broken wrist. He read from her journal — dates, times, events. He made them see that it wasn't a typical diary, not full of hopes and dreams, emotions and plans for the future. Just the facts, ma'am. The brutal realities of a life played out on autopilot. Of a woman who tried to survive each day without dying at the hands of the man who'd purported to love her and keep her from harm.

Rachel and George each took the stand and told of what they'd witnessed, of years of Cullen yelling, of thuds they knew where his fists on walls, or Mazie's body being thrown down the stairs. How they'd known what was going on but could not prove a damn thing. Until the day the cops and ambulance arrived. It confirmed their suspicions, but they were still powerless to save Mazie.

She wouldn't let them.

~~~~~~~~~

"Doctor Scott, why would a woman who is being abused by her spouse, who is being beaten on a regular basis ... why would she stay
~~~~~~~~~

with him?"

The woman on the stand sat tall and straight, her black, fitted business suit punctuated by a crimson scarf tied snugly around her neck. "Mr. Day, women who suffer from long-term abuse experience isolation, shame, humiliation."

"But can't she still leave?"

"It is often very difficult. Many abused women are not employed outside the home. They don't own property, often have no access to cash or bank accounts. They fear being a single parent without the means to support their child. And in most abusive relationships, there are periods of calm. Times when the abuser is contrite and makes up for their bad behaviour with gifts and kindness that lull the victim into thinking that there is hope. And there is always the fear that if they do leave, their abuser will stalk them, come after them, maybe kill them or harm their children."

"And are those fears reasonable?"

"Definitely. About twelve percent of all violent crime in Canada is domestic. And that is only what is reported. As has been made clear in this trial, much of it goes unreported. Most shelters for victims of domestic violence are full and turn women and children away daily. In eighty-five percent of spousal homicides, the victims are women. One woman is killed by her spouse or partner every six days. That is just in Canada."

"Thank you, Doctor Scott." Norman sat down.

"Cross?"

The prosecutor stood. "Doctor Scott, do all abuse victims kill their abusers?"

"No, of course not." The doctor tugged on her scarf and let it fall to her lap. A white scar snaked horizontally from under her left ear, across her neck, and disappeared under her blouse. "But I do understand why it happens."

Mazie touched her neck and swallowed against the lump in her throat. She eyed the jury. Three of the women were in tears, and one of the younger men had one hand clasped over his mouth.

~~~~~~~~

"Your honour," Norman gripped the sides of the podium with both hands, "I call Miss Ariel Reynolds to the stand."

The entire room filled with the shuffle of butts squirming in chairs and swishing of necks in collars, craning for a look. The gallery murmured and pointed at Mazie's beautiful little girl, now a full-fledged woman with her mother's hair and her mother's eyes and her mother's breasts. Ariel strode to the stand, held up her hand and swore to God to tell the whole truth. Her truth. The only truth that mattered.

Norman straightened his robe. He smiled at Ariel and gave a slight nod. "Ariel, can you please tell me about the time the police came to your house?"

Ariel nodded and bit her lip.

They'd practiced this moment, she and Norman. Mazie imagined his gentle manner easing her daughter's nerves. Making sure she told only the facts as she remembered them, no embellishments, no fibs. Just the honest truth, so help her God.

Mazie held her breath and clenched her stomach to ease the lurching in her gut. No version of her life that she'd ever dreamed or imagined included her daughter testifying in her murder trial.

"My father was angry that I got a low grade in math. Mom defended me. All my other grades were good. He sent me to my room. I could hear him yelling at her."

Mazie exhaled and closed her eyes against building tears. The tremble in Ariel's voice broke her heart.
~~~~~~~~

"Just him?"

"Yes. Mom didn't yell. Then there were loud thuds. I knew he was punching her. He kept screaming how he hated her and she was a," she turned to the judge, "pardon me, a stupid fucking bitch. I couldn't hear Mom anymore. I knew he'd hurt her before, I could see the bruises, see how she was with him, always so quiet, always doing everything he wanted. Even though it was never good enough." She shifted in her seat. "So I called nine-one-one."

"And what happened?"

"When the police came I went downstairs." She wiped her cheek. "Mom was lying on the floor, blood all over her face and on her shirt. She was unconscious. Dad was in handcuffs, his hands all bloody. There was even blood on his face, like it was spit on or something."

"Did you go to the hospital with your mother?"

"Yes. She was a mess, broken ribs and her face all bruised and cut."

"According to the police, his conditions of release included staying away from you and your mother until after his court appearance. When did your father come home?"

"The day after they released him. Mom told him he couldn't. That he'd be arrested. But he apologized. He cried. Next time he came he brought presents. After a little while, she gave in and he moved back home."

"Why do you think she let him come home again?"

"Probably because he would have killed her otherwise."

The prosecutor stood.

"Do you have an objection?" the judge asked.

"Yes, your honour. Calls for speculation."

"Sustained. Miss Reynolds, only answer what you know, not what you think might be."

"Yes ma'am."

The women on the jury and two of the men looked shaken. The implication was obvious — Ariel's father was an abuser and a manipulator who had no respect for the law, for his wife. For his daughter.

"Now, Ariel," Norman swept his gaze across the jury. "Did your father ever hurt you?"

The courtroom went silent.

"Yes."

"And what did he do?"

Ariel ran her hands over her skirt. Mazie could see them trembling from her seat in the prisoner's dock.

"He was mad because I didn't go to bed the second I was told, I wanted to finish watching my show. There was only a few minutes left. He grabbed my arms, left bruises on them in the shape of his hands."

"And what did your mother do?"

She looked at Mazie. "She stepped in between us, got me upstairs." She smiled. "She saved me from him."

Mazie smiled at her daughter.

"And then what happened?"

Ariel looked at the jury. "He backhanded her across her face." She looked at her lap. "He turned to me and I ran upstairs. I left her there with him." She wiped a tear from her cheek and looked at the jury. "I could see him punch her in the stomach from the landing." Several of the jurors looked aghast. "But she came and tucked me in anyway. That's the kind of mother she is."

"Ariel, did you feel safe in your home?"

"Sometimes. When he was nice. But no, not normally." She wiped her nose. "I never knew when he'd explode. It happened more and more often. And for the littlest things." She looked at her lap.

"Mom didn't know how much I'd seen. Not until after."

Mazie shut her eyes and hung her head.

"Thank you, Ariel." Norman turned to the judge. "Nothing further, your honour."

The prosecutor stood at the podium, sifted through some papers.

"Now, Miss Reynolds. I only have a couple of questions for you."

Ariel nodded.

"Did you love your father?"

Ariel hesitated. "Yes."

"Are you sad that he's gone?"

She scanned the room. "I don't know."

"You don't know how you feel?"

"It's complicated. I miss how he was when he wasn't drunk. When he wasn't mean. When he didn't hit me or hurt my mother." Tears streamed down her face. "I don't miss the rest. And that's who he really was, isn't it? The awful, drunk, angry, abusive bastard." Ariel wiped her nose with a Kleenex that she had balled up in her fist.

The prosecutor checked his notes. "Miss Reynolds, did your mother kill your father?"

Ariel squared her shoulders. "Yes," she said, her voice a near-whisper.

"And when you learned of this, were you afraid?"

She glanced at Mazie. "Yes."

"You were afraid of your mother."

Ariel's face contorted. "Of course not." Her voice filled the court.

"Your Honour I have no more questions." The prosecutor turned his back on Ariel.

She sat taller in the seat. "My mother wouldn't hurt anyone," she shouted. She turned to the jury, her brows furrowed. "I was afraid she'd be caught. That they'd take her away. Afraid of being alone." Tears streaked her cheeks.

"Miss Reynolds," the judge said. "That's enough. Mr. Day, redirect?"

Norman stood. "Ariel, has your mother ever spanked you?"

Ariel shook her head. "Never."

"Ever harmed you in any way?"

She sat taller. "Never."

"Thank you, Ariel."

The judge nodded. "You may step down, Miss Reynolds. Thank you for your testimony."

"I love you, Mom," Ariel called out across the courtroom.

Mazie burst into tears. "I love you too," she said through choked sobs.

<div align="center">~~~~~~~~~</div>

Each piece of testimony about Cullen's good nature was a punch in Mazie's gut. Each photo passed around, each diary entry read aloud, each secret of pain and humiliation she'd suffered at his hands told in that courtroom, that forum of public judgement, was another beating, another broken rib, another sink-side rape.

For two interminable weeks she sat on display in that box, her life laid bare. She got to know the jury well, but not in the 'hi, how are ya' kind of way. She studied their faces, their reactions to the evidence, to the witnesses. To the truth. The gruff man who left the courtroom each night and probably went home to beat on his own wife. He'd vote guilty. The three women who looked at her like she was a bloody idiot for not leaving sooner. They'd never have stayed, never allowed any man to beat, demean, control them. She'd get no pity from them.

It was the others she was counting on. The ones who cried when they saw the Polaroids, bloody fingerprints and all. The ones who looked at her with such sympathy. Nodded at her and wiped their snotty noses. They would convince the others of her innocence. They would be her salvation. At least, that's what Norman said.

The morning after closing arguments, the judge read instructions to the jury before sending them off to deliberate. They had four choices. Guilty of murder in the first degree. Guilty of the murder in the second degree. Guilty of the lesser charge of manslaughter. Or not guilty.

Mazie squeezed her eyes shut and rocked back and forth. Not guilty, not guilty, not guilty.

The sheriff led her from the courtroom and placed her in a holding cell. "If it goes into tomorrow, we'll take you back to remand," he said. The same sheriff each day. Sweet. Kind. Respectful.

"Can I have some water?"

"Of course. You hungry?"

"Yes. Thank you."

Norman stood outside the cell. The sheriff allowed him in as he exited.

"I called Rachel. They're standing by at her house. I'll text them when there's a verdict. Ariel wants to be here."

"What do you think will happen?"

"Impossible to predict."

Two hours passed as slowly as glacial ice melts. The sandwich and coffee the sheriff had brought sat like dead weight in her gut.

"What time is it?" Mazie couldn't keep her knees from bouncing up and down.

Norman checked his watch. "Four minutes later than last time you asked." He rested one hand on her knee and squeezed. "It might not happen today. Be prepared for that."

"How long does it usually take?" She stared at his hand on her nylons, his long fingers breaching the hem of her skirt. A slight tremor in his palm exposed his collected manner for what it was — a cover. He was just as afraid as she was.

"All depends. Sometimes it's quick. That could mean they sympathize and see your innocence."

She squinted at him. "Or?"

"Or it could mean that guilt is so obvious they don't need to deliberate for long." He ran a hand through his hair. "I'd hope for a moderate length. A couple of days, max."

She leaned back in her chair and emptied her lungs, pressed the heels of her hands to her eyes.

Two more days.

It may as well be a lifetime.

~~~~~~~~

Mazie sat in the box in the same damn chair she'd endured throughout the trial. The ache in her sacrum crawled up her spine and shot shards of pain across her shoulder blades. Public opinion hummed in the seats behind Norman. Strangers had already made their judgements. She was at their mercy. Control over her life was out of arms reach.

Just another normal day.

The faintest hint of strawberries floated by. She twisted in her chair and found black hair and emerald eyes. Since they'd returned to Calgary, Ariel had let her hair grow out. Quit dying it outrageous colours. Except for the fact she'd become a woman, she was back to her old self.
~~~~~~~~

Ariel waved and smiled at her, mouthed 'I love you.'

"All rise." The court clerk's voice echoed off the walls and brought her out of a small fantasy of her and Ariel together, shopping for a graduation dress, having coffee. Just being together.

The judge took her place and the jury filed in. Mazie made eye contact with the ones who were willing to look her direction. Most of them looked away, two of the women held her gaze. She had no idea what that meant.

"Have you reached a verdict?"

The court clerk's words were muffled by the pounding of Mazie's heart in her ears. The periphery blurred, and she trained her eyes on the jury.

"If so, please reply by your foreperson."

One woman stood, glanced at Mazie and shifted her feet. "We have."

"On the charge of first degree murder, how do you find?"

Mazie's entire future, written on one tiny slip of paper.

He cleared his throat. "On the charge of murder in the first degree, how do you find?"

Mazie closed her eyes and held her breath.

"Not guilty."

Her eyes flung open. The entire courtroom erupted in a buzz of voices and cries.

"But guilty of manslaughter."

The room spun around her and her knees weakened. She fell back into her chair, both hands on the armrests to steady herself.

"No, no, no!" Ariel's voice broke free from the din.

"Settle down, people." The judge jerked her head at the spectators and a hush overcame the room except for the whimpering and sniffing of a broken-hearted girl.

~~~~~~~~

"I am a victim. But not the victim of the woman you have in jail. Not a victim of my mother." Ariel focused on the single piece of lined paper in her hand.

Mazie blinked back tears and stared at the purple-inked lines of her daughter's tidy, vertical cursive, barely visible from the prisoner's box.

"I am the victim of my father's anger and abuse. Even with him dead, I remain a victim. I struggle to trust. I have difficulty sleeping." She wiped a tear from her cheek. "If my mother hadn't done what she did, she would be dead. And I'd be living with a monster who would continue to heap abuse on me." She turned and gazed at Mazie. "With my mother in prison, I am a victim once again. An orphan, really. I need her presence in my life. Need her guidance and her love." She scrunched the paper into a ball and looked up at the judge. "Your honour, I am pleading for her life. Pleading for mercy. She isn't a monster. She'd never harm me or anyone else. She acted in self-defence and in my defence and I love her for it. I thank her for it." She bowed her head. "Thank you," she whispered, and stepped away from the podium.

The public seats were almost empty, the circus that had witnessed Mazie's trial had pulled up stakes and moved on. Two months waiting for sentencing, waiting to hear her fate, had gone a long way to cool the attention. Newer cases had arisen. Worse offenders took centre stage. They could have it. She wanted to slip into anonymity and live out her life in whatever manner the judge foisted upon her.

The judge looked out at the court. "After careful consideration of submissions made, evidence presented, and Miss Reynolds' statement, I have made a decision regarding sentencing." The judge
~~~~~~~~

eyed Mazie over green reading glasses.

The hair on her neck bristled.

"Manslaughter is a serious offence. I believe that you had not planned to kill your husband, and that the jury made the right decision. But it is impossible to ignore the fact that you did plan to harm him." She waved a hand dismissively. "Yes, I know that he hurt you. Consistently. Horribly. For years on end. For that I wish the Crown had been given an opportunity to try and convict him. But we will never have that opportunity. The justice system cannot punish a dead offender.

"Despite your victimization at his hands, you went too far, and so the charge of manslaughter is appropriate. Having said that, I don't believe it is in the best interests of any party to this affair to lock you up for any extended period. I don't believe you pose any threat to the general public." The judge referred to her papers, stripped off her glasses, and tossed them on the bench. "Mazie Louise Reynolds, please stand."

A blur of scattered voices buzzed in Mazie's ears, half-muted by her heart, pounding and thumping like so many limbs tumbling down the stairs. She gripped the edge of the prisoner's dock and stood.

"You are hereby sentenced to time served. You will remain on probation for a period of three years from today's date."

Mazie stared at the judge. Three years. She could do that. Probation. Wait, what?

She found Norman's face, alight with a toothy smile. He looked like he might vault the pony wall between them. Behind him, Ariel's eyes were squeezed shut and her shoulders shook.

"Mrs. Reynolds, do you understand this sentence?"

Mazie faced the judge. "Yes, your honour." No, not really.

"Sheriff, please remove Mrs. Reynolds' shackles."

The sheriff opened the door of the prisoner's dock and unlocked her handcuffs. He placed a hand on her shoulder. "Way to go, Mazie," he said under his breath as he guided her free of the box.

She was free? Why wouldn't her feet move?

"Mazie?"

She turned to find the judge smiling.

"You're free to go."

Norman pushed through the gate that separated the public from the court officials, took Ariel by the hand and jogged to Mazie. Ariel fell into her mother's arms.

Mazie's head spun with the smell of strawberries and the feel of Ariel's sweet tears soaking into her blouse.

"Mazie?" Norman put one arm around her shoulder and kissed the top of her head. "Come on, baby. Let's get out of here."

Mazie closed her eyes to find Cullen looming behind the lids. She opened them to Norman's kind, smiling face. Her new reality. She touched his cheek. "I love you," she whispered. "But don't ever call me baby."

END

Thank you for taking the time to read *Mazie Baby*. If you enjoyed it, please consider telling your friends or posting a short review. Word of mouth is an author's best advertising tool.

ABOUT THE AUTHOR

Bean counter by day, novelist by night - Julie Frayn is the author of *Mazie Baby*, *Suicide City (a Love Story)* (winner of double gold medals in the Authorsdb.com 2013 cover contest), *It Isn't Cheating if He's Dead* (winner of the BigAl's Books and Pals 2014 Readers' Choice Award for women's fiction), and *A Trilogy of Unrelated Shorts* (always free on Smashwords.com).

Julie's fourth novel will tell the fictionalized story of her parents' love affair. *The Orphan and the Rose* will hit the virtual shelves in 2015.

Julie pens short stories and writes for her blog, www.juliefrayn.com, as mental floss between novels. She is mother to two wonderful adults, and keeps a roof over their heads by working as Chief Financial Officer for the largest living history museum in Canada.

PRAISE FOR JULIE FRAYN'S FICTION

It Isn't Cheating if He's Dead:

"Jemima, struggling to understand how she lost her fiancé and trying to make sense of her life after his death, is so utterly human that she blooms off the page." ~ Laurie Boris

"Jemima Stone, Jem for short, is one those characters I found myself caring about almost immediately. She isn't without faults (who among us is?), but she also has a way of taking a negative and turning it positive, which is a quality we could all emulate." ~ BigAl's Books & Pals

Suicide City, a Love Story:

"*Suicide City* is gritty, unrelenting, tragic, desperate, sad, heart-warming, heart-breaking, and gut-wrenching." ~ Sean P. Farley

"Hands down, the best ending line of any book I've read in the thirty-one years I've been a reader. Please, do not miss this exceptional novel!" ~ Amber Jerome Norrgard

A Trilogy of Unrelated Shorts:

"These stories are difficult to read, powerfully written, emotionally draining and awesome. Frayn's writing is flawless. There is nothing with which I can find fault. Frayn gives us a glimpse into a world that might seem bleak but is not without heroes." ~ Rabid Readers Reviews

Website/Blog: www.juliefrayn.com
Twitter: www.twitter.com/juliefrayn
Facebook: www.facebook.com/juliebirdfrayn
Amazon: http://www.amazon.com/Julie-Frayn/e/B00BH47C3G